THE WOUNDS THAT LINGER

a Regency Mystery

Managing Editor: Robin Shukle
Cover Design: Sandy Robson
Production: Liz Mrofka

ISBN: 979-8-9900489-6-6

Library of Congress Control Number
2024921041

THE WOUNDS THAT LINGER

a Regency Mystery

SANDRA & TAYLOR PREISLER

Dedication

For Jack, our dad and grandpa. Your unwavering belief in the women in your life gave us the space to dream big, and your belief in sound investments gave us the freedom to follow those dreams. Thank you for never doubting. You gave us wings. You are still missed.

London 1811

Chapter One

The familiar scent of soot hung heavy in the air around her as Lady Zoe Demas inhaled deeply. She turned with a smile to Mary Fletcher, her lady's companion. "Who knew it would be the London air I missed, of all things?" Last night's late disembarkation from the ship had left no time for a stroll through the London streets she so loved. And so, after a few restful hours in her own bed, she had awakened Mary for a dawn outing.

Mary took in a deep breath of her own, which was cut short by a hacking cough. "Who knew indeed, milady, as it calls into question one's sanity and health in a single breath." The night at home had improved her companion's spirits, but this early morning walk Zoe had insisted on seemed to be putting those renewed spirits to the test. "Regardless, time to put up stakes. Perhaps the rancid air will sit better after some strong tea."

As Mary gave a final dramatic cough, Zoe stifled a laugh. Despite her criticisms of London air quality, their months in America had done little to impress Mary. Zoe could hardly blame her—Americans' treatment of people of color left a great deal to be desired. Britain was hardly a shining example in that area, but at least slavery was no longer allowed in England itself. America had a long way to go to get even that far.

A propensity towards seasickness had only added to Mary's desire to never leave London again. The passage home took a full twenty-five days with rough seas, and Zoe was astounded a person with Mary's dark complexion could become quite so pale. She wisely kept these observations to herself, instead limiting her comments to those of a sympathetic nature.

Zoe herself never wavered, no matter the weather. It seemed as though she was born for rough seas.

As was young Gwen, their other companion on the journey. As a street urchin along with her brother Ezra, Gwen had navigated much worse conditions than the rough seas of the Atlantic. Employed by Zoe to care for her massive dog Brutus, Gwen showed equal fortitude at sea. If anything, the sea air had pinched some real color into her cheeks, and she'd put on some healthy weight as well. She and Brutus and Zoe had spent their time wandering the decks of the large ship at will, as most passengers were of a similar constitution as Mary.

The one thing Mary had developed a fondness for in her time abroad was American colloquialisms. But though fond of her new reservoir of quaint phrases, she rarely used it properly. Zoe didn't have the heart to correct her in regard to *pulling* rather than *putting* up stakes."

As Zoe acquiesced to Mary's desire to return to their home, she absentmindedly wondered if her mother had any candidates for a new lady's maid for her to review on her first full day home. Simone had promised to find her a replacement—it had, after all, been her mother's idea to elevate Mary to the status of lady's companion. Zoe's mind drifted back to the circumstances which brought the two of them together. Their meeting had been . . . unusual, to say the least. The year before had been marred by tragedy. Zoe's lady's maid at the time—poor Lucy—was shockingly and brutally murdered, and Mary was hired as a replacement. But it didn't take long for them to discover they were kindred spirits of a sort, and they developed a surprising bond of friendship. This breakdown of the social separation between employer and servant, in addition to Mary's naturally quick wit and inability to keep her opinions to herself, had made the occupation of maid a poor fit. Mary's elevation to lady's companion had been the perfect solution.

Though said companion was now moving at an accelerated pace that brought Zoe back to the present. She smiled at the sight ahead of her.

Dovefield Manor arose in view, the tendrils of morning fog adding charm instead of unease as they approached. It was not the most impressive home in London, but it wasn't without a feeling of prominence either. Her stepfather was not titled, being the second son of a lord, but he had forged a successful path as a barrister, and their economic comfort was reflected in the size of the home as well as the neighborhood in which it was situated.

Zoe felt a feeling of home wash over her as the long-standing butler, Quaid, opened the door with warmth in his eyes. She greeted him with as much affection as his formal bearing allowed before instructing him to bring up tea for Mary and coffee for herself. Exhaustion was clearly taking its toll on Mary, who chose to take her refreshment in her room. Zoe was instead drawn to the family dining room. The home had a more formal dining room for parties and dinners, but she and her parents had always preferred this smaller room with a sideboard the staff filled each morning. The window looked out over the charming square where they resided and was equipped with a table for eating, as well as armchairs in a group for casual seating.

Zoe was tired as well but had never managed the skill of being able to sleep while light shone. Besides, the late arrival had only allowed for a brief greeting with her family the night before, and she was eager to visit with them in more detail. She had not yet finished her first cup of the bitter brew Quaid had provided when her stepfather, Hugh Dovefield, and her mother, Simone, entered the cozy dining room.

Hugh paused to give Zoe a kiss on the cheek as he moved to pour his own coffee. He smelled of soap and lemon aftershave, as he commonly did. As a barrister he often prepared for cases at home, and through the years had taught his French stepdaughter much about British law. But their relationship had nothing to do with legality and everything to do with love. The two shared a strong connection, as well as a strong love for good coffee.

Simone, still French to her core, had managed to develop an affinity for English tea during her years in the foreign country. She helped herself while she glanced at Zoe. "How does it feel to be back home, *mon chou*? Seven months is a long time."

Her mother wasn't wrong. Seven months was indeed a long time to be away from her family and her friends. The trip had been unplanned. Her uncle Sebastian, Hugh's younger brother, had invited her along on his journey to America at the last minute, and Zoe had jumped at the opportunity to escape certain issues which had arisen in her personal life.

Sebastian was the kind of man who could liven up even the dullest of gatherings and was charming enough to make friends everywhere. Zoe couldn't deny the whole adventure had been great fun—an exciting distraction, exactly as she had wished. But she was terribly happy to be home.

"It was a lovely adventure, *Maman*. Uncle Sebastian's friends are very entertaining, and he did his best to make us feel welcome. But I was ready to come home—we all were."

"Well, it is fortuitous you are back not too far into the season. You haven't missed much yet."

"It is good to be back," replied Zoe, taking another sip of her coffee.

Truth be told, Mary had been the most homesick. The grand adventure to America had only made Zoe's outspoken companion more certain that London was where she belonged. As she'd said on the ship back, "There is no blessing place like home." Zoe had stopped herself just in time from telling her the proper word was *blessed.*

"We were also ready for you to come home." Hugh's gaze flickered to his wife before he continued. "A great deal has changed since you left."

A glance at her mother revealed the truth in her stepfather's words. She had missed them all—her mother, Hugh, and even her younger half siblings. But Simone was not the same woman as when Zoe left. Her mother looked the same on the outside—still beautiful, with only the faintest of fine lines appearing around her eyes to betray her age—but her countenance was different.

"Is there a new venture in your life, Maman? You look . . ." Zoe paused, searching for the right words. "Like you have a new *raison d'être.*"

Simone chuffed a laugh. "You have always been observant, *mon chou.* I am anew with purpose, as you say. The charity I started for mothers and children has done much good. It is fulfilling. I wrote you of its inception."

Thinking back to the weekly letters she had received from her family while abroad, Zoe smiled. "I remember. I didn't want to ask in case it was not successful. I am happy for you that it is."

"Your mother spends most mornings at The Haven, helping the mothers gain skills or find work." Hugh gazed at Simone with pride. "She comes home happy."

This development was pleasing to hear. Simone had been forced to flee France during The Great Exodus with young Zoe in tow, using all her resources and wit to keep them alive. That period of life had been a time with no place for weakness, and their survival depended upon her mother's rigid and unyielding determination. It was fortunate for them that Simone's natural disposition already leaned that way. But even after she had met and married Hugh, successfully pulling her and her daughter back up into high society and securing a future for them both, she hadn't seemed able to lower the walls she'd built up during those hard years.

But now she seemed softer—her natural angles still there, but rounded so that they were not quite so sharp. Simone had finally found balance. Perhaps those old wounds, which had lingered for so long, were finally beginning to heal. "And you, Zoe? Now that you are home, where will you find purpose?"

A fair question. If the events of last year had proven anything, it was that Zoe was built to have a purpose. She had thrived investigating Lucy's murder, stepping out of the mold that young women of her station were expected to hold, making friends across the spectrum, ignoring the traditional bounds of society. Of course the death was heartbreaking, but when the man who took Lucy's life was finally brought to justice, Zoe had felt great satisfaction in her role. As terrible as the circumstances which started her down that path were, those days had been some of the best of her life.

Though the next dead body had changed everything.

Zoe took a breath. "Purpose remains to be seen. Mary and I will take a few days to settle in, of course. The passage back was taxing, and Mary has yet to see her family. As for me, I was planning to call upon Mabel Anderson as soon as possible." She watched her stepfather carefully as she spoke.

Hugh frowned, his green eyes darkening with the concern she'd expected. "Are you certain you will be welcome? After last year's events they have quite cut us off. Understandably so, of course."

Understandable indeed. Mabel's darling younger sister, Margot, the diamond of that high society season, was the next dead body after Lucy. Hugh had defended the man accused of killing her, Thomas Chedrose. While he maintained the man's innocence at trial, it hadn't been enough. Zoe knew the conviction weighed upon him.

She thought back to the ball she'd attended last year. She'd been occupied with a plan to unmask Lucy's killer at the time, but she still chatted with Mabel that night while waiting for the pieces to fall into place. Mabel had been irritated with her sister's arguing with their father and storming off into the dark the night before, having not yet returned. Mabel was quite concerned news of her sister's actions would negatively impact her own reputation, perhaps resulting in her missing out on the only target a nobleman's daughter had in her sights—a suitable match.

But while Mabel and Zoe had been occupied with their own concerns, Margot was living on borrowed time. Her body was discovered not long after. Zoe sent a note of condolence to Mabel, but once Hugh was secured for the defense, communication between the families ceased. As her stepfather had said, understandably so. Which was why Zoe had been so surprised to receive a letter from Mabel while abroad.

"Actually Mabel wrote me around the time Sebastian and I decided to return and asked me to call when I arrived home."

The statement was met with shocked stares and concerned glances.

"Mabel asked you to call?" Simone's French accent always became more prominent when she was worried. "Why would she do that?"

"I'm not sure." Zoe shrugged. "As you know, we've never been close, although I suppose we were friends of a sort. But the year of mourning is almost up, no? Perhaps she's just ready to start receiving visitors."

Hugh shook his head with a sigh. "I doubt that. Rumor is that although both of her parents have taken to wearing lavender, Mabel still insists on dressing in black. She seems the least inclined of the family to put the whole tragedy behind her." He paused to look closely at Zoe. "Are you sure you're up to paying a call on someone who is still so distraught over a loss and who dislikes your family? You had a rather taxing year yourself."

That was an understatement. The investigation into Lucy's murder had been admittedly exhilarating but equally exhausting. Zoe had traveled the depths of London's squalor, attended a bull-baiting fight, acquired a bull-baiting dog, and actually purchased a child. Through it all she'd made connections with people who remained important to her, though admittedly eclectic. Mary topped the list, but a resurrectionist, a Bow Street Runner, and a criminal were also there. Then there was the inquiry agent.

Quinton Huxley.

A man who could both fascinate and exasperate her within the space of a single breath. Despite her best efforts, she'd spent more time than she would care to admit thinking about him during her time in America. Which was precisely what she had wished to avoid doing.

His connection to Margot's murder certainly complicated matters. Part of the reason Hugh had been so certain of Chedrose's innocence was because the poor girl had been strangled with a piece of cloth which strangely resembled the same cloth that had been used to end Quinton's mother's life eighteen years ago. Most considered this to be a coincidence, but Hugh and Quinton had been convinced there was a connection.

Zoe sighed. Though she'd passed her twenty-fourth birthday while aboard the ship home, the events of last year sometimes made her feel decades older.

"Last year was . . . complicated," Zoe admitted quietly. "I know you were both worried about me before I left, and I also know I did not always make things easy. It was a confusing time. After Margot was found, everything changed. But time and distance has helped. And Mabel did ask for me to call. If I have learned anything about myself over the course of events, it's that I'm not able to sit by when someone asks for help."

There was a pause, but then Simone smiled at Zoe. "*Mon Dieu*! It is good to hear you speak of helping others, Zoe. I have found a great deal of satisfaction doing the same. Perhaps another day this week I can take you to The Haven and introduce you. I had a small plaque made that honors Lucy and her son, Simon. It is really because of them that The Haven even exists, so other young mothers who have no support can find some within its walls."

Zoe nodded, accepting the change of subject with a smile fixed on her face, even while her mind drifted to other things the conversation had dredged up. Many things had changed while she was gone. But in her heart, some things had also stayed the same.

Chapter Two

Even in the state of dreams, Quinton Huxley kept a certain awareness. He had grown up learning in the school of life and death that was the streets. His guard could never be completely down, lest someone slit his throat and steal his boots while he slept.

That familiar feeling of uneasiness rousted Quinton from his slumber, pulling him from the depths of dreams into that hazy state between sleep and consciousness. His overdeveloped sense of self-preservation was ringing alarm bells, telling him he needed to open his eyes and be prepared to defend himself.

He finally forced his heavy eyelids open, only to start when he saw a pair of wide green eyes staring into his own mere inches from his face. The adrenaline hastened his journey to rational thought, and Quinton realized within seconds that the culprit was his own cat, Oscar. But not before he had thwacked his head against the wall in the initial panic.

"You stupid beast," he muttered, rubbing the now sore spot on his skull.

Oscar chirped a meow in response, unoffended by the insult.

She hopped off the cot, stalking to the other side of the room where her bowl sat empty.

A pang of guilt twinged in Quinton's stomach. When was the last time he'd fed her? It wasn't as if Oscar would starve without him; she came and went as she pleased, leaving a trail of dead vermin in her wake. Nevertheless, he had always supplemented her murderous lifestyle with leftover cuttings from the butcher. But recently he was a less reliable flatmate than she was accustomed to, and he couldn't blame her for being disgruntled.

He swung his feet over the edge of the cot, knocking several empty bottles out of the way as he did so. The sound of clinking glass rolling across the wooden floor seemed especially loud that morning—or was it afternoon? Quinton squinted at the light streaming through the window, trying to remember the events of the previous day. It was mostly a blur. He wasn't even sure of the exact date. Sometime in winter, he knew that.

A knock at the door redirected his musings back to the present moment. His confusion and guilt were quickly replaced by irritation and movement.

"What?" Quinton instantly regretted his decision to throw the door open quite so wide and so fast. He flinched away from the watery sunshine, the pounding in his head getting worse by the second.

His visitor was unperturbed by his reaction, brushing past him with a flick of the wrist. Once they were in the darkened room, Quinton could finally make out their features—it was Ezra, a street youth he employed regularly for all sorts of odd jobs.

The boy's lip curled in disgust as he glanced around the room. He shook his head, gesturing with his hands to communicate. In the past year, Quinton had picked up enough of the improvised language to translate the deaf boy's meaning . . . most of the time.

This place is a wreck. When does your housekeeper come?

Quinton used his hands to clumsily respond, speaking the words aloud as well. "She quit, remember?"

Ezra frowned and shook his head again. *"I thought Charlie paid her back wages?"*

"He did. But as you may have noticed, work is still slow for me." Quinton noticed the bulge in his satchel. "What's that?"

"Breakfast. For you and for the cat."

While even the thought of food was enough to turn his stomach queasy, Quinton did appreciate the gesture. Ezra never forgot about the cat. In fact, Oscar might have been the reason the boy first gave Quinton himself a chance. Ezra had been all of fifteen then, or thereabouts, nearly as tall as Quinton himself, but thin as a rail and filthy as the Thames.

Life had not been easy for Ezra and his younger sister, Gwen. He was angry and slow to trust, struggling every day just to keep the two of them alive. It didn't take long for Quinton to develop a fondness for both children, but that affection had nearly led to Ezra's death the year before. Though he'd escaped with his life, the boy had not come away from the madman who kidnapped him completely unscathed. The knife had left a small scar on his neck, and only in the last few months had the nightmares settled.

Ezra came and went much like Oscar, valuing his independence too much to take up permanent residence. But Quinton made sure the boy had a key so he could sleep by the fire whenever he needed a safe space. On those nights, it was Oscar, not Quinton, who calmed the boy as he lay there wrapped in a blanket and trapped in a nightmare. She would curl up next to him, kneading his arm until Ezra finally calmed.

The boy standing in front of him bore little resemblance to the memory. He was sixteen now, having filled out on a steady diet of actual food. He was still lanky, but the contrast between his height and his weight was less jarring. His confidence had grown as well, at least when it came to Quinton. Over the course of the last year, Quinton's reliance on the boy had increased steadily, to the point where a day rarely went by where he didn't see him for one reason or another. The film of grime that once caked the youth's skin and clothes was lessened as well, revealing a face that would one day be considered handsome—once he'd grown into his nose.

Quinton squinted, his thoughts finally catching up with his observations. Now that he was thinking about it, Ezra was especially clean that day. Even the dirt under his fingernails had been scrubbed away, and the dark hair sticking out from under his cap appeared freshly washed.

"Why are you so clean?"

Ezra rolled his eyes, pulling out a lump wrapped in grease-stained paper and setting it on the desk. *"You forgot, didn't you? Gwen got back yesterday. I'm going to see her when I leave here."*

"Oh. Right. Of course." Clearing his throat, Quinton shifted away from Ezra's gaze. It wasn't that he'd completely forgotten about the return of a certain someone—after all, she'd written not that long ago, asking him to tell Ezra the date of his sister's return. But he had pushed those thoughts and the feelings that came with them away, preferring to medicate his troubles with a liquor-induced haze. Now Zoe Demas was back and Quinton still wasn't ready to deal with the consequences of her return.

When through a ridiculous and complicated series of events Zoe had obtained a bull-baiting dog last year, Quinton had recommended young Gwen as a handler for the creature. Gwen was resourceful and he had been actively searching for an opportunity to find her a placement off the streets. When Zoe and her dog had abruptly left the continent for a holiday in the Americas, young Gwen had naturally gone along for the ride. These seven months were certainly the longest Ezra had gone without seeing his sister since her birth.

"Are you going to go see the lady?"

"What?" Quinton huffed. "Of course not. I'm far too busy. I have better things to do than pay social calls."

Ezra's expression was skeptical. *"Whatever you say. If you change your mind, I do have one piece of advice."*

"What might that be?"

Quinton didn't know the exact translation for the following series of rude gestures, but he could fill in the blanks.

———————◆———————

If only one good thing had come from his conversation with Ezra, it was that Quinton was inspired to clean up some of his sty. He started with the obvious—clearing out the myriad bottles.

When the bin of empties became precariously full, Quinton balanced it carefully, supporting it with one hand while he swung the door open with a single fluid motion. At the same time he swung his own tall frame through the open space, letting the door slam behind him. The carefully choreographed move came to an abrupt end when he slammed headlong into a man just outside his door. Quinton's temper flared as the bin dropped, the bottles clinking as they scattered, and, worst of all, the man laughed.

Quinton took longer than he should have to recognize it, but as the laughter cut through his still-hazy fog of a brain, he dropped his clenched hands to his side. Only one man he knew laughed like that.

"Rory!" exclaimed Quinton. "You're lucky your head is still attached to your body, you imbecile! Ought to know better than to sneak up on a man like that . . ."

His friend leaned back, still chuckling. "I am standing on a public street, my boy, not even walking. 'Tis you who ran into me."

Rory Stewart was older than Quinton by more than a decade, now just over forty, and wiser by twice as much. He was easily recognizable by his perfectly groomed reddish blonde hair, as well as his green eyes which usually glinted with humor and mischief. Not to mention his distinct Scottish brogue.

The Scotsman cheerfully helped gather and dispose of the array of empty liquor bottles, whistling a tune while he worked. After the chore was accomplished, Rory followed Quinton back inside and accepted a chair by the fire, leaning forward to enjoy its warmth. Quinton was glad he'd had the forethought to make a fire. Perhaps Rory would not notice the overall disarray of the place, or at least refrain from commenting on it.

"What brings you to my door today, Rory?" As Quinton asked the question, he spied another bottle he'd missed before and quickly kicked it under his chair.

"You've been on my mind, Quinton." Rory's face was serious. "Even when you don't need my professional services, you usually grace my door for an occasional chat, but it's been more than a while since I've seen you. Thought I'd stop by and check for myself you're still kicking. Had business this way anyway."

Seeing as how Rory made his living as a body snatcher, otherwise known as a resurrectionist, Quinton couldn't imagine what kind of business he would have during the bright hours of the daytime, but he chose not to comment on it. Instead, he answered the man with the same words he had used when John and Charlie and even Lord Dovefield had made their own inquiries. "I appreciate your concern, Rory. I really do. But I am fine."

Rory leaned back, his gaze even. "I think I'm done with that answer, lad. We've known each other too long for me to keep accepting platitudes."

That much was true. He'd known Rory a good many years now. Whether in matters of the heart or a head wound pouring blood, Rory always seemed to have the right bandage, listening or stitching with equal skill. Professionally and personally he was irreplaceable. But although Quinton truly did appreciate his wisdom, he simply could not manage to speak of what ailed him this time. "I can't give you more than that. Not yet, anyhow," said Quinton after a lengthy pause.

The Scotsman sighed. "I know you have things in your heart you'll have to sort out yourself. Lord above knows I've had a few times like these in my own life. But speaking from experience, I suspect your present state will remain much the same until you do so."

Rory stood, pausing for a moment before continuing. "I want you to know there are people who will still be here when your mind clears. I am one. My door remains open to you. When the time is right, you know where to find me."

Impassioned speeches were not unusual behavior for Rory. Quinton viewed him as a rare man who did not mind discussing feelings. Perhaps it was his penchant for Shakespeare that loosened his heart and tongue so easily.

"Words are easy like the wind, Faithful friends are hard to find," said Rory, right on cue.

Despite himself, Quinton smiled. Rory returned the smile and, with a final nod, let himself out.

Quinton spent the next few minutes quietly reflecting on the interaction. He still did not feel quite ready to return to the world of the living. But Rory had helped him see that the world was there for him if he changed his mind.

Chapter Three

Despite the confident words to her parents, Zoe had to admit to herself that she was nervous as she approached the Anderson manor. The family lived off Berkeley Square, a short carriage ride away. Zoe would have preferred to walk, and would even more so have preferred Mary's company, but her friend was still visiting her own family. Though Mary didn't often speak of them, Zoe had to imagine they too missed their daughter.

The carriage allowed Zoe to arrive unaccompanied and still honor the rules of society, or close enough to them. The driver helped her down, performing this last duty before wandering around to the servants' entrance. He would likely find a sandwich and glass of ale waiting for him in the kitchen, to occupy him until she was ready to depart.

Her knock brought the butler in a timely fashion. Upon receiving her calling card, he escorted her inside. The room he brought her to was near the back of the house, comfortable in size with a fire blazing in the grate to combat the dreary weather. Where a parlor would traditionally be used to receive callers, Zoe was surprised to realize she'd been shown to the drawing room, a space usually reserved for close friends and family, which Zoe didn't think fit her relationship with Mabel.

As she gave her wrap to the footman, Zoe took stock of the woman in black standing near the fire, her back to the door. There wasn't any easy way to start the conversation, but platitudes seemed like the best of her limited options. "Mabel! I hope you are well."

When the young woman finally turned to face her, grief itself radiated off her, like a terrible perfume no one would ever choose to wear. It wafted to Zoe, stopping her where she stood and infusing her with its powerful depth.

She instantly regretted her cheerful greeting. "Forgive me, I don't know why I said that. This must be terrible for you. I am so sorry."

As she took a single step in Zoe's direction, Mabel shook her head. "There's no need for apologies, Zoe. I know it's been a year and the time for acceptable grieving is coming to a close. But still I miss her so much, as if it all happened only yesterday." Mabel blinked, clearly trying to hold back a wave of emotion, but the wall only held for a moment, and then she began to openly cry.

The display of emotion was so unexpected coming from this girl of quintessential Britishness that Zoe was taken aback. But she only hesitated for only a moment before going to Mabel, wrapping her arms tightly around her.

She was, after all, French.

The sobs that tore from Mabel's throat racked her entire body. They came from her soul, from the essence of her very being. Zoe just held her, saying nothing because there was nothing to be said to ease such pain.

Time ceased to matter in moments like these, but eventually Mabel's body stopped shaking. As her breathing became smoother, she stepped back, resuming the more composed British air Zoe expected. "It's my turn to ask forgiveness, Zoe. My parents were uncomfortable with these displays of emotion, even when it first happened, and by now are quite exasperated with me. It's been quite some time since I wept for my sister."

Zoe's own sadness reached out, entwining with Mabel's. She had experienced grief over the loss of a family member, but it was the grief of childhood—simpler, with less definition, and without the pressure that came with adult expectations. The thought of anything happening to one of her young siblings, or to Mary, drove a cold stake of fear through her heart. She couldn't even imagine how she would react. And then the idea of Hugh or her mother chastising her for continuing to grieve . . . it turned her stomach.

With a deep breath, Mabel wiped tears from her eyes and did what all British people do when comfort is called for.

She rang for tea.

<hr>

Only after tea had been brought and poured did conversation begin again. Mabel asked about the trip to America, and Zoe was able to make her smile with a story about Uncle Sebastian and a high tea debacle. Once enough small talk had taken place to meet the expected quota, Mabel turned the conversation back to the only topic that really mattered.

"I do miss Margot." Sadness still tinged her voice, but Mabel was able to speak calmly this time. "We had our spats, as sisters do, but she was truly my best friend. I don't remember a time when she was not a part of my every day . . . until now of course." She swallowed hard, glancing at Zoe before continuing. "I remember that night at the ball, when I was complaining to you about her. It is one of those conversations a person plays over and over in their head, wishing each time they had the sense to say things differently. But each time I go over it, it all stays the same. I wish I had been kinder, less concerned with self. I just had no idea . . . if wishes were horses—"

"We could all ride to the moon," Zoe finished. "We all say things we regret, Mabel. But you had no idea of Margot's fate at the time, and it was the ball of the season. Of course you were anxious. You meant no malice by it."

Mabel shook her head sadly. "That all feels so petty and unimportant now. Dressing to the nines and parading before the sons and mothers of society like so many well-bred fillies . . . it all feels so distant, like that was another life. I no longer have any use for the rules of society that bind our lives as women. It all just seems so ridiculous now."

Zoe tried and failed to hide her surprise. She'd long ago realized she could not abide by the smothering sanctions of British society. Being French gave her some leeway as far as exceptions went. But she rarely met other ladies whose feelings mirrored her own. "Be careful, Mabel. The hawks of society may somehow hear and swoop down upon you, as if the soul of civilization is at stake. A woman who dares contradict the status quo. How scandalous!"

Mabel managed a faint smile. "You jest, but my parents act as if that is actually true. They demand I return to my life after this year of mourning as if nothing has happened, especially now that the season is once again upon us. My own feelings and opinions are disregarded as nothing more than frivolous womanly hysterics."

"That is most unfair, and I am sorry. I know you will heal in time, but the loss will always be a part of you. To think otherwise is ignorant." Zoe said the words with sincerity, thinking of her own loss.

The tears returned to Mabel's eyes, but she spoke with certainty. "What makes the cut run deeper is knowing there has been no true justice for Margot. I know the man convicted did not harm her, but no one will listen to me!"

That was even more surprising. Zoe did know some details of the case—how could she not, when it was so publicized and her own stepfather was the barrister who represented the accused. Everything had been well on its way to a resolution before she left for America. Hugh had also been convinced of the man's innocence and had pled his case masterfully. But some would only see certain facts and ignore the rest.

The man on trial, Thomas Chedrose, had seduced Margot.

That was undoubtedly true. They had met secretly on more than one occasion. Margot's father had discovered the seduction and instructed his daughter to break off the relationship. To seal his fate, Chedrose had no one to vouch for his whereabouts at the time Margot was slain. In the eye of the public, he was a monster who preyed upon a young, innocent society beauty, taking her virtue and then her life. He was convicted long before the trial.

It was easy to place all the blame at his feet, and Zoe had assumed the family would be grateful to do just that. If there was any silver lining to Chedrose's sham of a trial, at least it brought about a quick conclusion to the public firestorm. The family could move on.

Not everyone in the family, thought Zoe. Mabel was not satisfied. *How intriguing.* "Why are you convinced of his innocence? Did you know Thomas Chedrose?"

"Yes." Mabel shifted in her seat, but met Zoe's eyes squarely. "I know the press painted him as a monster, but he wasn't. He was common, and I didn't approve, of course, but if you'd ever met the man you'd know he's harmless. Besides, he was absolutely besotted by Margot. He wasn't capable of butchering a chicken, much less harming her."

This was an unexpected perspective, and Zoe couldn't just take her at her word. "I have found that we often don't know what people are capable of, Mabel, even people we know well. How can you be so certain of a man you only knew for a short time?"

Mabel crossed her arms and spoke bitterly. "You sound like my mother, and my father, the counsel that prosecuted the case, and every other person I have tried to talk to about this." Her words were clipped by barely suppressed frustration. "Every single person has disregarded my thoughts, my knowledge, my opinion—it is beyond infuriating! I was not even allowed to send a letter telling your stepfather what I knew."

Zoe was struck by the intensity in Mabel's words and in her gaze. She was not known as a great beauty—that had been left to

Margot, with her silky auburn hair and sparkling green eyes. But Mabel's eyes were fine as well, glinting behind the grief with a determination Zoe hadn't seen before.

"You are right." She reached over to lightly touch Mabel's arm. "I am in the wrong for trivializing your opinion. I'm sorry, it wasn't my intent. Please, tell me why you feel so strongly this man did not harm your sister."

The genuine interest seemed to catch Mabel off guard. Perhaps it sounded a great deal like respect, which she may not have been used to receiving. But this was obviously the moment she'd been waiting for. She hesitated only briefly before diving into her story. For over an hour, as the tea grew cold and was replenished, as she paced and sat and then paced again, the words poured out.

The picture Mabel painted of the man convicted of killing Margot was very different from the one portrayed in the papers. She explained how Margot managed to sneak out and meet Thomas, and her own reluctant role in covering for her sister. In her eyes there was no motive for Thomas Chedrose to kill her because Margot had no intention of ending the relationship. She said that when their father found out, he had been furious, but Margot was not willing to back down. She left that night in a fury, but still determined to stand by Thomas.

Zoe said little in return. She poured more tea and handed Mabel tiny sandwiches. She made sounds of understanding when appropriate and asked for clarification when needed. But mostly she let just the words pour from Mabel, watching as the young woman gained strength from the simple luxury of being heard.

When the words finally slowed, Zoe could see the weariness in the circles under Mabel's eyes. It was a taxing thing, bringing all that grief back up into the light. But she now exhibited a lightness that hadn't been there before, as if the sharing of the burden had lessened it as well. Zoe hoped it was enough for the woman to find some peace.

Any hopes along those lines were dashed by Mabel's next

words. "So will you help me find the real murderer of my sister? Will you help bring justice for Margot?"

"Justice? Me?" Zoe cleared her throat, lowered her pitch. "Mabel, a man is already convicted, whether right or wrong. I'm not sure what else can be done at this point."

Mabel's eyes narrowed. "Don't play the fool, Zoe. I was at the ball that night. There may not have been a trial or a conviction, but I know you found justice for your maid."

Zoe hesitated.

Mabel's statement contained a great deal of truth, but she certainly hadn't worked alone. Back then she'd had Quinton to help. Now things were very different between them.

Mabel was still speaking. "And you managed to go beyond the bounds of who women like us are expected to associate with. As the novels would say, you have connections that I simply don't."

Color warmed Zoe's cheeks. "You greatly overestimate my connections, Mabel. I hired an agent, that is true. But Lucy was killed only days before. It's been close to a year in your sister's case. If there were any pieces of the puzzle that could've fit together, you must see that by now they're likely gone."

"The puzzle pieces may be scattered, Zoe, but I do not believe they are gone—I can't believe that." Mabel sat on the couch next to her, taking Zoe's hands in her own. "I am utterly convinced Thomas Chedrose is innocent. His imprisonment is its own miscarriage of justice, but my motives are more selfish than that. If he didn't do it, that means the person who took my sister's life—my beautiful, stubborn sister—is still out there. They are walking free, thinking that they've gotten away with it. And that eats away at my soul, taking a little bit more every day. I fear that if I continue on like this, I'll simply waste away into nothing, but I don't know any other way to be. So I am asking you, please, will you help me?"

Zoe couldn't deny she was touched by the feelings behind the impassioned speech, as well as flattered by the confidence in her abilities. Though she thought there was little chance of success, she didn't have it in her to crush Mabel—not in that moment, when it meant so much to her. She wondered briefly if anyone had told Mabel the connection between her sister's murder and that of Quinton's mother. But if Quinton himself had been unable to find additional evidence in all this time . . .

"I cannot promise results, Mabel. Not even close." Zoe considered her words carefully; she didn't want to get Mabel's hopes higher than they already were. "You may have to accept that in some instances in life, there simply is no justice."

"But you will try?"

Zoe squared her shoulders, taking a deep breath. "Indeed. I will try."

Chapter Four

From the large picture window of her sitting room, Zoe's mother Simone had a perfect view of Ezra and Gwen in the garden. They embraced briefly, then stepped back and locked eyes. Their communication was fascinating to behold. They seemed to be connected on a level unknown to the rest of humanity. She watched their hands fly, hardly pausing for the other to have a chance with the gestures they understood to be words.

Simone thought of the few things Gwen had confided about their life on the streets. She had been very young when their parents passed. What details Gwen knew of her family were hazy at best, but she remembered feeling loved. One thing she knew was that Ezra was not born deaf but became terribly ill as a toddler. Their mother told them he was hot to the touch and delirious. It was expected he would die. But though his little body persevered, his hearing was lost. As he grew older, he learned to communicate with gestures instead of the spoken word, and in time the family developed their own language of sorts. Simone suspected that since Ezra was old enough to have learned some English before his world went quiet, that made it easier for him to understand people's meaning when he watched their faces as they spoke.

Gwen, born a year after Ezra lost his hearing, never knew him any other way. She easily understood his hand gestures, and in time the two of them could communicate on a deeper level. She became his voice, and as he grew tall, he remained her protector.

When Gwen was six and Ezra ten, another tragedy struck the family. Earning a wage as a dock worker, their father was killed. A year or two later their mother died from cholera, leaving the children destitute and without a home. But not alone. They had each other. Gwen became Ezra's ears and Ezra was his sister's protector.

Somehow they kept themselves balanced on the razor's edge that so many of the poor in London rode. They were forever hungry, but they had not starved. They were often cold, but they had not frozen.

While Simone had been reminiscing, the children had begun to head inside. She suspected they were headed down to the kitchen to look for fresh ginger biscuits. Simone employed a French cook, a master at her skill with a reputation for a quick temper. But for all her bluster, the cook had a soft spot for the orphans. Their quest would likely not be in vain.

Not long after, Simone heard a noise from behind. She turned to see a large dog regarding her, his massive head cocked to one side. His head was square and his eyes bulged, but Simone no longer found him repulsive—or at least not as repulsive. As she met those eyes, he sat down and wagged his tail.

"*Et voilà.* And what brings you to my rooms, Brutus?" The question was asked without malice. The beast immediately rose and came to sit in front of her, cocking his head again. She found herself reaching out to pet his massive head. How things had changed.

Brutus had not been a welcome addition last year when Zoe showed up with him. Her eldest daughter was mute about exactly how she had acquired a huge fighting dog, and for once Simone was actually grateful for the lack of information. But after considerable loud discussion, much of it heated and in French, it was agreed that Brutus could stay. The situation had evolved as a matter of practicality. The dog had clearly needed a keeper—someone to take him outside, to keep him clean and free of fleas and other pests, as well as to feed and water him.

Which brought them young Gwen. Though she'd been uncertain at the time, Simone was grateful for Quinton Huxley and his insight in sending them Gwen, ensuring they had a hard worker and Gwen had food and shelter. It was a further kindness that he then took Ezra under his own wing.

The clatter on the stairs signaled the imminent arrival of the children as they raced up, intent on finding Brutus and likely not expecting to find Simone. They both skidded to a stop when they saw her.

As they exchanged nervous glances, she smiled to reassure them. "Brutus has escaped your view, Gwen?"

Gwen's cheeks flushed with color, but she still faced Ezra as she spoke. Ensuring his inclusion was second nature to her. "I was just so pleased to see Ezra, and I took my eyes off him for only a heartbeat, Lady Dovefield." Biscuit crumbs fanned out as Gwen spoke, but even Simone had to admit Madame Favreau did make delicious biscuits.

Simone turned to Ezra, making sure to speak clearly. Even though he could not hear her, Gwen had told them that Ezra could better make out their meaning if he could see their mouths move as they spoke distinctly.

"I suspect you are quite happy to have your sister home, Ezra. We are also happy to have her back."

As Ezra's hands flew this way and that, Gwen laughed. "He said you're probably just happy to see the dog."

Simone laughed as well. No one was more surprised than she at her genuine pleasure at having the dog back in their household. Though he still ranked below actual humans in her mind. "Brutus does seem to listen better since the trip, Gwen."

Gwen nodded with enthusiasm. "Mr. Sebastian liked Brutus as Brutus would cause quite a stir among the travelers. Mr. Sebastian was always game for a bit of fun. Most were pretty wary of 'im, but on the way there an older gent took a real interest. He and Mr. Sebastian trained Brutus every day, as time was on our hands. Then they trained me, and now Brutus and I understand each other pretty well." She looked at Brutus fondly. "I ain't never had a dog before, or any pet that needed feedin'." Simone took mental note of her grammatical errors as Gwen went on. "Every now and again a street cat would hang around us. They liked to curl up and share our blanket, and they was welcome. We both got warm. Ezra is still partial to cats."

"They were welcome," Simone corrected her.

"They were welcome." Gwen repeated the words slowly, clearly taking the instruction seriously. "I been telling Ezra I been learnin' my letters, and nowadays I can read 'cept when I can't."

It took all her self-control not to correct every speech *faux pas*, but Simone didn't want to discourage the young girl. "It is lovely you are all home. When Zoe returns from her call on Lady Anderson, perhaps a walk in Hyde Park would suit you. For now, why don't you leave Brutus with me and do as you please with your brother while he's here."

They were no fools and jumped at the opportunity for some free time. As she watched them leave, Simone couldn't help but note how each child had grown. Ezra had filled out, no longer the rail thin boy with sunken eyes she'd first met. But the more obvious change was in Gwen. Seven months made a great deal of difference in a girl her age. The child was fading away, slowly being replaced by the young woman she would one day become. Her hazel eyes held a depth of understanding that hadn't been there before, and her long straight hair had lightened to a beautiful honey brown which framed her delicate facial features. Her slight body was also beginning to show the signs of womanly curves to come. Whether it was a sign of God's dark sense of humor or just a cruel twist of nature, it had always seemed particularly unfair to Simone that girls began to look like women when they were still children.

Brutus followed her to the window to watch the pair walk back to the garden. They evidently had exited through the kitchen, the fresh biscuits in each hand betraying them. As Ezra said something with his hands, Gwen threw back her head and laughed. It was a pure sound—the sound of innocence and youth. Good for them. For a moment, let them be children. Change would come soon enough.

Chapter Five

The second knock of the day came to his door when Quinton was well into his bottle of whiskey. Early evening had fallen by then, past the point of the day any potential clients would come around. That meant it had to be social.

He groaned, tempted to simply do nothing and let whoever it was go away. Then the knock came again, this time louder and more persistent.

"Come in then!" he finally growled.

Quinton expected one of his friends—perhaps John Smith the Bow Street Officer or Charlie Modi, a fixture of the criminal underworld, both of whom were his companions from childhood. That would be fitting, on the heels of Rory's visit. But they were not who walked through the doorway.

Zoe Demas stood there, her dark curls spilling down her back as she removed her bonnet. She looked much the same as he'd remembered—on the taller side for a woman, with a slender build and pleasantly arranged features. Her blue eyes took up a great deal of space on her face, and on another woman it might've lent to an innocent appearance, but there was too much intensity behind them to give that impression. Those piercing blue eyes haunted him the most—like a storm over the ocean, both beautiful and terrifying at the same time.

His mother had taken him on a trip by sea when he was a boy. They had sailed to an island and stayed by the shore, splashing in the waves and lying on the sand for days before the sail home. That was the only time he had ever left London, and the memory of the sea waves perfectly in harmony with his mother's laughter was etched in his mind. Each afternoon a storm would blow in, and they would race to shelter as the sea changed color.

Zoe's eyes always reminded him of the ocean, changing with her mood. Those memorable eyes took in his surroundings with a critical gaze; Quinton had never been so grateful to have taken the advice of another person. Thanks to Ezra's hurtful but accurate comment earlier in the day, he had made use of the bathing basin on his bureau and changed his shirt.

Storm abated. For now.

Finally her gaze came to rest on him. "Well, are you going to pour me one of those or not?"

He didn't say anything; even if he'd wanted to, the words seemed stuck in his throat. Instead Quinton gestured for her to take the seat across from him, pouring her a healthy drought.

They sat there in silence for a minute. A significant amount of time had passed since they last spoke, and much had happened, both before and after. It wasn't that there was nothing to say— trying to figure out where to start was where the trouble came in.

"Are you allowed to be here without a chaperon?" he said finally. It wasn't the cleverest thing, but at least it broke the stalemate.

She answered easily, unfazed by the question. "Technically it's frowned upon. But Mary is visiting her family and I didn't want to waste time waiting on propriety. I think the odds of being seen in this part of town are low enough to risk it, just this once."

"Mm." Quinton cleared his throat. "How was the colony?"

"They prefer to call it America." She took a sip. "And it was fine. I enjoyed my time."

For some reason that rankled him. "Good. Good. I'm glad you enjoyed yourself."

Zoe rolled her eyes. "Don't start. Should I not have had an enjoyable time? Would you prefer I was as miserable as you were?"

"Of course not," he snapped. "Not everyone has the luxury of a holiday on a different continent every time things become uncomfortable, though. Some of us just have to deal with our lives as they are."

"You are being completely unreasonable."

He was aware. "What of it?"

She opened her mouth, then abruptly snapped it shut. Taking a deep breath, Zoe continued. "I didn't come here to fight."

"Then why did you come?"

"To offer you a job."

That came as a surprise. "What job? Don't tell me another one of your servants has mysteriously perished."

Zoe downed the rest of her whiskey in one swallow. "This was a mistake. I'll return when you are less drunk."

"Wait." Quinton sighed. "What job?"

Those memorable blue eyes glared at him. "It happens to be in regard to the girl who died last year. Margot Anderson. Her sister believes the man convicted was innocent. She wants someone to look into it."

Quinton snorted. "Well I could've told you that. That man is just a patsy—a convenient way to wrap it all up with a bow. Of course he didn't kill her."

Zoe took a moment to respond. It seemed she wasn't expecting him to agree with her so easily. "You seem very sure of yourself."

"Well what do you think I've been doing while you were enjoying yourself in America? Nothing?"

"Well it wouldn't have surprised me!" Zoe stood, throwing her hands up. "Look, do you want the job or not?"

"No, I do not." He tried not to think about the bare cupboards not two meters away.

Her jaw dropped in shock. "You can't be serious."

"I'm very serious. I don't have time for this nonsense."

"Oh, because you have soooo many jobs right now." Zoe gestured toward the door. "I did see the queue when I walked in. Should I have them form two lines, or single file?"

Quinton slammed his glass down, the cool liquid sloshing over the edge and splattering onto his hand. Who did this woman think she was? To come here, after all these months, and treat him like this . . .

He spoke through gritted teeth far more calmly than he felt. "I can't accept this job because I've already done all there is to do. I have probed every angle, interviewed every witness, and investigated any lead I could find. I have expended as much time, energy, and resources as I can, and I've come up with absolutely nothing." Quinton took a deep, shuddering breath. "Tell your friend there's nothing that can be done for her sister that hasn't already been done. Now please . . . leave."

Zoe stood there for another moment, her angry blue eyes stirring emotions he did not want to consider, clearly debating the value of continuing the conversation. Finally she left, slamming the door behind her, and Quinton was once again alone with his whiskey and his thoughts.

Chapter Six

When the shirred eggs and coffee were served the next morning, Zoe was still fuming. A part of her had been holding out hope that the passage of time and separation of space would be enough to bring Quinton peace. She wanted "her" Quinton back.

If wishes were horses . . . Quinton was still just as selfish and inconsiderate as he had been when she left. Why she ever allowed herself to fantasize about a world where there was something more between them was beyond her now. His place was an absolute sty, and he looked like he lived in one. To top it off, the whole place smelled like p—

"Rough night, love?" Hugh's amused voice interrupted Zoe's mental evisceration of Quinton Huxley, and she looked up to see he had already helped himself to coffee and was sitting across from her.

"Let's just say yesterday lay bare some lingering wounds," she said with a rueful smile.

"You spoke with Huxley?"

Seeing no reason to deny it, Zoe nodded. "I did. It did not go well."

After taking a long swallow of his black coffee, Hugh spoke quietly. "After you left, Huxley spent quite a lot of time here."

That was a surprise. Zoe resisted the urge to interject, instead allowing her stepfather to speak his mind.

"As you know, the discovery of Miss Anderson's body brought back many unpleasant memories for Quinton. I'm not sure how much he shared with you. I assume you're aware of the connection to his own mother's murder."

She was aware. Quinton's mother had died when he was eleven—strangled to death by a madman. The case was never solved. But he remembered the unique cloth wrapped around her neck—the same cloth which was found wrapped around Margot Anderson's neck. He had never expected to find such a connection, and she could sympathize with his desire for the justice he'd long since given up on. But the line between desire and obsession was a thin one.

Hugh narrowed his eyes at her ever so slightly, then continued. "You can understand his interest in the case. He would come over to discuss the details, particularly in relation to Mr. Chedrose after he was arrested. He shared what was relevant about his mother's death. For the most part we stuck to professional topics, but I would be lying if I said our conversation never strayed into more personal territory. On more than one occasion we stayed up talking into the wee hours of the morning. Both of us felt strongly that Chedrose was innocent, and I still believe this to be true. I am sure he does as well." Hugh rubbed his chin thoughtfully. "But for Magistrate Holdsworth, the man would have hung. He made sure the sentence was confinement, not death. I'm still not sure how he did it."

Hugh rose to help himself to a plate from the sidebar, heaping grilled mushrooms and tomatoes on it, speaking as he went. "But as it became obvious that Chedrose would be blamed, Huxley grew increasingly despondent. The clues he hoped would be uncovered to definitively link this death with his mother's were elusive. It became obvious that although there were striking similarities, the powers that be were more interested in a tidy resolution than looking into the death of an actress from eighteen years ago. The magistrate did his best, even pointing to other cases over the years that fit the pattern. But no one wanted to hear it. Once Chedrose was convicted, that was that. When that last bit of hope that justice would be done for his mother was extinguished, it was as if Huxley's soul was extinguished with it. After that, he stopped coming by. When I've made inquiries with John about him, he does his best to be discreet, but I get the impression Huxley is not doing well."

Bow Street Officer John Smith was a long-standing professional acquaintance of her stepfather's and was boyhood friends with Quinton. In fact, John was the one who initially introduced her to the infuriating agent. As she pictured the disgusting state of Quinton's abode at her last visit, Zoe nodded grimly. "I can attest to that. It seems he spends much of his time foxed. Mary told me John is quite perturbed with his behavior, though his loyalty of course runs deep." Zoe paused, considering Hugh carefully. "However, there is more when it comes to your client. I paid that call on Mabel, and it seems she also believes Thomas Chedrose to be innocent. She's asked for my help in finding the real killer."

"Ah." Hugh's reaction was less extreme than she'd expected. "So that is why she asked you to call on her. Your mother will lose her mind if she finds you've gained a reputation for solving murders."

Zoe laughed. "I doubt it is the reputation she was hoping I would gain at this season of my life. But this is different than last time. Mabel is grasping at straws. She's not unlike Quinton, desperately hoping some sort of justice, any kind of justice, will bring her peace."

"Dare I hope you made it clear under no circumstances would you be a part of another murder investigation?" Hugh cocked his head as he eyed Zoe.

She glanced away. "Well, I did make it clear that there's likely nothing to be done at this point. It has been nearly a year. But she's determined, so I offered to take it to Quinton. As I said, that conversation did not go well." Zoe sighed. "On a positive note for you and Maman, there is little open for me to do without his help. I am currently dreading telling Mabel. She had such . . . hope. I think this will crush her."

Hugh ate in silence, his face thoughtful. Zoe sipped her coffee and remained thoughtful as well. She rose to gather the fresh pot of coffee, refilling Hugh's cup and then her own.

As she was adding the milk, he spoke. "I cannot pretend I'm not relieved that another murder is not at your doorstep. But I do understand finding it difficult to crush hope. I saw it with Huxley. Hope gave him strength—an anchor—and without it he is adrift. But life has a funny way of surprising us. For now, love, I am simply happy to have you home. I have missed our chats over morning coffee."

A sentiment she shared. Zoe gave Hugh a genuine smile, thinking not for the first time how truly blessed she was. As for Mabel, perhaps she could not keep the bad news from breaking her heart, but she could choose to avoid doing so today.

Chapter Seven

Her half siblings' faces brightened as they entered Hyde Park. Zoe's younger sister ran ahead, accompanied by Gwen and Brutus. The two girls seemed to have picked up where they left off. Phoebe was still at the tender age when social status was a distant concept and the lines between classes could be blurred. Zoe hoped she enjoyed it while she could.

In most ways Phoebe seemed the same—a happy young girl with little to worry about. She tossed leaves from the ground in the air over Brutus and laughed cheerfully as he shook his massive head to dispel them. She had her father's even temperament and her mother's blue eyes, and though she was eleven, she showed no signs yet of blossoming.

Her half brother Walter, however, had changed a great deal in the span of a year. He had always been a serious child, prone to worry, a trait Zoe suspected he got from their mother. But now he held the air of someone on the cusp of adulthood. The boy was solemn as he slowed to allow more distance to grow between the two of them and the girls.

He'd certainly grown physically—he wasn't quite as tall as Zoe, but nearly so. Though at fourteen he still lacked the broad shoulders he might someday inherit from his father. He already had Hugh's strong chin and thoughtful green eyes. Those eyes met Zoe's. "I don't want you to go away again, like you did to the colonies." She noted he already had a nobleman's air of stating what he wished as if he were entitled to it, believing it would happen simply because he wished it to be so. "*Maman* missed you."

That brought a smile to Zoe's lips. Though Walter had never left British soil and he was very much his father's son, he still called their mother the same thing Zoe did. His accent on the single word was impeccable.

It was no surprise, of course. Their mother had spoken to both the younger children in French since their birth. If her children were nothing else, they would be fluent in her native tongue. It was important to Simone that they succeed in British high society but still remember where they came from. They might have blue English blood in their veins, but their minds would work in French. If Simone had her way, Gwen would soon be multilingual too.

"*Je t'ai manqué, petit frère?*"

Walter cocked his head, his brow furrowed as he thought about the question.

"We all missed you, Z," he finally said diplomatically, carefully avoiding singling himself out. "But Maman missed you the most. Why did you leave so suddenly?"

He was the only one who called her Z. When he was first learning to talk it was as close as he could get to her name, and at times he still fell into old habits.

Zoe glanced at her brother, considering how to answer. He wasn't a small child anymore, and he was reaching a point in his life when he would become more of a peer to her than just a younger sibling. But as she continued strolling, she realized it wasn't his age that made her hesitate. It was she herself who was finding it difficult to put into words why she had needed to go.

The silence was too much for Walter, who despite his new-found height and growing maturity, didn't quite have an adult's patience for slow conversation yet. "Was it about the murdered girl? The Anderson girl?"

"That was a terrible thing, Walter." Zoe paused, thinking back to the previous year. "It was about that, but it's complicated. Do you remember my maid, Lucy?"

"I do, but not very much. She was very quiet and didn't say much."

The truth of Walter's words hung heavy on Zoe's heart. Lucy had kept everyone at arm's length, not just her younger siblings.

"I found out after she was killed that even though we spoke every day, I never cared to get to know her beyond what her job was to me. I didn't mean to be, but I was very selfish. So when she died, I felt awful. I wanted to make sure whoever killed her found justice because I felt I owed her that much."

"Is that why you left?" Walter's young eyes were thoughtful as he gazed at her. "You still felt bad about Lucy?"

"No. I felt good about Lucy, like I did right by her. I found a world where I thought I fit in, with people who liked me for who I am. But what I did . . . changed me."

He frowned. "Did you not fit in our world anymore?"

Zoe thought carefully before replying. "This world was built for you, Walter, and people like you. So it suits you fine. But for people like me, who are different . . . it's not designed to accommodate differences. So it doesn't suit me so well, and everything that happened just made the divide more obvious."

He was silent as he contemplated this. Zoe continued, "Regardless, then Margot was killed. And there was a . . . personal connection to one of my new friends. They fell into a deep hole of their own making, and at the time, no one could help them out. Certainly not me. They sank deeper and deeper and until they disappeared. It was very painful to watch and know there was nothing I could do to stop it. I suppose I thought our friendship was . . . special. But it wasn't what I thought. And then without them, I suddenly felt like I didn't fit in again. And it hurt a lot more because I knew what it felt like now to belong." Zoe paused for breath. "That's why I went away. Uncle Sebastian made me the offer, and the timing seemed right."

Walter pondered this quietly as they turned down Serpentine Road. Phoebe ran back to them excited, holding a lovely red leaf, fallen perhaps from a maple tree. She handed it to Zoe like a flower before heading back to find other treasures.

Walter waited until she was out of earshot to speak again. "What made you think your friendship was special?"

She glanced at him sharply. "Why do you ask that?"

"I guess I'm just curious." As he spoke, he glanced up at the girls before returning his focus back to the ground.

"Do you have a special friend, Walter?"

"No." His cheeks flushed red. "No, I don't."

Zoe looked at the two girls playing. Where Phoebe hadn't changed much, perhaps she hadn't noticed that Gwen had. She had been with her in America, so she hadn't noticed the subtle changes, but seeing her through fresh eyes . . . the girl had always been a pretty child, with a quick wit and sharp mind, and a hard life had given her an air of maturity for her age. But now her childlike body was beginning to take on the figure of a woman and her face was losing the baby fat of youth. Zoe didn't know why she was so surprised that Walter should notice.

She chose her next words carefully. "Friendships are important, Walter. Sometimes those friendships grow into something more. But people in our position have to be very careful—especially you, because you are a man. So you can make friends and leave friends, without many consequences for you. But sometimes the consequences for your friends are very harsh. So if you really care about them, then you need to be careful not to put them in a position where they'll get hurt." Zoe scrutinized him. "Do you understand?"

"Yes." His face was still red. "But I wouldn't leave my friend—my friends—behind."

"You say that now." Zoe sighed, placing a gentle hand on her brother's shoulder. "But despite your newfound height, you are still a boy, Walter. A great deal of freedom comes with being young. But soon you'll be considered a man, and when that happens, there will be a lot more expectations placed on the kinds of friends you have. It's better to accept that now."

Walter nodded, his eyes still pointed down. "I understand."

As she watched him walk off to join the girls, Zoe was not oblivious to the irony of her words. *Take my advice*, she thought. *I'm certainly not using it.*

Chapter Eight

The headache making its way from behind his eyes to the front of his head was getting steadily worse. John Smith rubbed his temples, attempting to ward it off. But there was no getting around the reality that this was very bad news, even for an experienced Bow Street Officer.

He stepped around the body of the woman lying in the dressmaker's shop, resisting his natural instinct to avert his eyes. The shop would soon teem with people—the coroner, other officers, the magistrate, and soon enough the press. It wouldn't take long for them to be followed by the morbidly curious masses, professing shock and sorrow but really only interested in taking their chance to gape at a dead woman.

He would not have a second chance to investigate the unaltered scene. John needed to observe everything he could while he still had the opportunity.

Kneeling next to the woman, a modiste by the name of Clarissa Amato, he imagined she had been an attractive woman in life. Her olive skin was now pale with the sheen of death, and her thick black hair was messy and dull, half covering her face. John stopped himself from brushing it away—she was beyond caring, and he needed to be professional.

He looked closely at the cloth that had been used to strangle her. It was wrapped tightly around her throat, tied off in an elaborate knot. It lay neatly and unwrinkled, as if arranged to show off the unique pattern embroidered on its surface. The fabric was dyed scarlet, with tiny elephants in shimmering gold thread forming lines across it. If one looked closely, one could see they were holding each other's tails with their trunks, showing the skill put into the detail work. It was by no means common, but John knew where the exact same type of cloth had been found before.

Around Margot Anderson's neck just last year.

Going back eighteen years, on Annie Huxley's neck.

John had never set eyes on Miss Anderson's body. She was discovered in an alley in the posh part of town by a night watchman. Since she was the daughter of a nobleman, the magistrate took a more than ordinary interest in the investigation, personally overseeing most aspects. But the details kept discreet during the investigation came out at the trial.

It was hard not to think back on the story Quinton had told him and Charlie many years past, when the three of them were just urchins struggling to survive each day to the next. He'd told them his mother was an actress who made extra scratch by sewing for the theater as well—curtains and costumes and the like. The night Annie Huxley died, she'd sent him away to play with the other actresses' children, telling him she had a friend coming over. When Quinton returned late in the night, he was afraid she would be upset he'd stayed out so long. His fears were unfounded, as Annie would never scold her son about anything ever again. He found her corpse in her bed, strangled by a piece of scarlet cloth decorated with gold elephants. Officers at the time had assumed it was from a costume she'd been working on for the theater. Quinton didn't remember very much after that moment, only his desperation in trying to remove the cloth from around her neck, but he couldn't make his fingers undo the elaborate knots.

The death of his mother forced Quinton out onto the streets, which is when John and Charlie came into his life. Charlie's mother was the only parent still living then amongst the three, and she had a soft spot for her son's friends, allowing them to occasionally sleep by the warmth of the hearth. More times than he cared to admit, John had heard young Quinton sobbing softly as he slept, begging his mother to wake up.

No one was ever arrested or tried in Annie Huxley's case. John suspected those in charge of her investigation had likely not put too much effort into the death of an actress, chalking it up to a consequence of the promiscuous lifestyle women in her line of work were known for.

The magistrate who took over three years afterwards was different. Mr. Ackerly Holdsworth was a man of honor, and he cared about each victim, regardless of status. He was the one who made the connection with the cloth and the death of another woman— then another.

Despite his suspicions, Holdsworth couldn't get anyone above him to acknowledge the terrible possibility. The killings were spaced out over the span of years, and the victims were women of a class which few cared about. It didn't help that the idea of a man taking lives at random, simply because he enjoyed it . . . that was too much for most to fathom. Far easier to file the pieces of cloth and similarities in manner of death under the category of strange coincidences and move on. His superiors had ordered him to keep his mouth shut and that was that.

Then Margot Anderson was killed, and suddenly everyone was paying attention. John hadn't even been aware of the possible connection to Annie Huxley and these other women until then, only that Holdsworth had a private theory about someone killing women and wanted the runners to keep an eye out for specific kinds of killings.

When poor Miss Anderson was found, Holdsworth thought he would finally be able to get people on board with his theory. He thought justice would finally be done, or at least that it would be acknowledged that justice was needed for these women. John respected him for that. But it wasn't to be. Instead, Thomas Chedrose was scooped up almost immediately and the murder of Margot pinned on him. The others weren't addressed, as if they didn't exist.

Holdsworth knew Chedrose didn't do it. If Margot was killed by the same man as the others, then he was far too young to be responsible. The man he was looking for would be at least forty years old, if not older. Chedrose wasn't a day over twenty.

When he was ignored once again, even with the irrefutable proof of the death of someone of Miss Anderson's status, it crushed the magistrate. John couldn't blame him. If only someone above Holdsworth has listened, maybe this latest tragedy involving Madame Amato could've been avoided.

Taking out his leather notebook, John made note of the fabric on the body, along with the blueish tint of her lips and the blood in her unfocused eyes. He noted the position of the body and looked for signs of a struggle in the shop. Most things seemed to be well ordered, indicating she either knew her attacker and hadn't feared him or that he was fast enough and strong enough to subdue her without much of a fight. The only thing out of place was a small round piece of metal with a break in the middle on the floor by the body. It was tiny, and could've just been missed when the shop was last swept. John still noted it just in case.

Her appointment book lay on the desk, and John took a moment to glance through it before slipping it into his satchel to review more thoroughly later. Then he heard the unmistakable sound of a carriage pulling up, followed by the footsteps of a person approaching the shop. He recognized the stride immediately, and John greeted the magistrate as he entered.

Ackerly Holdsworth was a short and stout man, running to fat in his middle age, with thinning gray hair brushed back in a semifashionable manner. His clothes were of moderate quality, clean and pressed. His wife had died some years ago, and he tended to his own needs, employing a cook and housekeeper but little else. He was an unassuming man, easy to underestimate, but that was a mistake. His brain was like a well-oiled machine, and John knew him to be a clever man who saw things others missed. He might have been discouraged that his theory was still ignored after the events of last year, but this would reinvigorate his determination.

He stopped inside the doorway, staring silently at the body. After a few moments he gave a long sigh. "I hate being right at times, Smith"

"Yes sir." It was the only proper response, but John knew full well Holdsworth liked nothing better than to be right. "Unfortunately, right you were."

"Make sure the coroner knows this body needs special attention." He looked at John with steel in his eyes. "God willing, this is his last one. We will catch the madman this time."

Chapter Nine

That infernal woman . . .

The next morning, Quinton was still stewing over his encounter with Zoe. He stalked down the street, hardly noticing the cool breeze.

His journey had no fixed destination when he started—he was just restless and unable to settle his racing thoughts. When he felt this way, he often found himself at Rory's home. His Scottish wisdom and penchant for quoting Shakespeare were usually the right tonic to smooth Quinton's nerves. But perhaps because he had already seen Rory, today his path led him elsewhere. Before he realized what was happening, his feet had carried him to Charlie Modi's door.

He pounded on the door until it jerked open.

"What is wrong with you?" shouted his friend, glaring up at him. "It is far too early for whatever this is!"

Quinton cared little for Charlie's discontentment. He brushed past his friend, the familiar home taking him into its dim, warm embrace. The faint scent of curry and spices lingered in the air, and he found it strangely comforting.

This wasn't the home his friend had grown up in—that hovel had long since crumbled into the ground, the last remnants having been erased by the relentless needs of population and progress. A new tenement stood in its place, with twice as many souls crammed within its walls.

No, this was the home Charlie had purchased in his adulthood as a place for his mother and sister to live safely and comfortably. The brownstone was two stories high and narrow, but spacious enough for the family of three. Its location was still adjacent to Whitechapel, where Charlie conducted his business and his mother carried on her work as a midwife, but in a more respectable neighborhood that he could be proud of situating his family in.

Quinton had been here many times over the span of his adult life, and though it wasn't the home he'd known as a child, he was still drawn to whatever space the Modi family occupied. Katyayini Modi had been the only consistent maternal figure in his life since the age of eleven. Though she had two children of her own to feed, she still managed to find room in her heart and hearth for him, as well as John, when the nights were especially cold. The three boys forged a bond in those formative years that remained strong to this day. For these eighteen years they had stood by each other as each forged their own path to manhood.

That bond was tested at times, such as when one showed up at the crack of dawn without warning or explanation. Quinton trudged up the stairs, with Charlie close behind, his stomps heavy and loud despite his slight stature. What his friend lacked in height, he made up for in tenacity and stubbornness.

When they reached the top of the stairs, Charlie gestured for Quinton to sit before storming into the kitchen. After a great deal of banging, clanging, and swearing, he returned with a pot of coffee, two cups, and a bottle of whiskey.

As Quinton reached for the bottle, Charlie swatted his hand away. "That's for me. You've had enough these past few months that I assume you'll go into your coffin pickled."

Grumbling, Quinton accepted the hot cup of unaltered coffee. The bitter liquid scalded his tongue and throat, but the painful sensation also grounded him in the moment. He sputtered, placing the cup down on the table and wiping with his hand at the wet brown spots on his shirt.

"Well?" said Charlie after he had taken a long swallow from his own cup.

Quinton didn't have a good answer. In truth he didn't have a good reason for rousting his friend at this early hour. He had just been . . . unsettled and still half drunk and in want of company. And there was something bothering him in the back of his mind—something distant and formless which he could almost grasp but not quite. It stayed just out of reach, only serving to further aggravate him.

He wasn't about to tell Charlie that though. "This coffee is too hot, and it tastes terrible. Where's your mother or Savita?"

"Babies are almost as inconsiderate as you. If you must know, they're working for a living. You might have heard of it, once upon a time."

"I have been working," Quinton snapped.

"You were working six months ago. And you haven't taken a paying job in nearly a year." Charlie took another sip, his one good eye appraising Quinton over the rim. "And it shows. You look like a corpse."

"I didn't come here to be insulted and drink poison."

"Well then why did you come?"

"I don't know!" The words came out louder than he intended, and the silence that followed was deafening.

They sat there for a moment, these two men who had grown up closer than brothers, bonded by childhood traumas and experiences. Both would take a knife to the gut for the other, but an unseemly burst of emotion was enough to make them shift in their chairs and avoid each other's eyes.

Quinton finally cleared his throat. "She's back."

"So I've heard." Charlie rolled his eyes. "That woman is a pain in the arse."

"Agreed."

"Yet . . ." He leaned back, his face thoughtful. "This is the first time I've seen the whites of your eyes in the light of day for quite some time. So I'll give her credit for that. Perhaps she serves some purpose after all."

"I don't know about that."

"Uh huh. What did she come to see you about?"

A deep sigh escaped Quinton's lips as he deflated into his chair. "She wants me to look into the dead noble girl. Again."

"What's her interest?"

"Apparently she's friends with the girl's sister and the sister is unconvinced. It's the sister who wants to hire me."

"Hmm. What did you tell the French woman?"

"I told her I had no intention of turning over rocks I've already looked under twenty times. There's nothing left to look into."

Charlie shook his head, rubbing his temples. "You really are a dense man, aren't you?"

"What?"

"Let me spell it out for you. You're a razor's edge from living under a bridge. You haven't had a paying case in months. How long has it been since you've paid rent to your landlord? I don't know what you have on that Lord Coleville, but it must be pretty juicy for him to have put up with you for this long. You are drowning, and John and I have already done everything we can to keep you above water, all while you fight us off at every turn. And here comes a lifeline, literally dropped in your lap, and you toss it aside. Who cares if you've already looked into it? Are you really so proud that you'd rather starve than make some easy money retracing a few steps?"

Quinton crossed his arms. "It's not that simple."

Though he was known for his quick temper, Charlie's voice softened. "Actually, it is. And you know it too; that's why you're here. You need a swift kick in the pants, and you know I'm the one to do it."

Quinton opened his mouth, then shut it. There was little to say in reply. If he was being honest with himself, Charlie wasn't wrong. But he'd spent so long wallowing in this mire, he didn't know how to start to move forward again.

Charlie continued. "I know this one's personal, and that makes it complicated. But you either need to keep searching or let it go. This in-between place you're living in . . . it can't go on. And since you can't seem to let it go, I suggest you get back on the horse and keep searching. Also, the sooner you get paid, the sooner you can pay me back." Charlie's glare reminded Quinton how people quickly learned not to test the man's patience. Though he wasn't cruel, his half-Indian friend's survival strategy rested on grit and a quick temper.

Despite his best efforts, Quinton chuckled. He stood up, walking over to the staircase. The sun had now risen high enough in the sky for the rays of light filtering through the windows to illuminate the way down—it was still dim, but he could see his way a bit better.

Chapter Ten

Zoe watched as the young woman carefully lay her sleeping child in the basket next to her own small bed in a corner of the room she shared with three other beds and three other baskets. The babe stirred, perturbed by this disturbance, but quickly stilled in the comfort of a world familiar to it.

"I don't know where we would be if it weren't for Lady Dovefield," said the young woman in a shy voice. "I didn't have nowhere else to turn."

As she continued to watch the sleeping infant, Zoe smiled. "She is beautiful."

The mother was still a child herself, with big brown eyes and long blonde hair held back in a simple braid. Zoe would not put her past seventeen, with the baby not far from a year.

Simone was reserved by nature, but she positively beamed at the young mother. "Grace has secured a position as a tweeny at the Ashton home. For now she will be allowed to return here each evening, a concession to be sure. As soon as Hope is fully weaned, Grace will split her evenings between here and at the Ashton residence. Hope will then be moved to the adjacent home here where she will be cared for by staff when her mother is at work. We were fortunate to be able to purchase two homes near each other—one for the expectant mothers and one for the young children." Her blue eyes darkened for a moment; Zoe suspected her mother was remembering Lucy.

The young woman had come to work for them as Zoe's lady's maid, but neither Zoe nor Simone had any idea she was desperately trying to support a child, housed at a baby farm. Both regretted the missed opportunity to help a young mother in their very employment. Much was revealed after her death, and they were able to find and provide for young Simon, but it was too late for them to help Lucy.

But it wasn't too late for Grace, and others like her. Simone had been galvanized to open a home for young mothers who had no other support. Some were girls from respectable positions in an equally respectable home who were unable to ward off the advances of the master of the house, then cast out with no references or options when pregnancy was obvious. Others were abandoned by men who offered flattery and promised marriage but had no intention of taking responsibility when a child came along. Then there were the ones like Grace, who suffered the worst kind of betrayal by those who they should be able to trust. In her case it was a friend of her father's who had had his way with her. When she told her father what happened, he believed his friend and not his daughter, turning her out to the streets without a second glance.

It seemed to Zoe that the men of this world had much to answer for.

She followed Simone to the sitting room of the large home, and her mother rang for tea. The girl who appeared was even younger than Grace. She held a tray laden with a simple tea, ginger cookies, fruit, small slices of cheese, and warm rolls. The girl poured tea before bobbing a quick curtsy and scurrying away. Her loose apron could not disguise the bulge in her belly.

The tea Zoe sipped was a fine blend. The spread might be

simple, but quality. The milk was served from a small, slightly chipped pitcher, but it was not watered down. The biscuits were fresh, and the rolls were truly divine. Simone nodded in the direction the girl had disappeared.

"Eleanor is in training to be a house maid of some sort. She is only fourteen, poor lass. By gaining skills now, before the baby is born, it will give her a leg up later, when she is able to seek out positions," said Simone once the girl was out of earshot. "And she will be able to apply with references." She paused. "She has agreed to allow a husband and wife adopt her child when the babe is born. They are a fine couple who live north of London, bakers by trade and not blessed with children of their own. She knows she is simply too young to do right by the child. But it does weigh on her."

"My hearts go out to them all, Maman." Zoe reached for a second roll. "You have worked a miracle here. Are the babies born here as well?"

"Thanks to the Modi women. Your recommendation of them was spot on." Simone took a delicate bite of an apple slice. "So far the births have gone fairly smoothly. The girls have been young and strong and the midwives are exceptionally skilled. The real issue I've run into, as with any charity, is money."

Unlike some families, Hugh and Simone had always spoken openly about financial matters. As a barrister, Hugh made a successful living for his family. He had also made wise investments with his earned money, and over the years his wealth had grown beyond simply comfortable. In most aspects of life, money was not an issue for the Dovefields. But Zoe could imagine the cost of running the two homes was significant.

But her mother was nothing if not resourceful. She would have a plan.

"How do you acquire funds?"

"Hmm. I have not always been the most popular lady of the ton," she admitted with a wry smile.

That was an understatement. Hugh Dovefield was untitled but known throughout the upper class as possessing a small fortune and good bloodline. Those two things had made him one of the more eligible bachelors at the time. When he chose Simone, his marriage to a French woman with a daughter in tow was not originally well received. But Simone was never one to admit defeat.

Zoe brought herself back to the present as she realized her mother was still speaking. "You know how hard I worked for our family to be accepted within society. Time has helped, but more than that, everyone loves a favor. A surprising number of nobles are in need of legal help from time to time, and I've always encouraged Hugh to extend a helping hand where he can. But there's no such thing as free favors, and recently I've begun to cash in on what we're owed. Most are grateful and willing to become benefactors when asked. Others need a little more . . . encouragement."

The thinly veiled reference to blackmail didn't faze Zoe, though she did smile. That was the woman who had raised her—once her mind was made up, nothing would stop her.

Zoe glanced around the room they sat in. It was decorated in a simple but tasteful fashion. The furniture was high quality, though clearly not new, and an eclectic mix to be sure. The walls were freshly painted in a soft green hue, with the curtains a contrasting darker green. Most sitting rooms with a feminine touch were bathed in pink and it was in fashion for all the fabrics to match. The style here was refreshing.

"I like the room," she said simply.

"*Merci*, Zoe. I like it also. The homes were in need of repair, and so we purchased them at a lower price. Several tradesmen actually donated their time—in exchange for some legal assistance, of course—though we paid for the supplies they used to make repairs. We changed the layout to suit our needs, and made the kitchen larger than a home this size would usually house. We often have thirty to forty mouths to feed each day, including the little ones. Each girl takes a turn in the kitchen to learn basic cooking skills. Being a cook's assistant would be an enviable job for our girls."

Simone paused to sample the ginger biscuits and smiled at the flavor. "It's not just working skills they spend their time on, though—each day our girls must find time to work on their letters. Literacy isn't usually required for a maid, but we attempt to broaden their minds as much as possible while they are here. If any come already knowing a trade, we teach them more advanced skills, such as sewing or pastry making. It increases their chance to gain a better position. One such woman currently here will make you a fine lady's maid. She was previously employed as a house maid, but she was in training to become a lady's maid. She is quite talented and personable. I think you will get along well with her."

The reference to "our girls" didn't escape Zoe's notice. Her reserved, bordering on cold, mother had certainly found her way— her purpose.

"How old is her child?" she asked.

"Old enough for her to leave during the day, and she will be allowed flexibility until the little one is fully weaned. It's a good situation as we have Mary who can step in when needed. Her name is Camille. *Un bon match pour tous.*"

It did seem to fit them all well. Zoe nodded with a faint smile. "How do girls find your Haven?"

"It wasn't difficult to put the word out. The first few were girls we personally knew. Word spread from there. We check each girl's story, to ensure there are no friends or family who could support them. Our space is limited, and we have to save our beds for those who truly have no one else." Simone paused, sadness in her eyes. "I only wish Lucy had told us of her predicament. I have certainly grown in my understanding of this situation, but even back then I would like to believe we would have aided her—worked out something."

"I would like to think that also, Maman." Zoe sighed. "I learned a great deal myself after Lucy died."

"We all did," Simone said ruefully. "I give everyone an opportunity to help a girl in their circle before we accept them as residents. If that had been presented to us when Lucy was in need, I cannot believe we would have turned her away. In any case, it's a problem that could find solution through many hands, not just ours."

"You are right, as usual." Zoe set her plate and teacup aside. "I would love to see the other house too, if it is possible, Maman. Let's go see the children."

Simone smiled at her and held out a hand that Zoe took with a smile of her own. Disagreement had always been a natural part of their relationship, but perhaps the time apart had softened mother and daughter. Zoe was surprised how much it genuinely touched her to see her mother so proud of her venture.

Her face glowing with pride, Simone led the way.

Chapter Eleven

Déjà vu. That's what Simone called it, the sensation of living a moment again. That's how Hugh Dovefield felt as he sat in his sitting room, listening to the Bow Street Officer explain the situation. A woman was dead, red cloth with gold elephants found at the scene.

He shook off the disturbing sensation and focused on what John Smith was saying.

"I thought you would like to know right away, Lord Dovefield, seeing as how you defended that Chedrose fellow. I don't know about anyone else, but seeing as how there's no way he coulda killed this woman, I'm thinking it makes it awful unlikely he killed Miss Anderson. You knew that already, but maybe this will help other people see it too."

It was a good idea. Hugh mulled his options over in his head. Perhaps an appeal could be launched . . . It took him an awkwardly long time to realize he hadn't said anything in reply to John's news. He stood up, crossing the distance between them, and grasping the man's hand in his own. "Forgive me, John. This is just so unexpected; I'm having a hard time processing. But you did the right thing to come here. Thank you so much for letting me know. Has Huxley been informed yet?"

John's expressive brown eyes couldn't hide his worry. "Not yet, sir. I am heading there next. He hasn't been particularly . . . himself lately."

"I'm aware. Would it be better if I broke the news to Huxley?"

"Sir, I'd give anything to hand over that job to most anyone else, but Quinton—he's like a brother to me. He's stood next to me when others turned away. Breaking the news is my duty, and I won't step away." He ran a hand through his thick, wiry curls and sighed. "I just hope this don't completely break him."

Before Hugh could reply, Zoe strolled into the room. Her face lit up when she saw John. They had known each other for a number of years, having met when Hugh and John's work overlapped. But last year their relationship had grown to friendship, and now they shared an affection for Huxley . . . though for different reasons.

She had entered with a smile, but when she saw the expressions on the two men's faces, Zoe's smile faded and her steps slowed. She always was an intuitive girl. Hugh watched as the shock in the room reached her and she stopped. "What has happened?" she asked.

It was John who answered. "We found another lady killed, Miss Zoe, like Lady Anderson from last year."

Zoe gasped out loud. "What kind of bedlamite could be loose who would kill women just to kill?"

"Such is the nature of madness," Hugh said gently. "To those of us blessed with sanity, it makes no sense."

The next question Zoe asked was the same question her stepfather had asked minutes before. "Does Quinton know yet?"

"My next stop, Miss Zoe. Good day to you both." John smiled softly, tipping his hat as he left.

Hugh watched him go, and the feeling of the *deja vu* teased his mind again. The feeling made him uncomfortable. He was a man of logic, a lover of the law, an upholder of principle. He shook his head, determined to throw off this odd feeling.

Continuing to muse, he turned and saw Zoe staring absent-mindedly at the door John had left through. She seemed to feel his own gaze upon her, glancing up and meeting his eyes, her own unreadable.

It was then he realized with a start that any order to his life was an illusion, and that as long as this unpredictable woman blessed his life, his world would contain chaos. It wasn't the first time he had come to this realization.

The first time was when he met her mother.

Deja vu.

Chapter Twelve

H e was in the middle of shaving when the banging on the door started again. Quinton jumped, cursing under his breath as the blade nicked his skin. He pressed a cloth against the wound to staunch the bleeding as he stormed over to the door. "Can I not have a moment's peace?" he growled, throwing the door open.

Given all the visitors he'd had in the last day, Quinton supposed it was only fitting to find John standing there, his hand still raised, an expression of surprise on his face. "Did you shave?" he asked with a squint.

"Clearly. Or rather, I was trying to when I was rudely interrupted."

"Huh." John, who was generally quick with a smile, shifted from foot to foot, his eyes downcast, wringing his hat in his hands.

It didn't take a master investigator to deduce something was wrong. "Come in then, if you must." Quinton moved aside to make room for his friend.

John stepped inside. "You cleaned too—I mean, at least partial. Is your housekeeper back?"

"No."

"Hmm. Miss Zoe's returned. You seen her?"

"John, what brings you by?" asked Quinton, avoiding the question. "I'm kind of busy."

John quirked an eyebrow at him. "You ain't been busy in three months, and all of a sudden you're busy today?"

"John. Please. What is it?"

Uneasiness rolled off the usually cheerful man in a wave that was almost palpable. Whatever he had to say was weighing on him. Finally he spoke. "We found another one."

"Another one—" Quinton didn't need to finish the sentence as his brain caught up to the obvious conclusion.

The weight that John had carried in transferred to Quinton all at once. He reached out a grasping hand toward the wall to steady himself as the floor seemed to sway beneath his feet. Slowly he lowered himself into the nearest chair. "Who?"

"A modiste by the name of Clarissa Amato, or at least that's what she was going by. She was found at her shop, over on St. James Street."

"The red cloth?"

"The same. It's the same killer."

Quinton processed the news in silence for a moment. "I knew there would be another one eventually. But with all the press last year, then the arrest and conviction, I just assumed he would lay low. If he had any brains at all, that would've been the smart play. But once the press gets wind of this . . ."

"They're trying to keep it quiet for now, but it can't last long, not anymore. There's too many eyes on this thing now."

As he closed his eyes and leaned forward, resting his head in his hands, Quinton took a deep breath. Much to his surprise, tears welled up behind his eyelids. As shameful as it was, he couldn't help the feeling of relief that washed over him.

"Q, you alright, friend?" John asked the question hesitantly, clearly dreading the answer.

"I thought I missed my chance." Quinton's voice was choked with emotion.

"What's that?"

He sat up, wiping away a stray tear. "I thought I missed my chance."

"Oh." John squinted. "Are you . . . happy?"

A pang of guilt twisted in his gut and Quinton scowled at John. "Of course not. But this changes everything, don't you see? He's back, and this time he's not getting away."

"I see—I mean, I see what you're saying." John's expression was confused. "But I'll be honest, I thought you'd take this a very different way."

Quinton shook his head, springing to his feet. "We don't have time to dawdle. I need to fetch Ezra."

"What do you need Ezra for?"

"To deliver a message. I need him to retrieve my retainer from that infernal woman."

Chapter Thirteen

The streets became increasingly narrow as Mary walked east, the crowded sidewalks making her invisible. *This feels good*, she thought. The sea of London poor reminded her of the firm earth beneath her feet, and the whole place smelled like home.

Maybe Zoe was onto something about the London air. Mary inhaled deeply.

A sudden coughing fit racked her body. Maybe it wasn't so special after all. But for its faults, it was home, and she was eager to see her family.

Her family's small home, jammed in with a hundred others, came into view, and she found her way to the front door. Much of her life had been lived in a third-floor tenement east of here, but a few years ago her parents had finally managed to rent this house in a slightly better neighborhood. Mary had lived here only briefly after losing her last job as a parlor maid.

She shook off the unsettling feeling of that difficult time and entered without knocking, calling as she did for her mother.

The woman herself was busy by the hob when Mary walked in, no doubt performing a miracle with bread and fishes. The living area was dark compared to the street outside, the furnishings weathered and worn but nevertheless scrubbed clean. Scattered around were children of various ages, down to a little one toddling about in a nappy.

Her mother, Cherry, looked up in surprise at the sound of Mary's voice and smiled. "Mary! You've come home!"

The reunion was cheerful, for a bit. As her mother bustled about making tea, Mary fell into her old role as the oldest and tended to the little ones. Her father was working, as were the older girls. Their combined wages, as well as Mary's contribution, had enabled the family to move to this crowded house.

When the tea was ready, both she and her mother sat to visit properly. Mary was pleased her mother seemed so happy to see her. Theirs was not always such an easy relationship.

After a few good American anecdotes, Mary concluded with her account of the transatlantic voyage. "The ship was just that big, Mama, and the sea so vast you couldn't see land for days and days. And let me tell you, this girl needs some solid land beneath her feet. That swaying ocean just does not agree with me." Mary mimed throwing up for good measure.

Cherry threw back her head and laughed. When her mother was happy, her whole body was happy. But Mary knew from hard experience that her mood could change with the snap of a finger. "Oh, Mary, it's good to have you home."

The conversation continued naturally, catching up with family news and gossip. After a time, her mother leaned forward, her eyes sharp. "You finally get tired of living with people not your own? You haven't forgotten your place, have you?"

There it was—the criticism Mary had been anticipating. She stilled, thinking carefully before answering. "I know my place, Mama. And I have lived with people not my own since I was nine and you sent me to work as a tweeny. The Dovefields are good folk, and I like my work with them." Mary knew she should end her words there, but she just couldn't help but say what else she was thinking. "And I am safe with the men of that house."

Cherry's eyes narrowed, and any cheerfulness disappeared from her demeanor. Mary instantly regretted her last sentence. She had expected this reaction. Now she'd have to weather the storm.

"You have brought those problems with men upon yourself, Mary, with the way you cannot control your mouth or hide your intentions," Cherry snapped. "Last time you had such a problem you brought great trouble to the doors of this family."

The words didn't shock Mary—she'd heard them before—but they still stung. She glared at her mother. "Do you mean when the son of the house where you sent me to work tried to attack me and take for himself what God gave to me? Do you mean when I fought to protect myself from his roving hands and worse? Or do you mean when I broke his nose with a candlestick holder and ran for my life?"

The image of bright red blood pouring down that man's face flashed in Mary's mind. An image she often saw when she closed her eyes. What her mother would never understand was the feelings that memory invoked—not just terror and anger, but also . . . pride. He deserved what she gave him, and Mary didn't regret it. Truth be told, she would do it again.

"Oh, don't be so dramatic." The cold edge in mother's voice brought Mary back to the present. "Sometimes you have to put up with a roving hand or two to put food on the table to feed your children. It is the way of the world in which we live. You have never known your place in that world."

Mary stood suddenly, barely containing her anger. "That's just it, Mama." She gestured to the sleeping child in her mother's arms and across the room where the others were playing. "These are not my children. I send money each week to pay for their food, but they are not my children. They are yours. To raise, and to teach, and to protect. As am I."

Mary could see no point in continuing the conversation. She reached for her cape, quickly pulling it over her shoulders as she walked toward the door.

Her mother rose as well, nestling the sleeping child into the chair as she did. "You are my girl, Mary, and I could have lost you. They could have arrested you, a woman with the color of your skin attacking a white man like that. They could have arrested you and they would have hanged you."

This time, instead of cold steel, Mary heard real fear in her mother's voice. She considered what her mother might have been feeling back then. Mary had run home that day, looking for comfort and receiving anger. She thought the fear she'd seen then in her mother's eyes stemmed from the lost wages. Could it have been fear over losing Mary?

Cherry continued. "I've tried to teach you your place Mary—to keep you safe. You get all above yourself, and in this world it leads to nothing but trouble. Now you're doing it again. Them folk are just using you like all the nobles use us common folk, and when they're done with you they will throw you out like the bones from the broth. I saw the hurt in your eyes back then, you think I didn't? I saw the hurt, and the only way to keep that hurt from happening again was to teach you to keep your place. You ain't above us, Mary. No matter how much you wish you were, you just ain't."

As much as the words hurt, Mary found herself thinking about them instead of snapping back. Some of her mother's fears might have been true—perhaps more than some. The world they lived in was often unforgiving. But now, things were different. Her life had changed when her cousin John had introduced her to Zoe. The world she lived in had expanded beyond anything she had dreamed of, and at this point, she knew in her heart she couldn't go back. Her mama was wrong. For better or for worse, her place was not the same as it had been two years ago.

Mary took a deep breath. "I know you love me, Mama, in your way." Mary shook her head. "You're right about a great deal of things, but not about this. I don't think I'm better than any of you, but I am different. I can't go back."

Her mother's eyes narrowed. "You do think you are better, Mary. I see it in the way you look around at our home. Poor as it is in your eyes, it keeps the weather off your family every day."

"I wasn't thinking that," objected Mary. "You're putting words in my mouth again." Exhaustion began to wash over her. Truth be told this was an old argument, older than her current position, though it had grown increasingly divisive since being hired by the Dovefields. Impulsively, Mary reached for her mother, drawing her into a strong hug. She spoke softly into the older woman's ear. "I will always be your girl, Mama. I don't have to agree or explain or justify to be the girl you raised. I love you, Mama. I'll stop back soon."

Even as she said it, Mary knew it wasn't true. She wasn't sure she would be back at all. As she let go of the embrace, Mary turned without waiting for Cherry's response. The door slammed behind her as she strode down the stairs and onto the street.

As she made her way back to the Dovefields', Mary stopped to buy a meat pie from a cart near High Street. She was less upset than she expected from the interaction. Her mother did love her—she believed that. Someday she hoped they would find their way. For now, she was content with the life she had found for herself.

Leaning against the wall of the nearby building, Mary stopped to enjoy every bite of the tender meat tender and flaky crust. She noted a pair of hungry eyes watching her from the shadows, hoping she would drop a crumb. Hunger and poverty and despair permeated this part of London.

That was another thing that had changed. Now she had the means to help, if only for a minute.

She stopped eating her pie a few bites in, and offered it to the urchin. The child hesitated, sensing a trap, but the hunger quickly won out and they snatched it from her grasp. The child ran, glancing back to see if a chase ensued. But Mary just smiled and continued on her way. She had a life to get back to.

Chapter Fourteen

Over her years as a part of the Dovefield family, Zoe had discovered a cure for the many ailments of life. Whether it be a sprained wrist or a broken heart, she always did the same thing.

She went to Aunt Theo's.

Known to the ton as the Dowager Duchess of Wentworth, Theodosia Bexley was still beautiful in her mid-sixties. Age had taken a toll in the lines which marked her face and her once-blonde hair which had faded to silver, but somehow the contrast only made her intelligent green eyes more striking.

Theo was Hugh's older sister, though the line between sister and mother had been blurred by the tragic death of their mother when Hugh was only fourteen. Already married and six years his senior, Theo had taken Hugh in when their father was busy ignoring his grief and acquiring a new wife. And she did this while navigating her own difficult marriage to a much older man

Then her husband died only four years later, leaving Theo with the freedom that came with being a young, beautiful, and very rich widow. Since the marriage had never produced children and she chose to remain single, Hugh remained the closest thing to a son she would ever have. When he wanted to become a barrister, Theo was the one who supported him, both in spirit and financially.

When later in his life he chose to marry an exiled French aristocrat with an angry daughter in tow, Theo was the first of his family to welcome Simone and Zoe into the fold. She'd taken a special interest in Zoe, becoming the nine-year-old's safe space in a time when Zoe had been desperate for any kind of stability. She still felt that way today.

When Zoe had heard that Theo was hosting a dinner party that evening as a welcome home for her and Sebastian, she'd jumped at the chance to arrive early for the day and spend the night after the party. Mary cheerfully came along as well, enjoying the perks that came with her position as a lady's companion.

The news of a new woman slain by the madman had Zoe at sixes and sevens, and there was only one place she wanted to be. She could not keep her mind from dwelling on both Mabel and Quinton. This would bring up most unpleasant memories for them both.

Of course, the dead woman was the real victim. She had been robbed of the opportunity to have an unpleasant memory ever again. And worse for that woman's own family and friends as well, people who would be broken by this tragedy in ways that could never be completely repaired.

Anyone who had lived through a tragedy couldn't help but be damaged by it. But friends did help at least keep the broken pieces together—like a shattered vase being kept in a box until such time as the pieces could be glued back in place. It would never be the same, but it could still be repaired, if someone was willing to put in the time.

When she and Mary arrived, Theo welcomed them in her library. Her aunt had always preferred this room to the parlor or sitting room others favored. A fire brightened the space, warming it to a comfortable temperature. After greetings, Theo motioned for the footman to pour them each a glass of single malt.

Theo had not only taught Zoe to appreciate whiskey but to appreciate the good stuff. This was the good stuff.

They spent some time catching up on the customary gossip, including Theo asking how her younger brother Sebastian had behaved himself on the American journey. Zoe gave all the right answers, sticking to the amusing anecdotes and carefully tiptoeing around Sebastian's more unorthodox activities. It was fairly easy, as Sebastian and she had carefully rehearsed her answers while on the boat home.

Being a third son of a baron with only the meagerest of allowances to sustain him, Sebastian had made his way in the world relying on charm, good looks, and the goodwill of his friends, of whom he had many. Sebastian was unorthodox and had never chosen marriage, which raised a few eyebrows, but most third sons had worse vices. A short rein on finances tended to bring about some unseemly behavior, such as visits to gambling hells, brothels, opium dens. Sebastian frequented none of those. That was enough for Theo to ignore any raised eyebrows about his friends or travels. She maintained how he made his way was no business of hers or anyone else's as long as he avoided outright scandal.

Eventually Mary brought up what Zoe had been waiting to discuss. "It's dreadful that another woman has been killed. Dreadful. I feel as if we are all living in some kind of nightmare." Mary took care with each word she spoke. She'd been practicing her prose and grammar, now that she was expected to actually converse with members of society instead of serving them.

Zoe knew that the transition wasn't always easy for Mary. Strict societal rules and expectations were second nature to the upper class, learned as they cut teeth. Even Zoe herself, though born in France, had lived long enough among the British upper class that she never questioned which fork to use or how to structure her sentence in the correct way, or how to address a particular nobleman. But to an outsider, the whole thing was ridiculous—even those on the inside could agree it was ridiculous. But the expectation was still there, so Mary still worked at it.

"Agreed, Mary, agreed." Theo shook her head before looking to Zoe expectantly. "Do we know more of the woman who was slain?"

"I do not know why you assume I know more of this than anyone else. I only know what the papers have reported. I haven't even heard her name yet." Zoe paused, eyeing Theo closely. "What do you know?"

"Nothing! Well, almost nothing. I did hear from Laura Corbyn that it was her dressmaker who was killed."

"That's hardly nothing, Aunt Theo. Did Lady Corbyn tell you her name?"

"Of course, my dear. She's quite torn up about the whole thing; it was her dressmaker after all. A good modiste is the most important friend a lady can have."

Zoe rolled her eyes and Theo noted the gesture.

"Well, perhaps not a friend in the way you might consider it, but don't think the relationship is trivial. No lady could survive without her dressmaker." Theo leaned back and clasped her hands, clearly pleased at the gossip she had to impart. "The poor woman's name was Clarissa Amato. She was an Italian dressmaker from the finest family, and skilled in her abilities to be sure. Laura was not the only member of society who appreciated Madame Amato's considerable talents."

"You mean to say this killed lady was an Italian lass?" Mary turned to Zoe, excitement distracting her from her precise prose. "Maybe it was some kind of Italian revenge? Those folk do love drama."

Theo cleared her throat discreetly. "She wasn't actually Italian, Mary. She was probably from somewhere as common as Yorkshire. But she learned an Italian accent and added an Italian name to be more sought out by the ton."

"Why?" asked Mary with a confused expression.

"Because no lady of stature wants to say they ordered their dress from a girl with a Yorkshire accent. But to say your modiste is Italian and tells you tales of Milan . . . it adds an exotic and fashionable element few can resist."

"I don't know if I'll ever understand all this." Mary sighed and shook her head.

"My dear, if you're looking for a logical explanation, you won't find it among British high society." Theo sipped her whiskey, assessing Zoe with a watchful side eye. After a moment, she apparently decided to take the risk. "Does Mr. Huxley have an interest in this newest death?"

As Zoe considered her answer, Mary tensed and averted her eyes, obviously preparing herself for some kind of explosion. But Zoe wasn't in the mood to fight. "To my knowledge, he does not. But my knowledge of Quinton could fit in a thimble and my understanding of him is quite a lot less. And neither is any of my concern." She ignored the look of surprise exchanged between Theo and Mary. "But I am worried about Mabel." She took the opportunity to impart the story of her visit with Mabel to Theo.

"This was before Clarissa was killed?" her aunt asked.

"Yes."

"Then there is hope for Mabel, my dear." Theo smiled. "Mr. Huxley may not have been interested before, but I would bet he is very interested now. He was like a dog in a fox hunt last year, until there was nothing left to hunt. He's been at the river's edge for some time, but now that there's a fresh trail, he will follow it. You should ask him again to take the case."

Zoe eyes narrowed. "You seem to know a great deal about Quinton's activities and well-being."

"I don't know why you should be so surprised, dear." Theo sat back with a smug smile. "I quite liked the little band of pirates you cobbled together last year. I've kept up with them, to a degree. Except for the Indian lad. I think he spent the whole time he was here plotting how to kill me in my sleep, so I've let that sleeping dog lay."

The description wasn't unfair. Charlie Modi had little use for the upper crust. Zoe wasn't sure he wouldn't kill her in her sleep, given the opportunity.

"—I've managed to take note of certain others. Young Officer Smith is always in touch with your father, and Hugh keeps me up to date. And as for your resurrectionist, Mr. Stewart and I have crossed paths a time or two."

"You're still keeping company with a body snatcher?" asked Zoe with a gasp.

Theo met her eyes squarely, clearly unperturbed. "I don't see why I shouldn't. He was quite charming during his visit last year, as well as intellectually stimulating, and his fashion sense is impeccable. A woman in my position can never have enough interesting friends." As Zoe stared, astounded at Theo's words, Theo paused and tsked. "Oh come now, dear. At my age I've learned people have inherent value outside of romantic interest. Mr. Stewart is good company." Theo continued. "As for Mr. Huxley, both Officer Smith and Mr. Stewart have insinuated enough for me to fill in the blanks. I believe this tragedy may be his salvation."

Taking one last swig of her single malt, Zoe contemplated her aunt's words. Perhaps this new killing would spark some kind of life back into the man she couldn't keep from thinking about. But she did not share Theo's confidence.

Mary too had finished her whiskey and was twirling the now empty glass between her fingers. "Is it impertinent to ask for another glass, Your Grace?"

"Very much so, Mary." Theo smiled. "Which is why I'm thrilled you did."

When the guest began to arrive, Zoe watched from across the room, putting off conversation as long as possible. She smoothed the muslin fabric of her burgundy gown, letting the texture distract her mind. The style was simple, but it suited her figure. Until the new lady's maid started, Mary was still working her magic with Zoe's dark curls, and both of them were particularly pleased with the effect tonight.

Despite her confidence in her appearance, Zoe would have given up a lot to be anywhere else. She quite disliked dinner parties. Her natural inclination towards speaking before thinking led her into enough hot water to make these intimate gatherings less than enjoyable. At the great balls she could fade into the wallpaper, drifting to the potted plants and hallways, or join groups large enough others would carry the conversational load. But at a dinner party there was no escape. She just had to pray for restraint on her part.

A strategy she had employed before without much success. The Almighty must have better things to occupy him.

Alexander Dovefield was the first to arrive. He was the son of Theo and Hugh's older brother, making him the future Baron of Newark and Zoe's cousin of sorts. They'd held a mutual distaste for each other from the moment they met as children, and the years had only deepened those feelings. He glanced her way, their eyes meeting for only a second before he turned to greet Theo. He always had been a master at the art of a proper dismissal.

Whenever Zoe found Alexander tiresome, Theo would defend him. He was her first nephew, and though she wasn't blind to his faults, she did have a soft spot for him. While Zoe thought him an obnoxious rake, he did seem to echo Theo's feelings. He visited regularly—a less generous person might say he came regularly to beg for money.

Her thoughts were interrupted when the other reason for a welcome home event arrived. Her Uncle Sebastian, now dipping his toe into his forties, was still a handsome man—to be fair, all the Dovefields leaned on the side of good-looking. He was still trim and strong, the only real concession to his age being the gray hair peppering his dark sideburns. Besides his looks, he was also gifted with a charm few could resist.

Hugh and Simone came in right after Sebastian, followed in

short order by Lord Felix and Lady Charlotte Fairfax. Charlotte was a widowed friend of Theo's going back quite a ways, and Zoe had had the displeasure of spending many a dinner party smothered by her critical presence. Her son, Felix, was less known to her. He was about Hugh's age and was enlisted as an officer in the Navy, so was often away from home. When he was in port, he lived in his family home along with his mother. It seemed to suit them both.

Two other couples came in whom Zoe did not know well, but Sebastian greeted them warmly. Lord and Lady Coleville completed the guest list. They had four daughters, the eldest enjoying her first season last fall. For this event, however, the couple arrived *sans* children. They were only acquaintances to her, but she knew of the Lord's generosity with Quinton.

Reluctantly, Zoe began to mingle. Sebastian sought her out first and they shared a few benign stories of America with the group, told mostly by Sebastian and eliciting laughter. He was an excellent storyteller. Then Zoe drifted to her mother and Hugh as a place of safety. They chatted amiably until one of the couples Zoe did not know joined the group. Introduced as Lord and Lady Burton, apparently he too was a barrister, and soon the conversation went down a legal path. The new murder was already well known among those in the field.

"Terrible business, this new murder," Lord Burton began. "So Dovefield, I suppose you think your boy deserves a petition of error? Guilty as charged, as far as I am concerned."

What a blustering old bag of air.

Hugh took it in stride. "My boy as you say, Charles, has been innocent from the beginning of this nightmare, and this proves it. He deserves justice." Hugh took a swallow of his claret. "I've already started the process and requested a writ of error to the lower courts. I plan to argue in front of the House of Lords in time."

Lord Burton planted his feet stubbornly. "I just don't see it. That boy killed that girl, we all know it. He was the only one with any motive, and the jury found him guilty. A few similar details with the new dead woman won't change the facts."

Hugh employed his usual trick of remaining silent when discussion was useless. Zoe recognized the tactic from many a debate of her own in her younger years. Actually, now that she thought about it, he had done it yesterday when she brought up taking Brutus to this very house. And here she was, sans Brutus.

The strategy proved to still be effective. Lord Burton blustered a bit more before excusing himself to refill his glass. Simone smiled at her husband and they shared a wink.

As Zoe turned to review the room, she almost ran into Fairfaxes. The lord had to jump out of the way, holding his drink up to avoid spilling it. Her cheeks flushed with heat at the embarrassment, but Lord Fairfax just laughed amiably. "Careful, young lady. Best keep that dress looking as beautiful 'til the end as it does right now."

His mother, a pace behind him, sniffed. "In my day, young ladies did not go racing about knocking guests off their feet." Lady Fairfax gave her a sharp look. "Though I suppose perhaps your French breeding may be to blame as well."

"She was hardly racing, Mother," soothed Lord Fairfax. "It was an honest mistake."

"I am so sorry, Lady Fairfax. You are absolutely right." Zoe forced a smile, all while wishing she could crawl in a hole. "I must watch myself."

Lord Fairfax returned her smile before ushering his mother along. Zoe glanced around to see her stepfather had witnessed the interaction. At first she thought his sour look was brought on by embarrassment of her actions. But then she realized his gaze was directed not at her but at the lord. Then the moment passed and Hugh's features were once again neutral. Zoe wondered if the two men had some kind of private issue. But then again, Hugh got to know many people when it was not their finest hour, and sometimes his view was colored by that knowledge. So perhaps it was nothing. Regardless, she had better things to worry about.

As she began to move toward the Colevilles, she was intercepted by Mary. In her hand was a slip of crumpled paper. Mary took her arm and guided her to the corner of the room.

A feeling of dread came over Zoe. "What is it?"

"A message." Mary smirked. "From Quinton."

Chapter Fifteen

"What do you mean, women aren't allowed?" The shrill question echoed against the stone walls and through the hallways of the building. It came from a voice which was all too familiar to Quinton. He didn't need to turn the corner to know where the indignation originated.

Zoe Demas stood at the guard station, hands on her hips and blue eyes alight with righteous fire. Though a bonnet covered most of her dark curly hair, a few stray pieces had managed to work themselves free in the commotion.

Beside her stood Mary Fletcher. Quinton had known Mary most of her life, though in his mind she was still a little girl hanging onto her older cousin John's shirtsleeves.

The two women were an unlikely pair, coming from vastly different backgrounds and both possessing a strong-willed disposition. When John told him last year that Mary was going to be Zoe's lady's maid, Quinton predicted it would never last. But they proved him wrong, taking an almost immediate liking to each other. If that wasn't enough, the following events had cemented their bond. Now they seemed joined at the hip.

A long, slow sigh escaped Quinton's lips. He was in no mood to deal with the dynamic duo in that moment, but now he would have little choice.

"What is going on here?" he growled.

As Zoe whirled around, the full force of her gaze hit him. "What do you mean, what's going on? I received word from you that you were going to be interviewing Mr. Chedrose."

"That doesn't explain your being here."

"Why would you send word if you did not want me to accompany you?"

"I sent word so you could forward my retainer," snapped Quinton. "Newgate Prison is no place for you."

"I see no reason why not."

"Naturally." Quinton pinched the bridge of his nose. "Why must everything be a fight with you?"

"Because you always insist on being unreasonable."

"Oh, I insist—"

"Well this is getting us nowhere," interjected Mary. "Being in this hellhole is giving me all manner of unsettlin' feelings, so if you don't mind, perhaps we could skip the squabble and go straight to the compromise?"

Quinton threw his hands up. "What do you want me to do, Mary? Newgate doesn't allow women past this point. In all honesty, I wouldn't go inside if I didn't have to."

"Now Quinton," Mary said with a no-nonsense look. "Let's not act like the rules apply to everybody the same. I'm sure you've got an angle you could use here, if you wanted to."

As much as he hated to admit it, Mary wasn't wrong. The right favor or palm greased made all the difference in situations such as these.

"Fine," he said finally with a huff. "Why is it," he said to Mary, turning pointedly away from Zoe, "when we compromise, she always gets her way?"

"Because you're a gentleman, Quinton, of course," said Mary smoothly.

"Hmm." He turned back to Zoe. "Get your coin purse out."

The amount the guard extracted from them was equivalent to highway robbery, but since Zoe was so determined to accompany them, she had little choice but to fork it over. She could afford it, but Quinton would remember that greedy little guard.

In the man's defense, he wasn't unique in this situation. Bribery was the way of life for guards at Newgate. Everything, from beds to blankets to food, cost something. Some even charged *not* to beat you. Life was easier for those prisoners whose family could pay, but for those at the bottom of the financial ladder . . . the rope was kinder. The system hinged on injustice and greediness, which did nothing to endear it to Quinton. The whole thing turned his stomach on the best of days, which this was not.

The three companions were escorted into the bowels of the prison. For someone of Quinton's bulk, the dim narrow hallways seemed impossibly tight. He imagined this was how a mouse walking into a trap might feel—not yet realizing it wouldn't be able to leave the way it had come, but still sensing a danger beyond its comprehension.

Cold moisture condensed on the ceiling and walls, resulting in random drips down one's back. Quinton flinched as another struck him just above the eye. As he reached up to wipe the dirty water away, he wondered if someone could get bad humors in their chest just from walking through such a place. This seemed like somewhere bad humors lurked. He tried to breathe through his mouth to limit the overbearing scent of mildew that hung in the air. The only thing he was more aware of than the atmosphere of death was Zoe's presence close behind him, her own breathing shallow.

They finally reached their destination. The cell door opened with a loud creak to reveal a small, dank room, but there were a few items within that were considered luxuries within Newgate: a cot with a thin blanket shoved into a corner and a plate on the floor indicating food did occasionally cross the threshold. On the bed sat the subject of their inquiry—Thomas Chedrose.

Nine months in prison hadn't been kind to Thomas. The last time Quinton had seen him, he'd been a strapping young man with ruddy cheeks and passion in his eyes. He'd been sad and anxious, naturally, but he was still a youth in the prime of his life.

Now the boy was thin and pale, his cheeks sunken and his eyes dull. With nowhere for it to dissipate, even worse was the truly unfortunate scent of unwashed body that wafted toward them as they entered.

Still, many prisoners had it worse. Thomas's face, though smeared with grime, was relatively unmarred by obvious bruises or cuts. The bed and food indicated his father was paying the price extracted by the guards for such necessities. Then there was the fact the boy should be six feet in the ground already, his body nothing but food for the worms—yet there he sat.

Thomas was the son of a well-respected coach maker, Howard Chedrose. The building and upkeep of coaches and carriages was considered skilled labor, and the Chedroses had gained enough of a following over the years from the nobility of London to do quite well for their family. Not well enough to erase their blue-collar roots, but well enough to hire a barrister and pay for their son's upkeep in prison. Quinton also suspected money had changed hands at some point to ensure the boy's lenient sentence. Prison was horrid, but a murder conviction almost always ended in a long drop from a short rope—and this wasn't just the death of some commoner. He'd been convicted of killing a noblewoman. By all accounts, Thomas should be dead. The fact he was sitting there with a confused expression on his face was nothing short of a minor miracle.

"Mr. Chedrose, do you remember me?" asked Quinton. "My name's Quinton Huxley. I spoke to you a few times during the trial last year."

"Yes, I remember you." Thomas's voice was barely audible.

"Good. I'd like to introduce Ms. Mary Fletcher and Lady Zoe Demas."

He blinked rapidly, trying to focus his eyes. "I didn't think they allowed women back here. I haven't seen my mother since . . . since it all happened."

Zoe cleared her throat and ignored the statement in characteristic fashion. "Mr. Chedrose, I believe we share a mutual acquaintance—Mabel Anderson. I understand you were close to her sister Margot."

"Yes, right, I remember Mabel. She didn't really care for me, but she kept Margot's secret." Thomas stared off sadly into the middle distance. "I was very fond of Margot."

"That's what Mabel said." Zoe looked him up and down, clearly appraising the character of the man in her head. "She believes you are innocent."

"Well she's in the minority." He shrugged. "Doesn't really matter. Margot's dead and I might as well be."

Quinton decided it was time for him to step in. "Actually there's been a development, Mr. Chedrose. Another woman was killed, similar to the way Margot was killed, likely by the same hand. Sad as it is, this might be helpful to your case."

Something flashed in the condemned man's eyes—for a moment, Quinton thought he saw a spark of the passion that had been there a year ago. But then the moment passed, and Thomas just shrugged again. "Like I said, doesn't matter. I'm never leavin' here alive. I've accepted that."

"But, Mr. Chedrose—"

"You're tryin' to give me hope, and I appreciate that. But I can't afford to go down that road again. It's better to just accept what is." His voice had raised an octave in his frustration, but now it returned to its soft raspy tone. "It's hope that'll break you."

There was little to say to such a statement. The room lapsed into awkward silence, with the visitors glancing at each other, seeking inspiration.

In truth, Quinton did understand the sentiment. A day ago he'd been languishing in a prison of his own making. But for him it was losing his hope that had broken him. Now that opportunity had come knocking once again, he felt invigorated. Yet, if this time also ended in failure . . . Quinton couldn't dwell on that possibility. But he did understand the weight hope could carry.

"Mr. Chedrose, I know you've lost a great deal." To Quinton's surprise, it was Mary who stepped into the void. "I don't blame you for your feelings—a person is entitled to that, if nothing else in this life. I sympathize, even if I can't completely understand what you're going through. And you're right, this might not change anything for you. But doesn't it grate on your soul?"

Thomas frowned, his eyebrows furrowed. "What do you mean?"

"Doesn't it keep you up at night, that one persistent thought burrowing its way into your brain? And no matter how hard you try not to think about it, I'll bet it's the one thing you can't get away from. All alone, with only four blank walls for company, and one constant thought, just going round and round in your head. No matter what you do, you just can't escape it."

Quinton had no idea where she was going with this. He glanced at Zoe, and she gave him an equally quizzical look. But Thomas no longer appeared lost. He looked at Mary, his eyes focused for the first time.

She leaned in closer, her eyes locked with his. "I'll bet the thing that haunts you the most, deep in your bones, is knowing that the man who took your Margot is still out there, free, just living his life and breathing air that should be hers."

The atmosphere in the cell had transformed with Mary's words; the air seemed thicker now, as if her words carried literal weight. Quinton held his breath, waiting for Thomas's reply.

Thomas straightened and his chest expanded as he took a deep breath. A light seemed to return to his eyes, and when he spoke it was with passion. "God willin' he'll burn in 'ell for what he did."

"Mm. We're looking for justice a little sooner than the grave." Mary gestured toward the other three. "Just answer their questions, alright? It's about Margot, not just you."

As Thomas nodded, Quinton exhaled the breath he hadn't realized he was still holding. He cleared his throat before speaking. "Mr. Chedrose, you told me last year that Margot was on her way to see you that night but she never showed up, correct?"

"Yes. She sent a message sayin' that her father had found out about us and she needed to see me."

"Do you think she was planning to run away?"

"No . . . no, I don't think she would do that to Mabel. I think she just wanted to talk. I waited at my father's shop for hours, but she didn't come. I thought her father must've stopped her. It never occurred to me . . ."

"Of course not," said Zoe. "Did you and Margot meet up often?"

"When we could," replied Thomas with a faint ghost of a smile. "It wasn't easy. But any time spent with Margot was worth it. We were meant to be together, her and me."

Quinton refrained from comment. It wasn't that he didn't believe the boy's feelings were genuine, and by all accounts it seemed the girl returned his affections. But by becoming besotted with a noblewoman so far above him socially, Thomas had set himself up for disaster. Even if the girl had lived, theirs was a relationship doomed for failure from the start. But Quinton was self-aware enough to know that now wasn't the time to voice such musings aloud.

He cleared his throat. "Mr. Chedrose, when was the last time you saw Lady Anderson?"

Thomas's face scrunched with thought. "I think it was about a week before. We met at a coffee house."

"And did she say anything that troubled you? Mention anyone who was making her uncomfortable or anyone she had a problem with?"

He shook his head, the passion fading from his eyes with each question. "No, nothin' like that. She seemed perfectly content."

It was a disappointing, if not unexpected result. Quinton had spoken to the boy before, and he hadn't known anything helpful then either. This visit was merely a starting point, to see if anything new might've surfaced.

As he and Zoe exchanged a look, Quinton could see she was thinking the same. It was time to leave.

"Mr. Chedrose, thank you for your time," he said. "I'm sure Mr. Dovefield will be in touch about your case."

"Sir, before we leave, is there anything you need?" asked Zoe.

"No. It was kind of you all to come." The faint smile returned to Thomas's face. "It hasn't been easy, since it all happened, but I have been surprised at the kindness of some. Your father, Lady Demas, he did his best by me, I know he did. And if it weren't for the magistrate, I know I would've hung. It's hard to keep everythin' in perspective, but I know there are things to be grateful for. Thank you for taking a closer look at Margot's death."

"This was a miscarriage of justice, Mr. Chedrose." Quinton reached out a hand, trying not to wince as the cold, clammy fingers wrapped around his own. "We'll do what we can to see it right."

His grip tightened. "I hope you nail the bastard."

The three of them spent the trek out of the prison in silence. It wasn't until sunlight fell upon their faces that anyone dared speak.

"Well, what now?" Zoe crossed her arms. "That seemed an utter waste of time."

"It was a long shot," admitted Quinton. "But it was necessary to see if the year spent in prison had jarred any new information loose. And while we were beating this bush, John has had the opportunity to pursue fresher trails."

Chapter Sixteen

John sighed, rubbing his temples. This conversation seemed to be going in circles. "So tell me again where Madame Amato was from?"

"Milan, Italy," parroted her assistant, a stout girl of about seventeen named Jane White. She stood near the front of the dress shop, feet planted but clearly ready to leave at the first opportunity. Her eyes darted about the shop but carefully avoided the area near the back where Amato had been found.

John didn't blame her. Most folks didn't relish the thought of sharing space with the spirit of one so recently departed. He would try to keep the interview as short as he could. "Right. But her name wasn't actually Clarissa Amato?"

The girl paused. "It was when she was working."

"What about when she wasn't working?"

"Well, we didn't really have a relationship outside of work." Jane shifted from foot to foot. "So I only knew her as Madame Amato."

The girl's dictation was flawless. Madame Whatever Her Real Name Was must've required it.

"I don't understand." That persistent headache was beginning to resurface.

The girl shrugged, finally meeting John's gaze "Look, all I know is that Madame Amato had a thick Italian accent and was from Milan. But when she left for the day, suddenly she had a Yorkshire accent. And once, I saw her open a letter addressed to Sarah something."

"I see." John pondered this. "Did she ever talk about her family, or anything in her past?"

"No. She was very private."

"Mm. Very well, thank you for the information." A thought occurred to John. "Do you know where the key is to her rooms upstairs? I'd like to see if she still has any of those letters."

Jane eagerly ran over to a desk in the corner and returned with a key in her grasp. "You can have the key and a look around, of course, but I doubt you'll find anything of hers up there. She rented rooms at a boarding house."

Now that was odd. Why would someone pay for a room at a boarding house when the shop space they were already paying for came with living quarters?

"Do you know what she was using' the upstairs rooms for?" he asked.

"No, just that I wasn't supposed to go up there." The girl nodded seriously. "Madame Amato was very particular on certain things."

John's ears perked up. "Hard to work for?"

Looking longingly at the door, clearly wishing to leave, Jane shrugged again. "Sometimes. But she was a good boss. She never made me or the other seamstresses work late, even when there was a rush order."

"She does sound like a good boss. I don't suppose you have the address for her boarding house?"

Grasping at the chance to be finished, Jane quickly wrote the address down. John waved her out the door and turned his attention to the upstairs.

It was as the girl said it would be—devoid of personal belongings. There were a few essentials, such as a bed and a couple of chairs, as well as a fireplace for heating and cooking. Art even hung on the walls, but John could find no clothes or letters or even a hairbrush. He could tell the furnishings were high quality, if a little opulent for his taste. Very strange . . .

It didn't take long for him to lock up and hail a hackney, directing the driver to the not-Italian's boarding house. The journey took them across the river, away from the sprawling homes of the gentry and the high-class shops and businesses that serviced them, and into a neighborhood John was much more familiar with. When the hackney pulled to an abrupt stop, he realized they were only about a block away from his own rented rooms.

This was the part of London where people like him lived—not rich enough for Hyde Park and not poor enough for Whitechapel. An in-between place for all manner of folk, from tradesmen to fourth sons of the gentry who'd gambled away whatever allowance they'd been gifted. It did seem a bit beneath someone of Madame Amato's supposed skill and reputation.

As the housekeeper showed him to the dead woman's room, John wondered what circumstances had driven her to change not only her name but her heritage as well. Perhaps it was only to further the mystique of her business persona, but if that were the case, why was she wasting money on these rooms miles away from her shop? Was she running from something—hiding from someone? Could it be that she'd committed a crime and was hiding from the law?

Speculation would only get you so far, John reminded himself. The magistrate had told him often enough to leave guess work at home and rely on facts in his work. He wouldn't be able to come to any conclusions without evidence. He could only hope a search of "Madame Amato's" room would provide him with something concrete.

Unlike the rooms above the shop, opulent wasn't a word that could be used to describe the living space John walked into. Spartan might be more accurate. Again, he found little in the way of personal things, but this time he did find some clothes and hygiene items to show a person actually lived there. Despite its lack of coziness, John did note that the room was clean and well kept. His mother, God rest her soul, had often told him that you could tell a lot about a person by the way they kept their home.

Though there weren't any letters sitting out in the obvious places, John had been a constable long enough to know most of the good hiding places, and his mother hadn't raised a quitter. Eventually he was rewarded for his persistence with a bundle of letters wrapped in twine, recovered from inside the mattress.

They were addressed to a Sarah Hammond. John sat on the floor, leaning his back against the bed frame, and opened the envelope on the first one.

My Dearest Sarah,

As I write these words, I find myself wishing that the news I had to tell you was better. Unfortunately, my wishes are not to be. I'm afraid Mother's health continues to decline, as it has ever since Father's death. I thank you for the money you sent last month, but I'm afraid the physician has already claimed it. Daisy has joined me at the factory in an effort to keep food on the table for the littlest ones, but with Mother's decline, I'm afraid it does not go far enough. I do not tell you this to worry you, or to increase any feelings of guilt you may process, as I know you and Mother parted under bitter terms, but only to keep you informed on the family's goings-on. If you are able to send more money anytime in the near future, it would be appreciated by all. I wish only for your happiness and well-being.

Your Loving Sister,
Edith Hammond

The other letters carried a similar tone—a family left behind, desperate for money and begging it from the only relative who could offer it. It was a sad state of affairs, and John felt a pang of sympathy for poor Sarah Hammond. From the regularity of the letters from her sister, it seemed she did send them money often and with increasing frequency, though according to Edith it was never enough.

It wasn't difficult to imagine the strain this burden must've put upon Sarah, but it did not explain why, when it seemed she was sending every spare penny home, she would spend any extra renting separate rooms.

John shoved the letters into his coat pocket and took his leave, mulling the mystery over in his mind. He would have to seek out other evidence to complete the puzzle.

Chapter Seventeen

Although Mabel was waiting in the same drawing room when Zoe was escorted in, the atmosphere was very different. Zoe felt the change immediately, not in the colors or the temperature but in the air itself.

Where before there had been only grief and despair and frustration, now there was a sense of . . . peace. It did not completely cover the other, but there was no denying its presence.

Mabel's eyes lit up when she saw her, and she spoke quickly. "I ordered tea already. Thank you for coming back. I have been anxious for news."

At least Zoe had some good news to impart—for that she was grateful to her bones. May God rest the poor woman's soul, Madame Amato's death meant movement in the investigation of Margot's.

"I have forwarded on the advance you gave me to my agent. He is already quite familiar with the case and has re-interviewed Mr. Chedrose. I am hoping for real progress, though we may need to be patient." She purposefully left out any involvement of her own—Mabel had proven to be surprisingly open-minded, but even she would likely balk at the knowledge of Zoe's visit within Newgate itself.

Her choices on what information to relay seemed to have the desired effect. Mabel sank into the cushions on the settee and breathed a long sigh of relief. "I was afraid no one would ever listen to me." Her voice was strained, as if holding back tears. "Don't think I'm naive. I know this won't bring Margot back. But I don't think you can understand how freeing it is to be heard when you've been ignored for so long. Thank you."

Zoe thought back on her stepfather's long hours helping to defend those without a voice and her mother's new project giving women without anyone else the assistance and opportunities they needed to thrive. Mabel wasn't wrong—you couldn't understand certain things until you had experienced them yourself. Seeing how her efforts had helped Mabel ease her pain had in turn eased her own. Lord knew after all the trauma she had endured through her life that Zoe had enough to spare.

Tea then arrived and conversation turned to other things. Mabel asked after Zoe's parents and Zoe found herself asking after Mabel's. Though she did not respect how they had handled their daughter's grief, she also could not imagine their own pain. To lose a child in such a brutal way . . . there were no words.

"At first my mother cried constantly and my father raged at all hours. But it wasn't long before he couldn't take it any longer, and he forbade even the mention of Mabel in the house." Mabel's eyes clouded at the memory. "He said grieving her was just making everything worse—that he had warned Margot of her association with Mr. Chedrose—that if she'd listened to him, she would still be alive. It was almost as if he was saying Margot deserved to die. If she hadn't crawled out into the street and been found by a nightwatch-man, her body would've rotted like a piece of trash in that alley."

"What?" Zoe sputtered some of her tea. "Margot survived the attack in the alley? I didn't know that."

"Few do. She did not live long. I thought it showed the fight in her, my stubborn sister, but Father felt any details of her death were unseemly, so he paid for the papers to keep it out." There was no hiding the clear sound of bitterness in Mabel's voice when she spoke of her father. That pot would only simmer for so long. One day it would boil over, and those closest would surely get scalded.

"Was she able to say anything when she was found?"

"She tried to speak but the words couldn't be made out. She had been . . ." Mabel's voice faltered, but after a moment, she continued. ". . . strangled. The cloth was still about her neck. The men who found her called for a physician, but she succumbed before any help arrived."

As the tears began to flow down Mabel's cheeks, Zoe reached over to grasp Mabel's hand. "I hope my agent can find real answers, Mabel. Hang on to that hope, and that someday Margot will rest in peace."

"I will. Thank you, Zoe." Mabel drew a shuddering breath before changing the subject to one of a more practical nature. "Are more funds needed for your agent?"

Zoe shook her head. "The advance you provided was already generous. I believe a balance will be required at the end of the investigation, but I am sure he will make it known if he needs an influx before then." Zoe suddenly wondered at where Mabel had obtained the money. "How do your parents feel about using their money to fund this investigation?"

"Oh, this is not funded with their money. Father would never stand for it." She chuckled, wiping away her tears and leaning forward. "I was the favorite of my grandmother. She left me a considerable portion when she passed two years ago. Not enough to support a lifestyle, but enough to give me choices. At the time I thought it wholly unnecessary and wondered what use money would be to me, as I hoped to make a suitable match. But now, it has proven to be a true godsend. I have freedom to spend it as I chose, with no permission needed. I'm not sure how she knew I would grow to appreciate this freedom, but I am forever grateful."

Zoe took a reflective sip of tea, considering the girl in front of her. The girl of last year no longer looked back at her. A woman met her gaze—still finding her way, but a grown woman certainly.

Growth often brought about equal parts gain and pain. She could only hope a change for the better was in store for both of them.

Chapter Eighteen

When John made his way back to the Bow Street office, Magistrate Holdsworth was waiting for him. Lady Luck was with them. The constables who had been assigned to canvass the area around the dressmaker's shop had yielded a witness. A huge lead, and John was pleased the magistrate gave it to him.

It was an undeniable fact that he was the magistrate's favorite. Ever since John had been promoted to a Bow Street Officer, Holdsworth had taken an interest. That had been a refreshing change; until that point, thanks to his mixed parentage, he had had to work twice as hard not only for his position as a Bow Street Officer but also for the respect of colleagues. Holdsworth, on the other hand, had seemed to like him immediately and had taken him under his wing in a professional capacity.

But with the discovery of Miss Anderson's body and the subsequent conviction of Thomas Chedrose last year, their relationship had taken a turn. After that he would let John stay late in his office, discussing his theories and frustrations over cheap gin. He talked about a killer who targeted beautiful women and left a signature behind, something so incomprehensible and unprecedented that most couldn't even acknowledge the possibility.

As he walked past the flower sellers and hot potato stalls on his way back to the dressmaker's street, John wondered, not for the first time, if the magistrate favored him for the work he did or if it was because he knew that John had the respect of Hugh Dovefield. It wasn't a secret that Mr. Dovefield had a soft spot for John, nor that the man was one of the richest and most prominent barristers of the day. Not often, but on a few occasions, Holdsworth would ask him what Mr. Dovefield thought on a matter, or if he had recently spoken to him. A man in the magistrate's position was always looking for a little leverage.

Unfortunately for Holdsworth, it wasn't in John's nature to share secrets. He had seen tough times, and he knew in the depths of his soul that his resilience wasn't the only thing that had saved him through those years, but rather his friends. If there was one quality he prided himself on, it was loyalty.

Besides, his relationship with Mr. Dovefield wasn't that of a friend he would meet for an ale at the local pub. Their standing was friendly, but still very much professional. Even if that wasn't the case, there wasn't much dirt to dig up on the man. He was a good sort . . . for a nob.

When he finally arrived at his destination, John took a moment to survey the street. The dressmaker's shop occupied the middle of the block. The corner held a coffee shop, which took his attention. Holdsworth said the witness worked there.

The first thing John noticed as he entered the shop, past the strong smell of good coffee, was the lass behind the counter, sturdy and clearly hard working. Her cheeks held a healthy color and her eyes were bright, indicating that her work must at least be able to keep her in regular meals.

She noted him immediately, no doubt identifying him from the red overcoat all Bow Street Officers wore. He met her gaze and gestured for her to sit at a table, which she did with a cheerful bounce.

"The constable told me a runner would be stoppin' by, but he dinna say you'd be quite so 'andsome," she said cheekily.

John laughed at that—she was a bold girl. "I'll take the compliment, lass, but you're far too young for the likes of me."

"That's not true!" she said with a sniff. "I'm nearly fifteen."

"That's lovely, congratulations. But any man my age who flirts back with you is a man to avoid." John leaned back in his chair, crossing his arms with an easy-going smile. "What's your name, Miss I'm-Nearly-Fifteen?"

"Agnes. Me name is Agnes Cooper."

"Nice to meet you, Agnes Cooper. Now I'm told you know something about Madame Amato across the street, is that right?"

Agnes' confident posture slumped slightly. "Yes, sir. She came over for a coffee every day at 7:00 when she closed up shop. She liked to sit for a minute and chat—sometimes she'd even chat with the likes of me." It obviously meant something to Agnes that Madame Amato had paid her attention.

"Did she usually sit alone, or did she have company?"

"Oh, sometimes she had a lady friend with her. A few times a fella would join her."

"What about the day she died?"

"Aye, that's what I told the constable." Agnes pointed to a table in the corner. "That evening she was right over there with a fella. Just talking, comfortable like. But then 'e said something she didn't much like and she got angry. Most of the time she was pretty soft-spoken, but this time she got real loud at the end. She told 'im if 'e wanted to find other arrangements, that was fine with 'er."

"Other arrangements . . ." John pondered this. "Did she say more about what that meant?"

Agnes shrugged. "Not that I 'eard. But the fella was right troubled, I can tell you that. 'e said she should calm down, but that just made her madder, and she was near shouting when she got up and left."

This was very promising. A man had an argument with the murdered lady the very night she was killed . . . John tried to temper his excitement.

"Can you tell me what this fella looked like?" he asked eagerly. "Was he older than me? How'd he dress?"

"He was older than you, a bit older than my da even. But not an old man. He weren't bad looking, though not as good as you." She said the last part with a wink.

"Agnes, please, try to focus." He said the words with a small smile to allay any criticism the words contained.

"Fine, fine." Agnes furrowed her brow as she concentrated. "Reddish hair and I think green eyes. He was a charmer for sure. Real classy dresser, too. Oh, and 'e weren't from London neither. He 'ad an accent."

A strange sensation began to come over John. A man in his forties, nice-looking and a snappy dresser, with red hair, green eyes, and an accent. There was something unsettlingly familiar about her description. But the odds . . .

"Could you tell what kind of accent?" A part of him hoped she wouldn't know.

She nodded proudly. "Oh, yes. My mama has kin there and they speak just like 'im. He was Scottish."

As much as he hadn't wanted the words to leave her mouth, John wasn't strangely wasn't surprised when she said it. He just happened to know a charming redheaded Scottish man in his forties. His clothes were higher quality than any body snatcher had a right to have, and he went by the name of Rory Stewart. More importantly, he was a friend. Still, London was not small, and maybe there were other well-dressed redheaded Scotsmen wandering around arguing with murder victims.

Agnes was still talking, oblivious of John's dismay. "I will say, he did seem real nice, up 'til the argument."

"Right, of course." John swallowed hard and cleared his throat. "Is there anything else?"

"Aye. I remember when she raised 'er voice, she called 'im by name."

The dread he'd been trying to ignore constricted in his stomach.

"She called 'im Mr. Stewart."

Chapter Nineteen

As he walked east from the coffee shop, John's mind moved so fast he felt as though it might catch fire, which made the numbness in his body even stranger by comparison. His feet carried him without conscious effort as he replayed the devastating revelation in his head.

His friend, Rory Stewart, a man he had known for years, was seen arguing with the victim the very night she died. As much as John would love to dismiss the story as ridiculous, he knew the witness was solid; the lass had no reason to lie, and she never changed her story or even looked nervous.

Of course, there could be a perfectly innocent explanation as to why Rory was arguing with Clarissa Amato less than a stone's throw from where her body was found that evening. If it were just up to John's personal convictions, he would state for a fact there was no way his friend could be responsible for the heinous act. At least . . . he was pretty sure he wasn't responsible. He didn't know much, but he knew that Rory was a good man. Good men didn't kill women at random, did they?

Of course they don't, he reassured himself. Rory could no sooner strangle a woman than fly to the moon.

But it wasn't up to his personal convictions. This would be tried in the court of public opinion and then again in the court of law, and in both cases, Rory would be found guilty. With the Chedrose boy last year, all it took was his station in life and the insinuation he'd seduced the dead lass to condemn him. As for Rory . . . as charming and stylish as he was, none of that wouldn't be enough to cover over his occupation as a body snatcher. The uproar would pull him under and drown him in its wake before any defense could be mounted.

Few things disgusted the masses more than a person digging up and cutting up a corpse. It wasn't actually illegal, but it was very frowned upon. Even John, though he was fond of Rory and understood the value of his work, still found the concept disconcerting. It didn't feel Christian, slicing a person up like that to take a look inside—but then again, it wasn't particularly Christian to allow murderers escape punishment or to let someone die of disease when it was preventable through knowledge. Whatever one's philosophies might be on the religious morals of it, as Rory often said, the dead were beyond caring anyway. But that wouldn't matter to the public or the courts.

Despite any good he did, a man like Rory would always hang if the opportunity arose.

Over an hour later, John looked up and realized where his feet had taken him. Not to Rory's house in the middle of London with the shed in the back that always smelt of blood and disinfectant. Rather, he stood in front of his friend Charlie's home in the east of London. His was a modest but decent neighborhood not far from the small piece of Whitechapel where he reigned. John hadn't often frequented the home as an adult, since the two boys had taken very different paths in life, but here was a place he knew he could go when he was desperate enough.

This is where someone went when they needed help outside the law.

As he raised his hand to knock, John hesitated. If he left now and went to Rory's place to question him, he would still have a job tomorrow. If Rory was convicted, he would have a healthy bonus on top of a job. That was surely the safest, not to mention the most legal, course. As an officer, he was committed to upholding the law, and he knew none of his friends would truly fault him for doing his job.

But though he did believe in law and order, John understood that what was right and what was legal did not always align. The world was more complicated than, and his loyalties, for better or for worse, would always be with his friends.

He pounded hard on the door.

A young boy answered and, after briefly looking John over, motioned him in. Though he did not frequent this home, he was no stranger to the Modi family.

As John entered the living room, his troubled mind began to clear, like clouds blowing off to reveal a crisp fall sky. Charlie sat on the settee alongside his sister Savita, and his mother Katyayini occupied an overstuffed armchair. The room reflected its inhabitants, with curios from India sharing space with the English furniture. The smell of curry spices filled the air, taking John back to simpler times.

Surprise registered on all three faces, and John couldn't deny feeling some satisfaction when the surprise turned to excitement. Savita was the first to recover, leaping from her seat and throwing her arms around John. The impact knocked him a step back, and John couldn't help but laugh. He gripped her by the shoulders and pushed her away gently, taking a good look at the young woman. The little girl he remembered trailing after the trio of boys was not so little anymore. There was no missing the amused glance Charlie shared with his mother, but John chose to ignore it anyway.

"John! We haven't seen you in ages!"

"I know, Savi. I apologize for not coming by more often." He cleared his throat and stepped away, meeting Katy as she rose to greet him. The tiny woman had stood between John and certain death more times than he could count after his mother died when he was a boy. They both knew she'd saved his life, and even though she didn't hold that debt over him, John also knew he would never be able to pay it back.

"You are looking thin, John. Have you eaten?"

That prompted another laugh. "Would it matter, Auntie? Not a single thing I've eaten since my last visit can hold a candle to the taste of your curry."

Though Katy smiled at the compliment, John saw the circles of fatigue under her eyes.

"A late night?" he asked.

"Indeed." She smiled and shook her head. "Why is it a fact of each day that babies prefer to arrive at night?"

"You're asking the wrong person, Auntie. Was it a difficult delivery?"

"It was not easy, but with the right food and rest, both mother and child will survive."

The use of the word *survive* instead of *thrive* was deliberate. Surviving was sometimes all the East End offered. Trained as a midwife in India, Katy had fallen back on her skill when the British father of her children abandoned them in the squalor of London. All these years later, she had not only provided for her family and brought hundreds of new lives into the world, but had also passed the skill on to her daughter, giving Savita the same opportunity to make her own way. John had nothing but respect for them both.

As Katy bustled into the kitchen to prepare some food, Charlie grumbled. "She doesn't need to work anymore. I make plenty of money for both her and Savi, but they must like leaving at all hours of the night and working in squalor for little more than pennies."

Savita swatted at him. "Don't be obnoxious, Charlie. Those

pennies kept us from starving, and you ought to show our mother more respect. Besides, those people need us, and you know that. Money isn't the only reason to help someone. Mother and I help because we can."

At the surprising maturity behind Savi's words, John spared another glance in her direction. Her hair was dark as a raven's feathers, thick and long, undone and spilling over her shoulders in the comfort of her home. The only marks her British father had left behind were shown in her lighter skin and eyes, which were a warm golden brown instead of her mother's black.

Those brown eyes were as stubborn as Charlie's in that moment, but John knew they twinkled when she laughed. As she turned away from her brother with a huff, John was struck for the first time by how truly beautiful she had become.

Savita Modi was not a little girl anymore.

After a brief stare down with her brother, she sniffed and went after their mother. As she stepped into the kitchen and out of earshot, Charlie turned to John. "Why are you here, and don't tell me it is to catch up. I see you every week or two at Quinton's. What is the real reason?"

By now there was no room for hesitation; John had committed to this course of action, for better or worse. "Rory is in trouble. I think the help he will need will be from you, not me."

Charlie squinted and crossed his arms, sizing him up, but it only took a moment for him to nod. "Well, there's no stopping that woman once she's decided to make a meal, but we will leave as soon as you've eaten. Whatever help Rory needs, he will have it from me."

Chapter Twenty

It was always a bit of a surprise to John when he turned the corner and Rory Stewart's house came into view. He'd had occasion to visit a few times in the past, usually regarding a post mortem, either officially or unofficially. Though John was fond of Rory, and vice versa, theirs was a friendship which tended toward a professional capacity.

The house, the second one into a rather nice neighborhood, was a brick cottage with a charming winding path that meandered its way to his front door. It branched around the back of the house as well, and John and Charlie followed that branch to its natural conclusion—a shed with thick vines growing up the sides and over the roof, as if trying to provide further shelter for the work which took place within. The solid door was open as John and Charlie approached, although the inside was still shrouded in darkness from their perspective.

John glanced at Charlie. His was often a stoic disposition, but he knew his friend well enough to recognize the clenched jaw and shifting eyes for what they were. Charlie was no stranger to death, not with his lifestyle. It wasn't something the two of them discussed, but John was not naive. His friend lived a violent life. He wasn't cruel, but he also wasn't above taking a life when he felt it necessary. More often than not, that happened in the name of street justice, the kind which the law couldn't or wouldn't bestow—rapists, abusers, predators. John felt certain such actions weren't Charlie's first choice, not when a good beating or talking-to would do, but there was no doubt Charlie would do whatever was needed to protect both himself and the patch of the city he claimed. John doubted he lost any sleep over those decisions.

But for all the things Charlie had done, somehow what Rory did was different to him. The trade of body snatching and dissection was deeply unsettling for Charlie. Where John found it uncomfortable but necessary, Charlie found it beyond distasteful. He too was fond of Rory, and he owed him a debt which couldn't be repaid, but he very rarely darkened this doorstep.

They stopped a discreet distance from the doorway and John called out. He was rewarded with a muffled reply from within. Moments later Rory popped out of the darkness, a leather apron covering an excellent cut of trousers. He was still wiping his hands on a none-too-clean rag when he spoke, his Scottish brogue pronounced. "John . . . and is that Charlie too? My, my, this must be important. To the heavens above and back, what brings you to my little world?"

"We need to speak about a matter, Rory." John nodded in the direction of the main house. "Any way we could go inside?"

Surprise registered in Rory's eyes, but he nodded. After he had closed the door to the shed and locked it, he motioned John and Charlie ahead, and they followed the charming path to the back door of the house.

"I'll put the kettle on." Rory gestured to the living room. "You boys are welcome to take a seat."

They followed his invitation, sitting in awkward silence while they waited for him to come through. Having examined the situation in detail during their walk over, Charlie and John had little left to discuss between them, and neither seemed inclined to break the silence, instead allowing the tension to grow in the room until John thought it might suffocate him.

Finally Rory came in, carrying a tray of tea and biscuits. His brow was furrowed, and after he put his tray down, he took a moment to gather his words. But he wasn't silent for long—it wasn't in his nature. "I've been ruminating on what could bring the two of you by on this fine day. John, you wouldn't bring Charlie if you were here in an official capacity. So either you're in need of a resurrection in the East End, or Charlie is in need of my surgical touch. How close am I?" His tone held a forced lightness to it, but Rory's smile faded as he watched John's reaction.

John sighed. "No easy way to say it, so I'll just say it. The madman is back. There's been another woman murdered. A woman I think you know—a Miss Clarissa Amato."

John's fears were confirmed when Rory froze at the mention of the name. There was no disguising the look of horror on his face. He'd definitely known her. John had already been pretty sure, but now there was no room for doubt. His heart sunk into his stomach.

After a few moments of absolute silence, Rory took in a shuddering breath. "Yes. I know—knew—Miss Amato."

"'Twas the same as the others. She was found in her dress shop, with the red cloth wrapped around her neck." John paused as Rory closed his eyes and leaned back. "I'm right sorry about your . . . about your friend, Rory. But I gotta ask you some questions."

Rory's eyes opened, comprehension dawning on him. "Me? Why would you want to ask me questions . . . unless you want me to take a look at the body? But then Charlie wouldn't be here . . . why are you here?"

"I'm here because you're in a right sticky mess," grumbled Charlie. He had been mostly silent on the walk over, but John could see the darkening storm brewing behind his eyes.

Rory looked nonplussed. "What are you talking about?"

"Rory, I know you argued with Clarissa Amato the night she was killed, at the coffee shop on the corner." John sighed. "A witness places you square in the middle of this, and I need to know how you knew her and what you fought about if I am to help you."

"Then I am a suspect."

"Yes." John didn't want to believe that Rory could have had anything to do with it, but he couldn't help himself from watching his reaction. But Rory's face gave little away other than his overall distress, which was to be expected. John forced himself to push the issue. "What was your connection to the woman?"

Rory's expression was pensive, no doubt weighing what he needed to weigh in his own mind. "I appreciate you coming here yourself, John, but I cannae tell you what you want to know. I will not speak of it."

John could nearly see the steam coming out of Charlie's ears. "John isn't here as a Runner, you stupid Scottish oaf. He's here as a friend, wanting to help, and he doesn't have time to play whatever game this is."

"I understand, Charlie," said Rory with a wince. "But I cannae speak on this matter. It's not a game, I assure you, and I do take this very seriously. But I have made my mind up and I will not be swayed by your shouting."

"You really are a stubborn piece of—"

"Charlie!" John snapped, interrupting the tirade before his friend said something he couldn't take back.

It worked, bringing Charlie back to reality. He took a deep breath before speaking again. "I'm also here as a friend, despite my better judgment. I'm still beholden to you for what you did for me that night."

He didn't have to elaborate on the night in question—they all knew to which he was referring. Charlie's left eye was still eerily white, and a prominent scar ran from his hairline to his jawline, a reminder of the single slash from a makeshift knife that had ended a fistfight those many years ago. Rory had been on his way home from one of his many nocturnal adventures when he heard Charlie's screams. He had carried the bleeding boy to his home, John and Quinton stumbling drunkenly behind him. When the night was over, Charlie was alive only thanks to Rory's medical skills, though the sight in his left eye couldn't be saved. A bond was forged, each of them becoming a thread in the tapestry of their lives. It wasn't a debt one forgot, and Charlie took his debts very seriously.

Charlie broke the weighing silence and continued, "I will find you a place to hide while John and Quinton look into this. Hopefully all will be cleared up quickly and that will be that, and you can go back to your little shed of death in the back like nothing happened. But should things not go that way, I can get you safe passage back to Scotland. I assume you still have a few shady characters there who can help you disappear for a time. Possibly a long time."

Rory stared hard at Charlie, standing suddenly, but looking lost he sat just as suddenly and shook his head. "You can't be serious. I've made my fair share of mistakes; however I can tell you with certainty: I did not kill Clarissa. I cannae just disappear. I have a life here—"

Time for John to weigh in. "Rory, you don't seem to understand what's happening here. Neither of us think you killed her, of course not." John said those words for Rory's benefit as much as his own. "But you were seen arguing with the dead woman on the day of her death. You won't explain what the fight was about, or how you knew her. That alone would probably be enough to convict you, but on top of it all you're a well-known body snatcher. The press will hang you once it becomes known you're a suspect."

Another long silence grew as Rory considered his words. Finally he sighed. "John, you are a man of honor to come to me as a friend and not an officer. I see it may cost you in the future, and I will not forget this. But I meant what I said. My relationship with Clarissa is not something I will discuss."

The persistent headache was settling in once again. "You must see how that makes your situation much more difficult."

"I do."

"Fine." John leaned back in his chair, his limbs suddenly heavy.

"Then you need to disappear, at least for a while. That's not something I can help you with, but Charlie can. Will you please let him help you?"

"Hmm." Rory crossed his arms, his brow still furrowed. "Very well. I will take you up on your generous offer, Charlie—to a point. However, for reasons of, shall we say, a personal nature, I cannae return to Scotland. Even if I could, I would not abandon all of you now. I can still help bring this madman to justice, even if it must be from the shadows."

"Rory, you need to be prepared for the reality of the situation," John argued. "I cannot keep this from the magistrate for long. As soon as I report to him what the witness said, you will be hunted. Quinton and I will do our best, but I can make no guarantees."

"I'm not asking you to."

"Alright, enough." Charlie rose, shaking his head. "Let's go before I change my mind, you stubborn mule. Pack your things— but only the essentials."

"Fine, fine. I'm going." Before he left the room, Rory looked to John. "The lad in the shed—I have some notes written down, but it boils down to natural causes. No one helped him leave his mortal coil. Could you see that his family is somehow informed? They'll need to make arrangements for his burial."

"I'll take care of it."

As Rory left the room, Charlie turned to John. "Avoid your magistrate for a time to give us a start. Get Quinton caught up, and for the love of all that is holy, find this madman. If Rory really won't leave England, then his neck depends on it." The look in his eyes was one of cold conviction. Charlie was a complicated man, and even John wasn't always sure what he was going to do. But he knew in that moment exactly where Charlie stood. Rory would not hang.

Returning a few minutes later with multiple bags, Rory set them down with a thud, accompanied by a distinct metallic clanking.

"No, no, no. Good grief man, do you not know what essentials means? This is far too much—"

"This is the essentials! I need clothes, and then what if I should need to perform a surgery or an impromptu autopsy, or—"

"You aren't going to need any of that—"

John slipped out of the house, leaving the two unlikely companions to their bickering. As he made his way back around the house to the shed to carry out Rory's requests, he reflected on his friends. Perhaps they were more alike than they would care to admit. They both knew how to walk a path outside the norm. They both were stubborn and loyal and dedicated to a morality unique to themselves. And as silence cloaked the house, and John glanced back to see an empty path, he realized there was one more thing they had in common.

They both knew how to disappear.

Chapter Twenty-One

The new housekeeper apparently had a policy of demanding the wages up front. She was unclear on if this policy applied to everyone or just to Quinton. He grumbled as he dug the coins from his pocket, but he had little choice. Three housekeepers had already turned him down. His current reputation evidently preceded him. More than a little offensive that a person had one rough patch and suddenly no one trusted them—though he would allow his rough patch had lasted a while.

While the woman counted the coins in her hand, she scanned the room. Heat crept up Quinton's neck as she took in his unmade cot, the heap of dirty clothes beside it, and the purring cat on top. Being sober and self-aware had its drawbacks.

"This first go around might be a bit of a job, Mrs. Reynolds, but I'll wager the rest will be considerably easier." His words rushed out in an awkward babble. "I'll drop my clothes at the laundress as those aren't your duties." He finished with what he hoped was a charming smile but suspected it was more clumsy than anything. Quinton didn't know what was the matter with him.

After a long pause, to his surprise, Mrs. Reynolds suddenly smiled. "I raised boys, Mr. Huxley. I know how it be. You'll have a square meal on the table for yourself and the mute 'fore I leave on the three days I'm here, and the place'll shine. You'll have food for the next day in yer larder, and I rate myself as a fine baker, so you'll have something in there for your tea. I'll start at noon the days I come and be gone by six o clock. Fer a little extra, I'd be happy to drop your laundry on my way home, though it'd up to you to pick it up."

"Ah, well, as long as it isn't any trouble . . ."

"Not at all." She walked past him cheerfully. "I think we'll get on just fine, Mr. Huxley. Seeing as it's only five past, I'll start now."

"Oh, yes, please. Thank you, Mrs. Reynolds."

Another pregnant pause filled the air as she looked at him expectantly. He took longer than he would've liked to realize she wanted him to leave. Quinton hurriedly grabbed his coat and headed out. She was welcome to the place.

It was a bit of mystery to him when he had become the kind of man who was downright intimidated by a solidly built middle-aged woman. As Quinton contemplated this, a flash of movement out the corner of his eye caught his attention. Ezra waved at him with a crumpled piece of paper clutched in his hand.

He waited as Quinton read the hastily scrawled note to see if a reply would be sent back. It didn't take long for Quinton to realize no reply would be needed, so he gave the boy a coin for his lunch and sent him on his way. The pleased smile and sigh of relief didn't escape his notice. Ezra appeared happy the coffers were replenished once again.

Quinton readjusted his course toward the Black Swan and found the sender of the note already there. John sat with two tankards of ale in front of him, one half empty. Quinton took the empty chair next to him and drank deeply from the full glass. He and John appreciated the quality of beer here, but he knew this was no social call. John never drank when he was working—until now, that is.

An exhaustion exuded from his friend that Quinton had rarely seen in John. He was usually a cheerful soul, with a twinkle in his eye. That twinkle was notably absent today. A deep worry welled up in Quinton's gut, but he made himself stay silent. John had sent for him, and he would tell him what was going on when he was ready.

It didn't take long.

"Rory is in all sorts of trouble, Q, and truth be told, so am I," John said, massaging his temple.

As his friend took another swig of his ale, Quinton reached out and grasped his shoulder. "Take a breath, John. Whatever is going on, we will face it together, like we always have. Tell me about Rory."

The story started slowly but then the words poured out, faster and faster. Quinton listened carefully, increasingly incredulous as John spoke of Rory's argument with Madame Amato. By the time John finished with the conversation at Rory's house, John had regained his composure. A burden shared was halved, it seemed.

In contrast, Quinton had become increasingly upset as the tale unfolded. His half of the burden had doubled. "Where is he now? Rory?"

"With Charlie. They left together, and not you nor I nor God above could find Rory now." John glanced at Quinton. "Of course, Rory couldn't have done this thing."

"Of course not." Quinton said the words confidently, but something in John's eyes gave him pause. He suspected John said the statement as much to convince himself as to convince Quinton. But they had both known Rory for years. He wasn't capable of cold-blooded murder. To believe otherwise . . . Quinton pushed such thoughts from his mind, turning his attention back to John with a deep breath. "But you are right he will hang if he is arrested. The only way out is for us to find this killer before the authorities find Rory."

Quinton was surprised how far his interest had shifted in the course of a single conversation. For years his only thought had been to find the person who took his mother from him. He wanted to see justice for that—he wanted to see someone pay for it. But now, with Rory's life in the balance, that motivation took a back seat.

Of the three boyhood friends, Quinton was closest to Rory. The older man had become a bit of a father figure to him—or perhaps an older brother or uncle. The definition for their relationship was murky, but it fell within the bounds of family. Even now, the thought of Rory hanging for this murder made Quinton feel like that lost boy from the past, desperately clinging on to any scrap of affection shown to him.

His mother was gone, and his father had been gone before he could remember. But this man was a living, breathing part of his life right now. He was the man Quinton went to when he faced moral dilemmas. When he faced physical altercations, Rory was the one to stitch him back together. Rory's presence was a pillar in his life. He knew in the depths of his soul that his already shaky world would not hold up if another pillar crumbled.

He wouldn't let that happen.

Another concern complicated the mix. "How will your job fare if it becomes known you spoke with Rory?"

"It can't become known." John eyes were dark. "I know the most important thing is justice for Rory, and the dead women, but truth be told Q, I right like having a paying job. Besides which, I'm good at it, and I don't mind eating regularly. If the magistrate finds out . . . I'll be out on my tail if I'm lucky."

"I won't let that happen."

"It won't be up to you, Q." John paused, and then surprised Quinton with a change of subject. "Been thinking lately maybe it's about time I settled down—find someone special. Maybe raise a family of my own. This job allows that kind of thinking, and I really don't want to lose it."

"Ah, I see how it is." Quinton leaned back and smiled. "Nothing wrong in wanting to get a bit ahead in this world, John. You deserve that life."

Color bloomed on John's light brown cheeks. "Aye, well, first I have to find someone willing to settle down with this ugly mug."

Quinton laughed. "Somehow I don't think that's going to be a problem. In regard to your job, Rory is long gone now. You should go to your magistrate and tell him what the witness said. Take him to Rory's home. It will look like you put the law above your friendship, and you'll win his favor and his gratefulness. If he finds you knew the man and didn't reveal it, you'll never shake off the stink of suspicion. Having you on the right side of the law might help us keep a step ahead of it."

John nodded and drew a deep breath. "Of course."

As Quinton stood up to leave, he turned back for a moment. "And John, thank you, for making sure Rory gets a fair shot at clearing his name. You could have handled this all kinds of different, but you chose to follow your heart. It's the kind of man you are, and whatever happens, that loyalty will follow you."

A hint of twinkle made it to his eyes as John looked back at Quinton. "The only real truth a man has is in who he shares his life with. Rory, you, Charlie. What would that make me if I didn't have your backs when you needed me?" John downed the last of his ale. "I'm off to play my part, my friend. I'll find Ezra or go to your place if there's anything you need to know."

Quinton left the pub, knowing exactly where his feet would take him next. God above might not be able to find Rory, but Quinton knew exactly where Charlie would have taken him.

The direction he headed was not east to Charlie's home, but rather south. Few knew all of Charlie's real estate holdings—sometimes he wasn't sure if even the man himself was aware of everything he'd acquired through the years. But Quinton knew more than most, and he had a pretty good idea where to start looking.

Though Charlie loved his mother and his sister, the reality of living with them did drive him a bit mad at times. Sometimes he needed his own space. A couple years back, Charlie told Quinton he finally found the best of both worlds. He bought a house, in a modest neighborhood of London not frequented by the Modi midwives. Truth be told, Quinton wasn't sure if "bought" was the right word. In Charlie's world, acquiring assets was not always so straight forward. But regardless, Charlie owned a small house tucked behind a bigger house in a place few would think to look for him. One had to know it was there to find it. It even had a back entrance through the garden that was unseen from the neighbors.

A space like that had many uses—amorous pursuits, private business dealings, or, in this case, perhaps hiding a fugitive. It wasn't someplace John would know about, but Charlie used to let Quinton take meetings there, before he'd landed at his new office and residence, courtesy of Lord Coleville. Charlie would remember that.

Quinton found the front house and worked his way around to the small dwelling behind. He didn't have to knock—Charlie had been expecting him. He opened the door and stepped aside to allow Quinton to pass.

"Finally." Charlie shook his head, glancing toward the back rooms. "Maybe you can talk some sense into the bloody Scot."

As if summoned by the words, the bloody Scot himself wandered out, hair in disarray and clothes rumpled. His disheveled appearance was surprising even though Quinton was well aware of his abrupt departure. He'd seen Rory in many situations, including awakened from a dead sleep, but never so . . . lost.

"Figured you would show, lad. I won't tell you my secrets any more than Charlie, let's get that out of the way now. So what's the plan?" The look of desperation in his eyes allowed Quinton to realize what Rory needed. He needed to know that this wasn't the end—he needed to know there was a plan in place.

Both the body snatcher and Charlie looked expectantly at him. In the space of a day Quinton had gone from the lost boy to the man with the plan. Fortunately the walk over had hatched one.

"When was the last time you actually robbed a grave?"

Chapter Twenty-Two

As John shifted uncomfortably in his chair, he glanced over at the magistrate. Ackerly Holdsworth was in the midst of rummaging around in his desk drawer. Finally he found the object of his search and pulled out two glasses and a bottle. He poured a generous finger of gin for both himself and John before leaning back in his chair, a contemplative expression on his face. "It won't be long before we find this grave robber. Then perhaps this madness will end."

"Yes, sir. Let's hope so." His job was to agree with Holdworth, and this wasn't the time for alternate theories.

"Indeed, indeed." Holdsworth turned an appraising eye towards him. "I know you worked with this Stewart before, in an official capacity. I also know you were on friendly terms with him outside of work. You handled this matter correctly, and I appreciate your honesty. Your loyalty to the law and to your fellow officers won't be forgotten."

"Thank you, sir." John ignored the twist of guilt in his gut. Only a few hours before, Quinton had been telling him almost the same thing. He didn't regret his decision to put his friendship before his profession, but that didn't mean he was blind to the irony of the magistrate's words.

An awkward silence filled the room, and John found it impossible not to fill it. "When did you first figure it was a single man killin' multiple times, sir? No one else was clever enough to catch on to it."

It was a story John had heard before, but he knew Holdsworth never tired of explaining how his insights were right. He needed to grease the man's ego, stay in his favor and his circle of trust so he was kept in the loop on the investigation and could keep one step ahead. He promptly squashed the rising guilt further down.

"Well, Smith, that is a story unto itself," started Holdsworth, easily falling into the trap John had laid. "I was a magistrate in Cambridgeshire for twelve years before my wife and I moved to London. We didn't get many murders out there, not like that. Occasional highwayman, maybe, or a thief. But not murders."

He paused to sip his drink. "Once I came to London, that changed. One of my first was a lady's maid who'd been killed, a red cloth wrapped around her neck, tied in elaborate knots. The girl didn't have much in the way of kin, and the family she worked for just wanted the whole thing to go away . . . so it did. That never sat right with me. But as I spoke with the runners, a few remembered seeing a case like it before, three years previous. It was an actress found dead that time—I would come to find out later she was the mother of your friend Huxley—strangled with a red cloth. It seemed a very strange coincidence to me, but there wasn't much to be done about it at that point, so I let it lie. A few years passed, and life moved on. Then we found the next lass, a market girl, and the whole thing came back into focus for me. This one was the same as the others, with that infernal red cloth around her neck. Those little gold elephants on it, very distinctive—too distinctive to be a coincidence any longer, at least in my mind. I kept that piece, to show it was the same. I thought it proved all the women were killed by the same hand. Of course, I was the only one who thought that."

John nodded, knowing the words Holdsworth wanted to hear. "That was right smart of you, sir, to put that together."

"Perhaps, but it did little good. Then we found another, you remember, you had just been promoted to Officer. Same cloth, same knots. Still no one believed me. But I just couldn't let it go. Every time I tried . . . I just couldn't get those girls out of my head.'" The alcohol was beginning to do what it did best, softening the magistrate's inhibitions. "I think about your friend Huxley sometimes. That must have been perfectly terrible for that boy to find his own mother dead like that. Perfectly terrible."

"Yes, sir. I'm sure it was." Bloody understatement of the century.

"For years I made noise, Smith, and no one would listen. The lasses that were killed were either too unimportant or worked for people too influential, and no one wanted to believe such a killer existed. And it wasn't just the madness of the theory, but also the years in between which poisoned those above against me. It was always long enough for everyone to simply put it out of their mind and move on. Couldn't get any of the government lackeys to take me seriously. Swept under the rug, all of it. But I knew . . . I knew there would be another."

"I wish to God I hadn't been proven right by Margot Anderson, may her soul rest in peace." The statement was spoken sincerely, but Holdsworth's face soured. "Shame it had to take the death of a nobleman's daughter to get people's attention. A real shame. Without her . . . who knows how long these killings would have continued. That death was a gift—a terrible, terrible gift. Might not have been immediate—everyone focused on the Chedrose boy. But now . . . things are different." Holdsworth abruptly downed the rest of his glass and slammed it to the desk.

This was John's opening. "Any success finding the trail of Mr. Stewart, sir?"

"Not as of yet. We have constables canvassing his neighborhood—it won't be long before we find him." His eyes were alight with righteous fire. "I can't believe he was under my nose all this time, but it all makes sense. As helpful as those anatomists can be, there's no way around the fact it is deviant behavior. And now he's finally slipped up. This time, he'll be captured."

"Of course, sir." John felt the heaviness in the pit of his stomach gain weight. "Has any other evidence turned up?"

"As a matter of fact . . . " Holdsworth paused to pull a piece of paper out of his desk. "Take a look at that."

John quickly scanned the document—wrinkled and yellowed with age, but still readable. The first line read Passenger Manifest 1792.

"What is this?" asked John, confusion mixing with the dread which was already haunting him.

Self-satisfaction practically dripped off the magistrate. "Never let it be said I don't do my due diligence. That there is the manifest from the ship which brought Rory Stewart from Edinburgh to London. Note the date."

"1792." John tried to say the words without emotion, but as the magistrate had been speaking John had been putting the pieces together. "The year before Annie Huxley was murdered."

"Precisely. Proves the man was in the city when the murders were happening." Holdsworth snatched the paper back, returning it to his drawer. "Just trying to get ahead of any clever barrister antics for the trial."

"Of course, sir," repeated John hollowly. "Very clever, sir."

Holdworth smiled. "I've left word to have him brought in alive. I want everyone to have the satisfaction of seeing him swing."

Chapter Twenty-Three

Beneath his woolen hat and scarf, Rory's voice was muffled. Even though it was well past midnight, Charlie had insisted the man at least feign at covering his features. His sketch was in the paper, so now anyone on the street might recognize him and they still had several blocks to go before they reached their destination.

"What?" muttered Charlie.

Rory spoke again, much clearer this time. Charlie turned to see the scarf now slung around his neck in a semblance of fashion, rather than subterfuge. He gritted his teeth but said nothing.

"I don't usually do my own digging these days, lads. I have men now for this part, while my skills are saved for the blade." Rory paused to gather the shovel and pick into a different grip. "Honestly it feels good to be back in the game."

Charlie took a firmer grip on his own shovel, his mood dark. "When you are a wanted man in all of London for brutal murders stretching back years, there are precious few men to trust. Let's just hope we find the body quickly and get this whole endeavor behind us."

He knew he was being surly. He had a reputation for being harsh, even deadly when necessary. That's what it took to survive. But some things were beyond even his tolerance for the gray areas of life. He wasn't a man who believed in any religious faith, either Hindu or Christian, but his mother's Indian heritage had still made a strong impression on him. It wasn't death that made him so uncomfortable—it was touching the corpse. A shudder ran down his spine just at the thought. Charlie knew it was irrational, but that didn't change his feelings. In all his years of knowing Rory, this was an aspect of his life he'd always managed to stay separate from. It was a testament to what he owed the resurrectionist that he had agreed to be part of this escapade tonight.

Ahead in the dark, he heard Quinton stumble and swear softly under his breath. "It had to be the dark of the moon on the night we rob a grave."

The night was indeed black as pitch, but that would lend to their favor when they actually began digging.

White, uniform smudges of shapes began to come into view as they approached the graveyard—the stones, all lined up in row after row, marking the final resting place of those in the ground like faithful soldiers. At least, that's how some might perceive it. Charlie had little time for such philosophical thoughts. Even if he did, it wouldn't be for the supposed restfulness of the earth. When he died, probably at a young age in a violent way, he hoped they didn't put him in the dirt. It was likely the dead didn't really care, but something about being buried that felt like being trapped. He didn't want to be enclosed in a coffin, alone in the dark with six feet of earth pinning the lid shut. If it were up to him . . . they'd take him out of the city, maybe to a nice hill overlooking the surrounding farmland. Let his body burn and the ashes float away in the breeze, carried in death to places he never saw in life. But of course, he had no time for such thoughts.

Quinton paused at the graveyard's edge, silently counting the rows. With a quick nod he continued in a straight line, with Rory and himself trailing behind. Finally his friend paused again, then pivoted, following a row down to a freshly dug grave.

The stone was not yet marked, but they all knew whose corpse lay beneath the overturned dirt. Since Rory refused to reveal any information on his relationship with the seamstress, nor his known argument with her, Quinton had suggested he at least examine the body. Whatever Charlie's personal feelings on the matter, he knew there was no one better at reading the language of the dead.

"Let's get this over with." Rory's tone was unusually subdued.

"I thought this was what gets you out of bed every day—the chance to slice into a fresh corpse." Charlie planted his shovel in the soil, running a hand through his thick hair, which was already beginning to stick to the sweat beading on his forehead. "Why so low, old boy?"

Even in the dark, there was no mistaking the spark of irritation in Rory's eye as he turned. "It's one thing to cut into a stranger. It's another to cut into a friend. The fact I'm one false step away from the noose is the only reason I'm here, and that reality does little to soothe my conscience. Perhaps move your shovel more than your mouth."

"Relax, Rory. I didn't mean nothing by it." Charlie's reply was casual, but he felt a pang of guilt at his callousness. He'd been so wrapped up in his own discomfort, he'd forgotten about Rory's. He still didn't know what this Clarissa Amato had meant to his friend, but whatever their relationship had been, he was clearly affected by her death.

As the three men began to dig, the only sound to be heard was the scrape of metal against dirt. The freshly turned soil made the work relatively easy, and it wasn't long before they found the casket. Charlie swallowed hard and glanced away as Quinton and Rory gripped the deceased by her shoulders and ankles and lifted the body out. They quickly wrapped it in the blankets they had brought while Charlie went behind them and closed the coffin's lid. He quickly scrambled out and began to unceremoniously shovel the earth back into the hole.

"Hurry along, Charlie," Quinton muttered. "Constables could happen by at any time."

"Oh, I'm sorry, did we want everyone to know we removed the lady from her grave?" Charlie shook his head and continued throwing dirt on the casket below.

"Of course not." Quinton scowled at him. "But it wouldn't kill you to hurry up."

"Do my eyes deceive me or is that a shovel by your hand? Get over here and help if you're in such a hurry."

"Gentlemen!" Rory interjected. "Please, let's just get this done. We need to get her to Charlie's place before dawn."

Charlie froze. "My place?!"

"Shh, keep your voice down!"

"My place?" Charlie repeated, his tone lowered to a strained hiss.

"Well, where else did you think we were taking her?" Quinton hissed back.

"I don't know. I assumed anywhere but my house."

"I just assumed you understood the obvious here." Quinton pinched the bridge of his nose, then grabbed his shovel. "There is no other place, Charlie. This is not the time to be arguing about this—the body is out of the ground and we are on a clock."

"Now see here—"

"Stop. Complaining. And. Grow. Up." Quinton punctuated each word with a shovel full of dirt thrown on top of the empty casket.

Despite the serious circumstances, Rory started to laugh softly. "This does indeed present a conundrum, lads. But whatever we decide, we cannot do what needs to be done here."

"Well then come up with an alternative, because you are not cutting that corpse up on my kitchen table."

Rory's expression became thoughtful. "Actually, as it happens, we are not far from my own little shed."

"You can't be serious, Rory." Quinton shook his head. "You can't go back there."

"Why not? It's already been searched and all my tools are there. Sometimes the best place to hide is in plain sight." Rory nodded, his mind clearly made up. "Finish up lads, and follow me."

Chapter Twenty-Four

As Quinton stood in front of the door, the brass knocker in his grasp, he found himself hesitant. The dead of night events the night before seemed surreal as the glare of day brought a new challenge. Once he knocked and the sound echoed through the home, he would be committed to this path. The urge to simply walk away before his presence was perceived appealed strongly to him.

After several long moments spent caught in the purgatory between choices, Quinton sighed. As much as he was tempted to leave, he also knew he'd already committed in his heart. Sometimes one had to swallow one's pride for the greater good. As reluctant as he was to darken this particular doorstep again, he knew he would regret it more if he took the coward's route now. He swallowed hard and knocked.

The door swiftly opened, revealing the Dovefields' butler, Quaid. He was likely thirty years Quinton's senior, but his back stood straight and his eyes still glinted with sharp intelligence. "Ah, Mr. Huxley. It's been some time. Is Lord Dovefield expecting you?"

"No, Quaid, he isn't." Quinton paused for a moment before forcing himself to say the next words. "But actually, I'm not here to see him. Is Lady Demas home?"

The butler appraised him with a bird of prey's candid gaze. Quinton understood the calculations he was doing in his head. On the one hand, a man of his station had no business calling on the single daughter of a gentleman. But on the other hand, he was known to the household, and the lord of the house himself had entertained him socially on more than one occasion. His presence and request did not fall into a clear category of yes or no, forcing the butler to make a judgment call in the moment.

Finally Quaid made his decision. "You may wait in the entryway while I enquire if the lady is receiving visitors."

Quinton inclined his head to acknowledge the allowance and stepped over the threshold. Though this was not his first time crossing it, he still felt like a stranger within these walls.

When the Anderson girl was killed the year before, he'd spent several late evenings going over the case with Lord Dovefield. At first they met at his solicitor's office or at a gentlemen's club, but after Zoe left for America, the barrister began to invite him back to his home. They would sit up talking and drinking whiskey for hours, poring over the details.

But the months passed, Chedrose was convicted, and the official investigation ended. As the leads faded away, so did Quinton's visits. In truth, he was grateful he didn't have to face the lord that day. He could only handle the disappointment of one Dovefield that afternoon.

Not long later, he was ushered into the sitting room by a young footman, indicating Zoe hadn't immediately insisted on his removal from the premises. It wasn't much, but it was a start.

The sound of footsteps in the hallway announced the woman's imminent arrival. She swept into the room with the force of a storm on the ocean, her lavender gown swirling around her legs with a soft swishing sound. Her dark curls bounced with each step, while her eyes flashed with unreadable emotion. "Has something happened?" Her voice was breathless, as if she'd ran down the stairs.

"What?"

"Has something happened?" she repeated. "Is someone injured or dead?"

"I have no idea what you're referring to. No one is hurt."

"Then what are you doing here?"

Quinton blinked. "The only reason you can think why I would be here is if someone were seriously injured or dying?"

Zoe scowled at him. "You never call on me . . . not anymore. I assumed Ezra had been hit by a carriage or perhaps John was stabbed by a suspect. I don't know, I just assumed something terrible must've happened for you to be here."

"Well it's nothing of the sort."

"Very well."

"Very well."

The two of them stood there for a tense moment, staring at the other, unsure what to say next. Then Zoe broke the standoff and pulled a rope on the wall. Within thirty seconds Quaid appeared at the doorway. Zoe had left the door open for the sake of propriety.

"Could you have the cook send up a tray of tea, please? Mary will be joining us shortly."

"Of course, milady."

As the butler left, Zoe gestured to a plush armchair. "Take a seat, if you're going to stay."

The chair only protested with a mild creak as Quinton settled into it. The tea was served in the next five minutes. Zoe poured him a cup, adding a generous amount of cream and honey to the brew. The Dovefields as a whole did not support the sugar trade, protesting the loophole in the new law that allowed British colonies to continue relying on slave labor even though the practice was illegal in England itself.

Once he was settled with cup in hand, she spoke. "So if serious injury did not bring you here today, what did?"

He took a sip before answering. "John obtained an appointment ledger from the dressmaker's assistant. Due diligence would indicate someone should interview the women who had appointments on the day of the murder."

"Indeed." Zoe took a sip of her own tea, her stormy eyes appraising him over the cup's rim. She didn't say anything else, instead letting him fill the space.

It was a good interrogation tactic, and Quinton obliged her. "John and I discussed it, and since the higher classes are already so reluctant to speak with the constabulary, lest they be associated with scandal, we felt it might be best if they were interviewed by someone less . . . intimidating. Perhaps in a more relaxed setting, where they might not even realize they were being . . . interviewed." Quinton shifted in his seat, avoiding Zoe's gaze.

She grinned like a cat who'd eaten a canary, as he'd known she would. "I see. So you have come to ask for my help?"

Quinton scowled. "Well, I suppose under certain circumstances, one might say something like that."

"Something like what?" Zoe leaned forward on her palms, her voice sweet with false innocence.

Little point in delaying the inevitable. He swallowed a sigh along with his pride. "I need your help, Zoe."

"That's all you had to say." She sat back with satisfaction, much to his annoyance. "Give me the list of names and I will have Theo arrange something—perhaps a lady's soiree."

"Mm. Thank you. Be sure to ask what ask if anything unusual happened that day. Perhaps the dressmaker mentioned something or they saw someone lurking around. But be subtle—don't make it seem like an interrogation."

She waved a dismissive hand. "I am always subtle. Besides, as much as they might hate being associated with scandal, there's nothing the upper class loves more than talking about it. I doubt I'll even have to bring it up."

It took a great deal of self-control to refrain from commenting on her first statement. He was getting better at letting Zoe be Zoe. "That may be true. But this is important. Rory's life may hinge on something they witnessed."

Zoe's brow furrowed. "What's this about Rory?"

He briefly outlined Rory's murky connection to the case. It didn't take very long, since he himself still didn't really understand it. He had intended to keep certain aspects to himself—such as his own role in hiding the fugitive—but with a warm cup of tea in his hand and a soft pillow at his back, Quinton found himself telling her nearly everything. Who knew a few creature comforts and a woman hanging on his every word were all it would take to loosen his tongue?

"Well that does complicate things," Zoe said when he had finished. "Where does Rory say he was that evening?"

"He admits that he argued with her, but he refuses to provide any explanation for his presence, even to me. It is extremely frustrating, and puts the rest of us in an impossible spot—especially John. We need to come up with something—anything—that might provide an alibi for him, while at the same time pursuing the real killer. I know it is not his intention, but his stubbornness has doubled everyone's work."

The initial shock which had been etched into her features quickly faded to a pensive expression. She seemed to hesitate before speaking her next words. "I know you're terribly fond of Rory. But you're sure he didn't do it?"

"Of course I am!" The exclamation came out harsher than Quinton intended. "I've known Rory since I was sixteen years old. He's eccentric, certainly, but—"

"Eccentric is one way to put it." Zoe sipped her tea calmly, seemingly unfazed by his reaction. "I know you are close to him. I myself enjoy the man's company—he's clever and witty, not to mention helpful in all manner of needs. But you cannot deny he lives his life on the moral and ethical fringes. How well do you really know him? How well do we really know anyone, for that matter?"

"I know him a great deal better than you," Quinton snapped. But though he didn't want to admit it, even to himself, her words struck a nerve. When John had informed him of the passenger manifest, Quinton had been quick to dismiss it. He didn't want to doubt Rory. He didn't want to even consider the possibility that his friend of over a decade—a man he looked up to and had turned to over and over again in times of need—could be this terrible thing. If it were true, it would mean that Rory had not only killed Clarissa and Margot and the others, but also that he had taken Quinton's own mother's life. Quinton couldn't have misread the man that much . . . could he?

No. Quinton had made mistakes in his life, but his friendship with Rory wasn't one of them. This was a man who couldn't bear to drown an unwanted litter of kittens. He may have his own idea of what was moral or not, but deep down, he was a good person. Quinton was sure of it. He had to be.

"I know Rory isn't capable of this," Quinton began. "I know you don't know him as I do, but I am asking you to trust me on this. I need you to trust me."

Zoe was silent for a moment, those blue eyes of hers unreadable. "Very well."

Quinton let out a deep breath he hadn't realized he'd been holding. "Thank you. For this, and for agreeing to assist with the interviews."

"I promise I will do my best." Her face had lost its self-satisfied expression, instead taking on a more sympathetic countenance.

"I would not have asked you for this if I didn't have confidence in your ability." Quinton said the words before he could stop himself, surprising them both. Nevertheless, he did mean them, which surprised him even more.

Chapter Twenty-Five

Theo didn't take much convincing to agree to host a soiree for the women on John's list. She gleefully sent out the invitations, mixing in a few random ladies so as not to be too obvious when it came to intentions. She never could pass up an opportunity to be in the middle of the action, something Theo understood was both a blessing and a curse.

She set the date for two days later. It was short notice, but time was of the essence according to Zoe. Besides, it wasn't as if the ladies of society had too many pressing appointments at two o'clock in the afternoon.

The RSVPs came in swiftly, with all the ladies on the appointment ledger agreeing to attend. Theo wasn't surprised. The untimely death of their modiste was likely the most interesting thing to happen in their vicinity in ages. They were no doubt dying for an opportunity to tell their tale. Never mind the fact that their temporary spotlight came at the cost of a human life.

However, if she was being truthful, Theo knew she was not completely innocent when it came to profiting off the tragedy. She too was eager for a spark of intrigue to liven up her monotonous life. It wasn't that she didn't care about justice for the poor murdered woman, but she couldn't claim her motive was entirely selfless either.

When Zoe and Mary arrived early on the day of the event, Theo greeted her stepniece enthusiastically. Though they were not related by blood, they were bonded by spirit.

From the first moment she'd set eyes on her, Theo had pegged Zoe as passionate and intelligent and bold—all the qualities a young woman should have. Society all too easily stomped out any sign of passion in a lady. Theo saw it happen more often than not. Then there was the other side of the coin—the danger of letting a child grow up with no direction on social tact, resulting in a rude and unlikable creature which no amount of good breeding could make up for. Theo had taken it upon herself to encourage and guide those qualities in her niece, striving for a balance that would suit her well. Now she was an adult, and although she was far from perfect, Theo was very proud of her.

Her recent hobby of investigating murders was an . . . unexpected development, but Zoe seemed to find it stimulating, and the challenge had certainly helped her mature. She'd acquired an eclectic group of associates along the journey, some of whom Theo approved of more than others, but as long as Zoe kept her in the loop, she tried not to be overly critical. If there was one thing she'd learned raising her brother Hugh, it was when you told a young person not to do something, they would likely do it anyway, the only difference being they'd keep it to themselves next time.

"Are you ready, Aunt Theo?" asked Zoe, her eyes sparkling.

"The canapes are all prepared, the tables set up in the garden, and Benson is hovering over a wine glass with the claret, ready to pour as soon as the first guest arrives." Theo smiled at her niece. "If you are referring to the other matter, I am confident in our abilities."

"Well it looks like we won't have to wait long to test your confidence." Mary was peeking out the window curtain. "Lady Pemberton is early."

Mary was one of the associates Zoe had picked up near the top of Theo's positive list. She was a dark-skinned girl, her hair thick with tight curls, the bulk of which was held back in a bun by a brave hair ribbon. Theo sometimes caught herself wondering what the volume of hair would be if freed.

Though she'd started off as a lady's maid, Mary had a temperament that was clearly better suited to being a companion. She too was a bright young woman, with a sharp wit and natural boldness that complimented Zoe. The two had quickly become thick as thieves, much to Zoe's benefit. Zoe had spent too long feeling like an outsider, and every woman needed a friend to support her, as well as keep her grounded. Theo hoped Zoe was as much that friend to Mary as Mary was to her.

"Lady Pemberton is always early," Theo grumbled. "Even worse, she's one of the extras I mixed in to create the illusion of randomness. She'll do her best to bore us to death recounting a tale of boiled vegetables if she has her way."

"I think I'll go check on Benson and that claret," said Mary with a wink.

"Mary, don't you dare leave me," Zoe hissed, but it was too late. Her companion abandoned her without a backward glance, leaving Zoe to face the tedium of Lady Pemberton with only Theo for assistance.

"Chin up, my dear. This is where British fortitude comes in handy."

"You forget, I am not British."

"You are my niece, which makes you close enough."

By this time Lady Pemberton had been shown through to the garden. She was a stout woman nearing her middle age, with a plain countenance and a dreadful lack of social awareness. Most were willing to overlook this unfortunate personality trait because her husband was the Queen's cousin, making her not quite royalty but certainly royalty adjacent. In a culture where social standing meant everything, that was enough to cover most of her shortcomings.

"Ah, Your Grace. It's so good to see you," said the stout woman.

Theo inclined her head. "And you, Lady Pemberton. How is the count these days?"

"Fine, fine." The lady waved her hand dismissively. "I swear ever since he visited Ireland, all he's wanted to eat is boiled cabbage. I've heard all about the miracle health benefits of cabbage—Plato himself advocated it—but I must say it leaves a lot to be desired in regard to digestion."

Zoe snorted, trying to disguise her laugh with a discreet cough. Theo carefully avoided looking at her, lest she too lost her composure. Despite her years of practice in controlling emotion, even she felt a twinge pull at the corner of her lips.

She decided a lack of comment was the safest path forward. "You recall my niece, Lady Zoe Demas?"

"Of course! It's your fifth season, isn't it?"

An awkward pause followed. "Sixth."

"Well, it's a good thing you're still so lovely, darling." Lady Pemberton gave a slight sigh. "I suppose there's not much to be done about your complexion."

Another pause, during which Theo held her breath.

"Of course. Thank you, Lady Pemberton. It was lovely to see you. If you'll excuse me." With those words, Zoe turned on her heel and stalked off. Well, "stalked" wasn't quite correct. Her head was held high and she didn't stomp like a child. In truth, Theo thought she had handled that better than expected. If nothing else, she'd finally learned the painful adult skill of holding one's tongue.

Although Lady Pemberton seemed oblivious to the rudeness of her words, she did tsk at Zoe's sharp departure. But Theo was able to sooth her nerves with a glass of sherry.

As more guests began to arrive, Theo fulfilled her role as hostess, assuring that each of them was settled with food and a beverage. She made the rounds, flitting from one group to another, keeping the conversation light and neutral.

After about an hour of congenial conversation and several glasses of claret, she caught Zoe's eye. It was time.

"That is a lovely gown." The compliment was directed toward Lady Soarington, whom Theo knew was among those who had an appointment with the modiste the day of the tragedy. "You must send me your dressmaker's information."

The viscountess paled. "Oh, well I thank you very much Your Grace, but I'm afraid I cannot assist you. A terrible accident befell the modiste who made this gown not four days ago, and I am afraid she has passed on to God."

Theo feigned shock. "Oh my dear, how terrible! What kind of accident?"

"It was no accident." One of the other women, a Lady Doringfield, interjected. "I heard her death was at the hands of another."

"A murder, you mean?" Theo gasped, covering her mouth with a gloved hand. "How terrible."

She didn't ask another question—she didn't need to. It was the chance they'd all been waiting for to discuss the tantalizing bit of gossip.

"I heard she was assaulted in the alley." "Of course she was assaulted; she was killed." "No, I mean . . . in an indecent way."

"I heard her skin was covered in Satanic ramblings." "Well I'm not surprised. She was after all Italian, and we all know foreigners are less God fearing. She was probably mixed up in some dreadful devil worship and God struck her down." "Please, Lady Callum, don't be ridiculous. She wasn't even Italian."

Theo let them squawk among themselves for a few minutes, just listening to their comments and theories for anything useful. Most if it was untrue. She knew from Zoe that the poor woman hadn't been raped and that there were no Satanic writings on the body. But a few gems might be hidden in there somewhere.

"I saw her the day she died, God rest her soul."

That was what she'd been waiting for—Theo zeroed in on the

speaker. "Really, Lady Soarington? What a spiritual experience for you, to be one of the last people to speak to someone before they passed on." Theo leaned forward. "What did you talk about?"

The woman looked surprised to be addressed directly. "Oh well, nothing of note. Just about making some adjustments to one of my gowns."

"Naturally, of course. I wonder if the poor woman knew whoever it was who took her life. I don't suppose she said anything revealing?"

"I'm not sure what you mean by that." Lady Soarington's face seemed to have gone a shade paler, if that was even possible for someone with her natural lack of color.

It was a risk, but Theo decided to push further. "Well, something that at the time seemed ordinary enough, but upon further reflection, together with the context of what we know now, might stand out as unusual?"

"No, I don't think so." The viscountess stood. "If you'll excuse me, Your Grace, I am feeling a bit faint. I think I'll go for a turn about the garden, if you don't mind."

"Of course, feel free my dear."

Another one of the ladies jumped up, taking her arm in hers, a look of concern on her face. Theo watched them depart, the two figures soon obscured by the foliage. Soarington's reaction had been . . . odd. She was new to the circle of married women whom Theo interacted with—the younger woman had secured a match less than a year ago, so Theo was less familiar with her normal countenance. It was difficult to tell if her behavior was suspicious or if she was simply a nervous creature by nature. Then again, being a newlywed, there was also the distinct possibility her reactions were more physical than disposition related. Perhaps a happy announcement was on the horizon.

The conversation of the ladies continued to revolve around the death of Clarissa Amato, but nothing of any particular note was said. The ones who had seen her that day reported nothing out of the ordinary. By all accounts, she was a talented seamstress and popular among her clientele. Some found her a bit radical in her political and social views but chalked it up to her "foreign blood." No one had any real complaint against her, despite one persistent attempt to convince them all it was God's wrath that struck her down.

Finally the conversation drifted to other topics and Theo excused herself. She caught Zoe's eye, moving to a quiet corner where they could compare notes discreetly.

"Well?" she asked.

"Well nothing." Zoe's tone was decidedly discontent. "Apparently not one of them saw or heard anything important. And I've been stuck in a group with Pemberton *and* Fairfax!"

"Ah, I forgot about Charlotte." Theo glanced in the direction of the plain woman whose face was pinched as she examined a scone. "Remind me, is she one who had an appointment that day, or one of the extras?"

"She did have an appointment, but it was the day before. She deemed it extremely vital information to tell me in excruciating detail about how her coachman was sick, so her lady's maid hired a hackney to take them both there. Honestly I don't know how you endure these people."

"Well, I know Charlotte can be a little dull. But she means well. She came out a few seasons ahead of me, but we've spent a great many years in the same social circles." Theo shrugged. "Shared history isn't everything, but it isn't nothing either."

"You may share history, but you have nothing else in common." Zoe crossed her arms with a sigh.

Theo sighed as well. "Your father would agree with you, dear. He hasn't much use for the Fairfaxes, though I believe it was her son he disliked."

Zoe's reaction to that was to roll her eyes. She had a low tolerance for small talk, and apparently she'd exceeded her limit for today. "I think we might've learned as much as we are going to."

The definite whiny pitch in Zoe's voice confirmed Theo's deductions. They would need to wrap this up before Zoe did something uncouth.

"Perhaps." Theo paused.

"What is it?"

"Well the only thing that happened that stands out is Lady Soarington's reaction."

Zoe raised an eyebrow. "Elizabeth? I know her a bit. She got married last year, to a much older man, if I recall correctly. She was getting a bit long in the tooth for her parents' liking. Rumor is she spent more time in their library than practicing the art of congenial conversation."

"Mm. Well, I wouldn't know either way. I've hardly spent any time with the woman socially. It may or may not be out of the ordinary, but she did seem very anxious. If she had gone any paler, she could've been mistaken for a ghost."

"That is interesting." Zoe contemplated this. "I don't know her very well, but she did always strike me as a bit retiring, bordering on mousy. Perhaps discussions of death are too much for her disposition. Although . . ."

"What?"

"Now that you say it, a few of the women in my group reacted a bit strangely too. When everyone else wanted to sink their teeth into the gossip, Mrs. Lorant and Lady Brightlingsea seemed more uncomfortable. But I just thought they were squeamish."

Theo snorted. "If there is one thing Lady Brightlingsea is not, it's squeamish. If women were allowed on hunts, she would be the one to make the first kill. I've never seen her shy away from a subject for fear of sensitivity or poor taste."

"Well you would know more than me. Perhaps it is worth you following up with them." Zoe glanced around. "Have you seen Mary?"

"Not lately. I suspect she's downstairs . . ." Theo noted the stumbling steps of one of the footmen. "Participating in a servant's drinking game behind Benson's back, if I were to guess."

Hands on her hips, Zoe huffed. "Well, she's supposed to be helping me."

"In her defense, dear, this has been quite a change. Mary's still getting used to interacting on a social level in settings like this."

"I suppose."

As if summoned by the use of her name, Mary came bounding up next to Zoe, an excited expression on her face.

"Where have you been?" Zoe raised an eyebrow. "Are you drunk?"

"Absolutely not!" replied Mary with a hiccup. "And before you get too irate, just remember that it's not only the blue bloods who notice things."

Zoe rolled her eyes for the second time of the evening. "What are you talking about?"

"Just wait until you hear what these fine lady's coachmen had to say . . ."

Chapter Twenty-Six

Quinton let out a slow, deep breath, his thumb repeatedly rubbing against the cool metal surface of the watch in his pocket. That was the thing about gold—no matter how long you held it in the heat of your hand, the metal stayed cool.

The texture of the design etched into its surface was intimately familiar to him. Years of constant friction from his anxious rubbings had worn it down until it was nearly smooth, but the design was still there, faintly visible. It had already been fading when it came into his possession all those years ago. He wondered if his own father had found the same sort of comfort in the repetitive motion, as if the golden watch were a touchstone in times of stress.

He tried not to think of his father often—what was done was done—but Quinton did occasionally catch himself wondering about the man. His mother had always portrayed the relationship as a happy one, but it was sometimes difficult to separate the fantasies of boyhood with the realities of adulthood. Though Zoe's Aunt Theo had once offered to help him discover the truth of his parentage, it hadn't been something Quinton was interested in learning at the time. But he wondered if knowing the man's name might provide him answers about himself—answers that could only come from understanding one's heritage.

There was no good to be had in going down that path, Quinton reminded himself. The reality was his mother had been an actress and his father one of her patrons. Quinton had turned Theo's offer of information down for a reason. His father was dead, and the only thing to be gained by learning the truth was resentment toward whatever relatives remained on that side of his family line. In this case, he thought it better to keep the fantasy in place, rather than go searching for answers that would no doubt only bring him pain.

His musings were interrupted by the arrival of his expected companion. Lord Montgomery Coleville greeted him with a smile and a firm handshake, taking a seat in the armchair next to Quinton's own. Though the gray had creeped up a little further along his hairline since the last time Quinton had seen him, Coleville was still a fit man with broad shoulders and a trim waist. When they were standing, he came up almost as tall as Quinton, if not quite there.

The current viscount and future earl ordered a drink and then turned his attention to Quinton. "Well, how have you been, man? Your eyes seem a bit clearer than the last time I saw you."

"Yes, quite." Quinton shifted in his seat, his neck suddenly warm. "I apologize for my behavior over the previous months. You've always treated me fairly, and I'm afraid I behaved quite badly towards you."

Coleville waved his hand dismissively. "Water under the bridge, Quinton. I had no doubt you would sort it out eventually. I'm just pleased you've found your feet again."

"That is kind of you, my lord." The heat had moved up into his cheeks—Quinton didn't know if he would ever not feel embarrassment over his breakdown. "I have the back rent I owe you, plus interest."

"Ah, very good. I assume that means you've taken up working again?"

"Yes." Quinton took a sip of his beverage, considering how much of his case he should reveal to someone on the outside of it. "I've recently taken on a new client."

The lord appraised him shrewdly. "I don't suppose it has anything to do with the death of that dressmaker all the papers are talking about?"

"You're a clever man, my lord," said Quinton, committing to nothing.

"I've found, living in my world, it's a necessity if one wants to survive with their hide intact."

The envelope of cash was handed over, and with that, the "business" gentleman found so distasteful could be concluded. Quinton often thought it ironic that the upper-class world relied so heavily upon having money, and yet the concept of acquiring money through any means other than inheritance was considered so uncouth. He supposed it wasn't something he would ever fully understand, since he was among the members of society who worked for a living.

Suddenly the viscount's expression darkened as he glared at something beyond Quinton's field of vision.

"What is it?"

"What? Oh, it's nothing." Coleville shook his head, as if trying to shake off whatever feelings had come over him. "I suppose it was inevitable."

Now Quinton's curiosity compelled him to look. He'd never seen Coleville so obvious with his emotions. He turned around, catching sight of a man in his fifties dressed in a navy uniform. The gentleman was distinguished—a woman might even say handsome—if perhaps a little over groomed.

"Are you acquainted with the officer?" he asked.

"I'm aware of him, as I suppose he is of me."

Quinton weighed his curiosity against discretion, but in the end curiosity won out. "Bad blood?"

Coleville sighed, taking a long swig from his beverage. "No, not in so many words. We have personally never had any disagreement." He paused for a minute before continuing. "I've told you of my brother?"

"Yes. I remember he died some years back."

"Indeed. I was just a boy of fourteen when he passed. But I was very fond of him." Coleville chuckled. "I suppose you must think that an inappropriate expression of emotion from a British man."

"No. Not at all."

"Hmm. Well it's the truth. Graham could do no wrong in my eyes, which looking back, I realize that was the rose-colored glasses of youth. But I do know he was a good man, and I trusted his opinion."

Quinton said nothing, waiting for Coleville to fill the silence in the heavy pause.

"He had hardly a bad word to say about anyone. But Felix Fairfax . . . I know my brother detested him."

The lord trailed off after that, so Quinton prompted him with a couple questions. "I assume the navy man is Felix Fairfax? Is he a noble?"

"Unfortunately. Earl of Dristoll, last I checked."

That was a surprise. "I thought it was only second or third sons who bought military commissions. Did he have an older brother who died?"

Coleville snorted. "No. The fact that his father shipped his only heir off to war should tell you everything you need to know about the man."

As Quinton opened his mouth to reply, a shadow fell over him. He glanced up and was surprised to see Alexander Dovefield—Zoe's stepcousin and more often than not a downright nuisance. Though the man was only a few years his junior, Quinton struggled to remember ever being so immature.

"Mr. Huxley." Alexander acknowledged his companion. "Lord Coleville."

"Lord Dovefield," started Coleville with a genial smile. "Is there something we can help—?"

"I wish to speak with Huxley," he said quickly, cutting the lord off.

Quinton raised an eyebrow, but once again curiosity was his enemy. With a nod and the promise to return in a few minutes, Quinton excused himself and followed Alexander over to another table a few yards away.

"If you're here to start a fight, I would suggest waiting until we're outside," said Quinton, taking a nonchalant sip. "It would be a shame for you to lose your membership at another club."

Alexander looked at him sharply, no doubt wondering how Quinton was aware of his troubles. He would have liked to have said it was a brilliant investigation on his part, but Alexander's behavior—drinking, gambling, fighting—was public enough, at least to men who frequented the clubs, that it was hard not to be aware of it.

"I have no interest in starting an altercation today." Alexander stayed an arm's length away, perhaps recalling the time he'd miscalculated in antagonizing Quinton and been pinned to the wall by his throat for his trouble. It wasn't one the moments Quinton was most proud of, but these things happen.

"Then what is it?"

"I wish to know what your intentions are in regard to Zoe."

Quinton blinked. "What? Surely you can't be serious."

"She was seen leaving your lodgings not more than a week ago—alone."

He could feel the blood draining from his face. "I don't know what you're talking about. Are you . . . following her?"

"Don't be ridiculous. A friend of mine happened to be in the area on business and saw her. Fortunately he only told me in confidence and will not spread the information further. But should this happen again, I cannot guarantee it will be another friend of mine who sees." Alexander looked him square in the eyes. "So I'll ask again—what are your intentions?"

Quinton met his gaze evenly. "I have no intentions, not that it's any business of yours. Nothing untoward happened."

Alexander rolled his eyes. "As if that matters. In this game, all that matters is perception, not reality. Normally I'd be content to let my eccentric cousin hang herself, but in this case her behavior affects the rest of us. A scandal like this would drag the whole family through the mud."

"That seems extreme."

"Perhaps. But whatever collateral damage may occur in the wake, you cannot deny her reputation would be irrevocably destroyed."

There was little to say to that. He wasn't wrong. But Quinton wasn't one to back down. "Lady Demas is a grown woman and her decisions are her own."

"Miss Demas still thinks she's in France and that life will bend to her will simply because she wishes it so. But this is England, and here, there are consequences for one's actions." Alexander's fists were clenched tightly. "If you care for her at all, I would suggest you keep your distance."

Quinton snorted—he was done with this. "If I have any questions about consequences, I will be sure to seek out someone who has actually experienced them. Good day, my lord." His words were confident, but as he turned his back on the young man, Quinton couldn't help but feel a distinct pang of doubt in his chest, twisting like a knife. Could he live with himself if Zoe's life was ruined because of her involvement with him?

Not that there was anything untoward about their relationship, but Alexander was correct that the perception was all that mattered. And if that fool was able to arrive at such a conclusion, then there were sure to be others.

As he glanced back at Alexander, Quinton saw another man already speaking to him. His back was turned, so he didn't recognize any features. It seemed to him all the toffs dressed alike—not an original thought among them. But his petty musings came to an end when he looked past the stranger and saw Alexander's face.

Alexander Dovefield appeared stoic, keeping up the appearance of the stiff upper lip the British were known for, but Quinton was skilled enough at reading people to see the strain on his features. Alexander clearly didn't want to be talking to that man. In fact, if he didn't know better, he might think the young obnoxious heir was afraid.

If it were someone else, Quinton might feel obligated to step in or at least wonder what the conversation was about. But he knew enough of Alexander's dirty laundry to fill in the blanks. If he were a betting man, he'd place his money on debt collection. Alexander was a betting man, but clearly an unskilled one.

Lord Colville cleared his throat, bringing Quinton's attention back to his own reality. He sat down as a man filled both their drinks. When he glanced back, both Alexander and his companion were gone.

Perhaps the young man was going to have some experience when it came to consequences after all. Scandal could come to the Dovefields' doorstep from more than just Zoe.

As he mused on these dark thoughts, Quinton's hand slipped back into his pocket, his thumb moving across the surface of the watch, over and over again.

Chapter Twenty-Seven

With the second glass of whiskey, Zoe began to feel herself settle. As the stiffness in her shoulders eased, she breathed deeply and leaned back, taking a glance around. This time Quinton's place was spotless, smelling faintly of lemon and bleaching powder. His cot, discreetly pushed against a far wall, was neatly made, and there was not a sock out of place. Oscar was curled up on top of the tallest bookshelf, eyeing Brutus from her perch. There was certainly no trust between the two beasts, but for the moment they tolerated a fragile truce.

Last time she came here, Zoe had left Brutus at home, but Hugh had pointed out it defeated the purpose of having a large protective dog if he only had the opportunity to protect her from the maids. She wasn't sure the sarcasm was necessary, but he had a point. This gathering at Quinton's was late in the evening, well after the sun had disappeared from the horizon. If she was being honest, Brutus was a welcome addition to her and Mary's travel here.

The three human companions had drunk their first glass of whiskey in relative silence, but it wasn't heavy. Instead it felt peaceful, as they decompressed to the sound of the fire crackling in the hearth. None of them wanted to be the first to speak—to be the one to break the silence and end the moment. But every moment eventually ends.

Finally the door opened again, breaking the unspoken agreement, and Charlie entered. John was not long after him. A tiredness clung to both of them, but they accepted their drinks gratefully.

As they settled in, Zoe took a moment to compare the three boyhood friends. Though they were close as brothers, the three men couldn't look or act less alike. Quinton was tall and broad shouldered, with light skin and dark hair which fell in wavy curls into his brown eyes. The way he survived all those years on the streets was by being adaptable, able to blend in with most classes and groups of people. He was cautious and controlled in his actions and reactions, and when he wasn't spiraling into a deep pit of despair, some might even say he had a good sense of humor.

Charlie was a different story. The top of his head barely came to the middle of Quinton's chest, and his half-Indian heritage was apparent in his dark skin tone and thick, straight black hair. He was known for his temper and his evident distaste for the upper classes. Zoe had never been quite certain exactly what his employment was, but she knew he was involved in the East End's criminal underworld.

That left John. With his light brown skin and hair, his mixed heritage was no secret. Mary had confided in her that he was the product of a white nobleman taking advantage of his black maid. He undoubtedly had plenty of experience with being on the outside. But his disposition and easy nature usually turned strangers into friends. That's how he had survived, by learning how to build bridges. Even his speech changed depending on his company. With Hugh his diction was quite decent, only a hint of the street boy creeping in. With his friends, the street boy held his place, and a hint of toff keeping pace.

After the newcomers had taken a few sips of their drinks, everyone knew the time had come.

Charlie had chosen to stand near the fire, his face contemplative as he gazed into the flames. "Rory is safe, for now. I think everyone in this room knows he's innocent, even you toffs." His gaze flickered to Zoe, but his eyes held less antagonism than usual, and he carried on smoothly, his dictation careful and well spoken. His derelict British father, for his many faults, had taught him to speak *toff* pretty well.

She suspected he took great pride in his speech—Charlie took great pride in many things about himself. He wanted to be taken seriously and hated for anyone to think him stupid or inferior. The cockney accent he'd grown up surrounded by only slipped in occasionally, when he was distracted by something else.

"The stubborn mule refuses to discuss any personal goings-on with Madame Amato. He will not budge, despite repeated . . . encouragement from me, which is bloody ridiculous. But he has had some use, in doing what he does, examining the body."

"How did he examine the body? I thought she was already buried." Zoe shared a look of surprise with Mary.

Charlie held her gaze without speaking, allowing the truth to dawn on Zoe without assistance.

"Oh. Of course."

Sometimes it was hard to reconcile the man with the occupation. It was easy to forget that the Shakespeare-quoting, sharp-dressing Scotsman had made his small fortune grave robbing. She knew she ought to be repulsed, and there was a time she had been. But last year had changed her view of many things. Rory provided a necessary service as a resurrectionist. He spoke the language of those who could not speak for themselves.

She really did like Rory. Zoe had come to accept the oddities that made him who he was. And they never would have found Lucy's killer the year before without his assistance. But where the others in this room had known him for years, she didn't have that luxury when it came to assessing his true character. She didn't want to believe he was capable of killing any of these women. She had been consistently squashing any doubts that popped up, as Quinton had asked of her. But sometimes Zoe couldn't help but wonder, just for a moment, if they might all be wrong about the charming Scotsman.

"What did he discover?" asked Zoe, dismissing the line of thinking as she had before.

After a sip of his whiskey, Charlie continued. "I think we all know the same fabric was found wrapped around the necks of the dead ladies. Red, with gold elephants."

Zoe couldn't resist glancing at Quinton to see his reaction to the words, but his face gave away little in the way of emotion. Only the whites of his knuckles as he gripped the fabric of the chair betrayed him. She turned her attention back to Charlie.

"However, Rory discovered that this cloth is not used to kill the women, as we'd always thought. The seamstress was strangled by a long, slim chain. Rory says the marks on her neck were unmistakable."

Mary interrupted, her brow furrowed. "If that's true, how come nobody figured this out before?"

"Well the chain must've been removed, and apparently some bruising only shows a day or so after death." Charlie threw his hands up. "I'm not entirely sure, I'm just telling you what Rory told me. You know I don't understand all of this anatomist nonsense."

"I just don't understand how he can know the fabric wasn't used to strangle them," insisted Mary. Zoe glanced at her, wondering if perhaps she harbored some of the same doubts about Rory's innocence.

"Fine, fine." Charlie turned to Zoe. "May I see one of your gloves? Please?"

"Um, yes." Zoe was surprised, but she wanted to see where this was going. She pulled off the glove and handed it to him with one graceful motion. "Here."

"Thank you." Holding it flat in his hands, Charlie showed the article of clothing to each of them. "See how it's lying flat here, all smooth and such?"

After they indicated they did, he took John's arm and wrapped it around his wrist. "Now see what happens when I pull and twist it?"

The fabric stretched as he pulled, straining under the force.

"Ow! Charlie!" snapped John.

"Sorry. Don't be such a child." Charlie released the tension, pulling the glove back and then showing it to his audience again. "Now see how it looks?"

Zoe grasped his point. "It's stretched out and wrinkled."

"Exactly. He had me check with John, and the cloth he saw on Amato's neck was pristine." He handed the glove back to Zoe.

She took it with a sniff. "Hmm. Well, I'm glad my glove was ruined for a good cause."

Charlie waved a dismissive hand. "I'm sure you have others. But do you understand now? For most of us, if we saw a piece of fabric wrapped around a dead woman's neck, we'd probably assume it's what was used to kill her. But this cloth around the seamstress's neck was smooth and hadn't been stretched out the way it should've been. Rory thinks it must've been placed there after death."

As he massaged his wrist, John inclined his head. "Well demonstrated, Charlie. Even if you did nearly break my arm."

Charlie's cheeks darkened at the compliment and he shifted from foot to foot. "If I'm being honest, I didn't come up with it. That's just how Rory explained it to me when I asked the same question."

John was nodding thoughtfully. "When I discovered Miss Amato, I found a small metal link on the ground, as if lost when a chain broke."

"This is all very interesting." Mary leaned forward, chin in her hands. "But what does it tell us?"

Quinton spoke for the first time that evening. "It sometimes seems to me as if there's no subject Rory doesn't have at least some knowledge of. It's not something he speaks of often, but he fought in the war. Most men who go to war kill because they must—because it's necessary for their own survival. But Rory's told me that there are a few who learn to enjoy killing. Some even came already having a lust for blood. For some, the killing can become almost like . . . a ritual." Quinton paused, his grip still tight but his face unreadable. When he did continue speaking, his voice was without emotion. "Rory thinks the piece of cloth ties these murders not just to each other, but back to my mother. The killer keeps the cloth pristine, not twisted or rumpled in use strangling someone. He leaves it there because it means something to him, not because it's practical. Rory thinks it's a sign of a man who kills for pleasure. The fabric is a token, like a thread he's desperate to tie back to my mother."

He paused again, as if the next words were stuck in his throat. Finally, Quinton continued. "I believe the killer likely knew my mother personally."

Her stomach twisting, Zoe frowned. "What makes you think that?"

"When I think of that day, I usually think about finding her . . . about struggling with the knots. I couldn't get it off, no matter how much I clawed at them . . ." Quinton shook his head, as if physically dispelling the image. "But in dragging all this up again with Rory, I remembered something else—something that happened the day before."

No one spoke as they waited for him to reveal the memory.

"My mother received a package. It was brought by a special courier, so I knew it was expensive. That wasn't too unusual— actresses often received gifts from men. But when she opened it . . . her whole face went white. It was as if she'd seen a ghost. I only caught a glimpse of what was inside. All I could make out was that it was red and gold."

Quinton shook his head again. "She must have known whoever sent that package and she was afraid of him. I don't know why I never thought of that before. It seems so obvious now and I can see it so clearly. If I had thought of it sooner, maybe things would have been different."

"You were a child," said Zoe quickly. "It was a horrible trauma. You cannot blame yourself for not remembering all of the details of the surrounding days."

The words were true, but she could tell Quinton didn't believe them. Zoe opened her mouth to say more, but she couldn't think of anything else to say. After a moment she closed it, glancing away so he wouldn't see the tears forming in her eyes. She didn't know why she would be so emotional. It wasn't as if it were her mother's death they were discussing.

The rest of the group was also silent. It was a lot to take in. As if on cue, all five of them took a long swallow of whiskey.

This time the silence was broken by John. "There's something odd."

"What do you mean?" asked Quinton.

"Well, I never laid eyes on Miss Anderson herself last year. But I saw the cloth that was found on her. It wasn't pristine and smooth the way you just explained. It was definitely twisted and stretched out."

"Perhaps he didn't have the chain with him that day, or something else interrupted him. It doesn't really matter either way." Charlie shook his head. "I don't claim to be a saint, or anywhere near, but this man is a demon. I don't think we can understand how he thinks, or what his madness might compel him to do. But Rory was sure about this with the latest lady."

"So how does this help us actually get closer to the killer?" asked Zoe.

Charlie sighed. "I'm not sure yet."

Mary glanced her way before stepping in. "Well now we know there's some kind of ritual to his killing, is there any other part of his mad ritual that we can infer?"

"Excellent question, Mary." Charlie paused. The weariness which had clung to him all evening was still there, even heavier now, as if he was wearing a thick wool coat soaked with rainwater. Finally he continued. "Rory suggested that perhaps the women have something in common, and that's why he chooses them. Perhaps they look like Ms. Huxley, or remind him of her in some way."

Quinton flinched, but this wasn't the time to shy away from sensitive subjects. Zoe reached out a hand, resting it gently on his forearm. "I know this must be difficult, Quinton, but I never met your mother. None of us did. What did she look like?"

They held their breath, waiting for his reaction. Quinton was quiet a moment, and then, to Zoe's surprise, a soft smile came over his features. "She was beautiful, my mama was. She had many admirers during her time in the theater. She was tall and willowy, with an olive complexion. Her hair was raven colored, as black as black could be, and she was proud of it. It was long and thick, and she only wore it up when she was sewing. At night she would brush it as we talked, getting ready to go to bed."

As he spoke, Zoe imagined the woman he described coming to life in her mind. She would've loved the chance to draw her.

"Her eyes were blue, like a sky with no clouds, and most of the time they sparkled. She loved life, even though there was also a sadness to her. I don't look very much like her. She told me I take after my father in looks."

Mary glanced from Zoe to Quinton as he was speaking, a queer look on her face. Zoe squinted at her, but Mary just shook her head discreetly.

John sighed. "I can't speak for any of the other murdered ladies, but I do know Margot Anderson didn't have dark hair—it was reddish or something like that. She was supposedly beautiful, though. Could the ladies he kills remind him of your mama in some way besides looks?"

Charlie spoke first. "No doubt, but it could be anything. There's no telling how his madness has twisted his mind."

Zoe spoke slowly. "His mind truly was twisted." She turned toward John. "Perhaps you knew this, John, but Margot Anderson survived the attack. She managed to crawl for help and was found, but succumbed to her injuries before a doctor could arrive. Mabel told me."

John shook his head, a rare sheen of anger glassing over his eyes. "I did not hear that. It seems almost more beastly to picture her desperately searching for help as she was dying. The bastard."

A change of subject was called for, and Zoe was grateful Mary stepped in. "On a different note, we found out a bit about Madame Amato. Zoe and the Dowager talked to each of the ladies who had appointments the day she was killed."

She paused, glancing at Zoe, who understood her cue and continued for her. "They had little of interest to add, but several were quite uncomfortable discussing the woman at all, when one would think they would be thrilled to gossip about a murder of someone they knew."

Mary picked the thread of conversation up. "The coachmen were more willing to talk about who goes where and when. Two of them told me the ladies of the house went to Madame Amato's at all hours of the night, when the master of their house was away. Doesn't take a lot of imagination to put together they weren't there to get fitted for dresses. More likely to be removing them."

John's cheeks colored, but he didn't reprimand his cousin. They were a very open family when it came to such things. "That does make sense. We have discovered that Madame Amato did not live in the rooms above her shop. She rented rooms near Gannet Street, though her own upper rooms were furnished. Her real name was Sarah Hammond, and she had a family in Yorkshire that was desperate for money. Seems she was sending as much as she could and it still wasn't enough. By all we officers have been told, she was an astute business woman. I'm not surprised she was willing to explore additional sources of income. If what you're saying is true, it sounds like she found a lucrative one, renting out her upper floor to women who wanted a discreet place for meeting lovers. Though I still don't know why she would pretend to be Italian."

"Sarah Hammond sounds like the reverend's daughter. Clarissa Amato is exotic and exciting, and most importantly, fashionable." Zoe shrugged, as if Theo hadn't just recently educated her on this subject. "The persona was part of what made her so successful."

"Regardless, that brings us back to Rory." Zoe saw Quinton's expression was one of relief, and his shoulders had relaxed. "He must be protecting someone—a woman."

Perhaps Quinton had not been as confident in Rory's innocence as he had led Zoe to believe. She shared his sense of relief. At least this theory about Madame Amato's second income stream provided some explanation as to Rory's behavior.

"A married woman," Charlie added. His face held no judgment, but the fact was important. "Because it would not be Rory who would suffer for an affair with a married woman, had it become known. He would weather it easily. The woman's life, on the other hand, would be ruined."

Their conversation was interrupted when Zoe's chair was suddenly shoved. She looked down to see Brutus, his rear end backed up against her chair. "What is it, boy?" she asked as she glanced around the room, trying to find out what was making him so uncomfortable.

The source was quickly identified. Oscar was making her move, on the ground, moving closer to Brutus instead of away. She moved slowly, her back in the air as if invisible strings held her up, walking sideways instead of straight on. Brutus whined and looked up at Zoe with an obvious plea in his eyes.

She laughed, reaching down to pat his enormous head. "Don't look at me, you're bigger than her."

This did little reassure him. As Oscar continued closer, Brutus turned his head away, watching her out the side of his eye. She came within a meter, then deliberately leaped to Charlie's chair, never breaking eye contact. Still glaring, she turned in a tight circle, finally curing up in his lap.

The cat had staked her claim. This house was hers.

"Aren't you full of yourself?" Charlie's tone was fond as he stroked Oscar.

"Good for you. Never let anyone take that from you, Oscar." The words were muttered by Mary, barely audible. Zoe suspected there was a story behind them.

Quinton's pride was clear when he spoke. "I guess it's not the size of the dog in the fight after all. Well played, Oscar."

His amused eyes met Zoe's, and she felt a long-buried flutter in her heart. He was uncommonly handsome when he smiled, she would allow that. He almost seemed like "her" Quinton again.

She smiled back. "Your beast wins this fight, Quinton."

<hr>

Much later in the evening, when Zoe and Mary were sharing their hackney home, Zoe asked her companion about that queer look.

Mary shrugged. "When Quinton was talking about his mother . . . it just surprised me is all."

"What did?"

"Well, it's just . . . he could've been describing you."

Chapter Twenty-Eight

That stupid, bloody Scot . . . only he would get himself arrested doing something so foolish . . .

The outcome was inevitable, but John still felt the metaphorical blow. The whole city of London had been on the lookout for Rory —his name and description known to everyone from newsboys to the Prince himself. It had only been a matter of time before he was recognized and arrested. Keeping him hidden forever would have been impossible.

At least that's what John told himself to ease his frustration with the Scotsman. Possibly if Rory had stayed put and kept his head down as instructed, things could've been different. If he hadn't decided to go for a stroll, maybe they could've delayed this a few more days.

If wishes were horses . . . no changing the past now. John shook his head, thinking about what the magistrate told him not an hour before. Rory had been walking down the back streets in broad daylight—granted, wearing a disguise, but a poor one. He was in baggy, unfitted clothes with a ratty hat tucked low, and he'd done a shoddy job dyeing his red beard black. Overall the description would sound comical if his friend's life wasn't on the line.

Rory had been recognized nearly immediately by a woman whose young son Rory had stitched up just a month previous. She had no money for an actual surgeon and, like others who knew of him, had sent for Rory.

Without Rory's skill, the boy would've died from his wounds, caused by a carriage rolling over his legs. But that was last month, and a mother's gratefulness would not feed her children.

The forty-pound reward was life-changing for a young widow. Righteous indignation meant little to the hungry and desperate. She had two other children besides the one Rory saved, and in the end her children would come before anything else—certainly before a cheerful Scottish grave robber she paid with thick soup.

His thoughts came to an end as John reached his destination. He knocked on the front door of the Dovefield home. Most of the other gentlemen John dealt with made it plain constables and officers should use the servant's entrance, and it wasn't uncommon for John to cool his heels for an hour or more—if they saw him at all. But Mr. Dovefield was different. He had no problem with John using his front door, and had left instructions with Quaid to inform him immediately when someone such as John arrived.

Of course, Mr. Dovefield was not just a gentleman but a barrister. He and John's professional relationship stretched back years, starting in the courtroom. It was only last year, when the maid was murdered, that the two had gone from friendly to something more like friends.

John was brought directly to Mr. Dovefield's study. He always appreciated the mahogany panels on the walls and how the flickering light from the fireplace danced upon them. The furniture was a soothing blue tweed, and the maps on the wall and books on the shelves lent an impression of intellect. The air of dignified masculinity reflected the room's occupant.

In the rare moments when John allowed his imagination to

carry him away, he could see a world where he'd been born into a different life. In that life, he had a room like this one. But of course, such dreams were ridiculous and there was no use dwelling on the impossible.

Mr. Dovefield rose, gripping his hand in a firm handshake before motioning him to one of the neatly placed chairs in front of his desk. "I thought you might swing by, John. Mr. Stewart was bound to be apprehended sooner or later. We are fortunate he was apprehended alive."

"Indeed." John thought carefully on his next words. Mr. Dovefield had always treated him as an equal, and their personal and professional relationship was something he valued. He didn't want to strain it by asking for favors that would put the barrister in a difficult spot. But he also didn't see that he had much choice.

"You likely know what I am here to ask, Mr. Dovefield," began John. "I don't believe Rory killed this lady, but it's going to take a miracle to convince the rest of the world. He's gonna need some-one to make that case."

"I suspected as much." Mr. Dovefield sighed, leaning back in his leather chair. "I know he's a friend of yours, John, but just how certain are you of his innocence? From what I've heard of the evidence, the magistrate has a compelling case."

John didn't answer immediately. Mr. Dovefield wasn't entirely wrong. There was real evidence against Rory, and John couldn't pretend he'd never had his own doubts. But at the end of it all, Rory was his friend. Discovering the reason for his unwillingness to share an alibi had helped alleviate some of John's doubt. And even without that . . . it really came down to whether he believed his friend or not.

"You're right, Mr. Dovefield. Some things I can't deny. Rory did have an argument with Madame Amato. He doesn't have an alibi, at least not one he will provide. The manifest proves he was in the city when the first of the women were killed." John considered his next words. "But that's it. There's no witnesses who saw him kill Amato. No red cloth was found in his home. The magistrate is relying on the reputation of body snatchers to win this case. I could sit here all day and tell you what I believe, but if there's one thing I know about you it's that you believe in justice for the accused and you wouldn't want to see a man hang when the biggest piece of evidence against him is simply public opinion."

"Hmm." The barrister's expression was difficult to read. "Have you spoken to him yet?"

"Not yet. It's a madhouse round Bow Street. I'm headed there next, but I know the magistrate would give weight to you representing Rory."

Silence followed the statement. John could see the wheels turning in Mr. Dovefield's head as he considered, weighing the pros and cons. He was a man of logic and reason, but also of compassion and justice, and no answer he could give here wouldn't complicate his life in one way or another.

John understood this wasn't an easy decision to make. "I know you weren't well respected for your decision to represent Chedrose. I wouldn't ask for your help if the stakes weren't so high."

Mr. Dovefield laughed, but the sound rang hollow. "That's an understatement, John. For months merchants refused to deliver to the house—the staff had to pick up wares under a false name. And socially . . . I couldn't begin to count the number of invitations refused or not extended."

Silence fell as Mr. Dovefield rose and poured himself a glass of whiskey. He nodded in his direction, but John shook his head. He really did try to limit his drinking while working.

Mr. Dovefield continued as he made his way back to his chair. "It was harder on Simone than me. She's worked so hard over the years to establish this family in society—to pave the way for our children's futures. But she took solace in the fact that Zoe was to be in America for most of it, and the younger two have some time ahead before they'll be introduced to the masses. We could afford to be shunned for a year or two, until the righteous indignation faded. In the meantime, I had my work and Simone had her new charitable endeavors."

With another heavy sigh, Mr. Dovefield sat back down. "Things were just beginning to return to some semblance of normal. Stirring all this up again won't be pleasant."

It was a blow, but not altogether unexpected. John began to rise. "I understand, my lord—"

"Sit back down, John." Mr. Dovefield waved his hand dismissively. "I didn't say I wouldn't do it, I'm just saying Simone is going to be unhappy. But we've weathered worse and we'll do it again in the future. Even with the public disapproval of my actions, my flow of clients never faltered. So you see, there are a few benefits to being a notorious barrister."

A wave of relief washed over John. "Does that mean you'll represent Rory? He'll pay you handsomely, I can assure you of that."

"Well, I'm not one to turn down a paying client, especially a friend of yours." Hugh gave him a wry smile. "Besides, I've always had a soft spot for hopeless cases."

Every little bit helped, but having Hugh Dovefield on their side gave them a significant leg up. John didn't know if it would be enough to save his friend from the noose, but it was a good start. Although all of his little tribe were adults in their own right, having overcome significant challenges and made their way in the world, Mr. Dovefield's assistance felt strangely like they had an adult on their side—at the very least, someone who knew what they were doing.

"Thank you, Mr. Dovefield."

"Of course. Now, on to our next step." Mr. Dovefield downed the rest of his whiskey in one movement, setting the glass down with a distinct thud. "Let's go see Mr. Stewart."

Chapter Twenty-Nine

"You cannot be here."

Zoe ignored the statement, brushing past Quinton into his lodgings.

"I'm serious, Zoe, you can't be here alone. What if someone sees you?"

"In this part of town?" Zoe laughed as she removed her bonnet. "I find that unlikely. Anyway, I brought Brutus for a chaperon." Her hand reached down to find Brutus's head, a gesture which had become habit.

He said something else under his breath, but she couldn't quite make it out.

"What's that?"

"Nothing. Where is Mary?"

"She's just outside, chatting with Ezra. She'll be along in a minute." Zoe raised her eyebrow. "What's gotten into you?"

Her grumpy retainer made no reply. Quinton just shook his head and grumbled again under his breath. She wondered with a pang of concern if the pressure of Rory's arrest had set him back.

If he backslid into that pile of self-pity and booze . . . it would be a tragedy—for everyone, of course.

Dismissing her concerns for the time being, Zoe pushed forward. "Regardless, I'm here because I had a thought, but I'm not quite sure how to turn that thought into a plan."

While she was speaking, Mary entered the room. Her lady's companion glanced between Quinton and Zoe, her gaze appraising. "What's up with you, Q?"

"Nothing," he snapped. "Absolutely nothing is the matter with me. Now what thought are you talking about?"

Zoe hung up her cloak and bonnet on the hooks by the door before helping herself to a glass of the whiskey Quinton kept in the bottom left drawer of his desk. Not the top right, where he kept the rotgut—no, this was the good stuff he didn't think anyone knew about. She offered a glass to the other two, which Quinton accepted despite the annoyance etched into his features.

"Well, I was thinking," began Zoe as she settled into a chair. "We know Sarah Hammond, as Madame Amato, was renting out her rooms to a few discerning noblewomen for rendezvous, but we haven't really talked about the implications, beyond what it means for Rory. In fact, I think we've all gotten so wrapped up in Rory and the mind of the killer, that we've hardly thought about the poor dead woman at all." She knocked back the dram in one swig, the golden liquid burning her throat, and then refilled her glass.

"I'm not sure I understand your meaning." Quinton snatched the bottle from her grasp, which Zoe allowed as she already had her refill.

"Why did someone want her dead?"

"What?"

"Why did someone want her dead?" she repeated. "We know whoever killed her has killed other women before, but why did he specifically want Clarissa Amato dead?"

"You mean did she have something common with the other women?" Quinton held the bottle up higher, out of Mary's reach.

"Didn't we already discuss this?"

Zoe snapped her fingers and pointed at him. "Yes, exactly! We talked about if maybe the women looked alike or something like that, which has some possibility. But even if that's it, that still doesn't explain how he's finding them. Why Clarrisa and not one of the thousand other dark-haired women in London? What if the reason he killed her is because he knew her before? What if he knew all of them before?"

Quinton swirled the glass in his hand, sinking into an armchair and tucking the expensive bottle in next to him. "I suppose it's possible. We already suspect he knew my mother, at least to a degree, based on Rory's reasoning about the cloth and my own recollection of the day before."

"Right. So if that's true and he knew her, maybe he knew all of them. He might be someone in their lives." Mary crossed her arms, her expression thoughtful. "One thing we know more or less for sure about Madame Amato is she helped women with powerful husbands have affairs."

Zoe had already discussed these possibilities with Mary that morning. Zoe was so excited she could burst. But she tried to contain herself, allowing Quinton to put the pieces together for himself.

"Hmm. A jealous husband is a motive old as time. It just feels so . . . ordinary when compared with the murders."

Zoe shrugged. "Maybe. But we don't really know why he's killing, just that it might have something to do with your mother. We don't know what sets him off. There's a reason jealousy is a motive old as time."

Mary interjected. "There's also the possibility it has nothing to do with the affairs but perhaps is a little closer to the poor woman's own heart."

"You mean a lover?"

Mary nodded. "What we do know of Madame Amato—Miss Hammond—is that she was skilled in her trade and shrewd in business. Her social and political ideas bordered on radical, and we know she had no objection to love outside a marriage. No reason to believe a woman like that wouldn't take a lover of her own—even more than one."

Quinton was silent for a moment. Zoe held her breath, waiting for his response.

He took another sip. "You make some valid points. Rory being caught up in all this may have been more distracting than I cared to admit. I'll get the address of the assistant from John and see if she knows anything about the men in Miss Hammond's life."

Satisfied in her theory and Quinton's response, Zoe leaned back and sipped her whiskey, enjoying its smooth yet complex flavor. The man did have good taste in some things, she would give him that.

He was quiet for a few moments, as if considering his next words. "Mary, could you give us a minute?"

The request was a surprise to Zoe, but Mary seemed unfazed. "The bakery across the block has the most delicious pork pies. I think I'll go treat myself."

With that, she was gone, taking Brutus with her, leaving Quinton and Zoe alone. Normally Zoe wouldn't have been uncomfortable, but there was something about the way Quinton was holding himself—leaning forward but not making eye contact, his hand tightly gripping his glass—which made her nervous. A tension thick enough to cut with a knife settled over the room.

"If you have something to say, say it," she said, unsure if she really wanted to hear whatever it was.

Finally he spoke. "Do you ever think about the future—your future?"

She blinked. "I suppose. Sometimes. Why?"

"Right now you are unchaperoned in a room with a man, and you haven't batted an eye." Quinton finally met her eyes, the full intensity knocking Zoe off balance. "Where do you think this path leads for you?"

"You are the one who asked Mary to leave!" she protested.

"And you didn't object!"

"Well how was I to know you'd suddenly turned into an old biddy aunt!"

"Zoe!" Quinton took a deep breath and let his eyes fall before continuing. "Like it or not, you are held to different standards than I am. If even a rumor were to start about your character, it is not only you who would face consequences—your whole family could be sucked into the mire. You gallivant along as if you have not a care in the world, but the truth is you have everything to lose just by being here."

She squinted, studying his face. "Where is this coming from?"

He sighed. "Does it matter? You know what I'm saying is true. And as if that weren't enough, you also insist on inserting yourself into every dangerous situation you possibly can. So you are under constant threat, both from physical and societal harm. Doesn't that frighten you, even in the slightest?"

Finally comprehension dawned on Zoe. She hadn't been able to recognize the strange energy radiating off him because it wasn't an emotion she associated with Quinton, but she finally understood—it was fear. The great and stoic Quinton Huxley was afraid, and she was the cause.

"Of course it frightens me . . . sometimes." Zoe carefully considered her next words. "Only a fool doesn't value their own life, and contrary to what you may think of me, I am not a fool. I have no desire to die young and tragic. And though I may not agree with the rules of society, I do understand how they work. I know the consequences if I fall."

"I do not think you are a fool, Zoe." His voice was soft.

"Then you are in the minority," she said with a slight smile. "Quinton, I know you may not always understand why I make the choices I do. But you may forget I was not raised in the lap of luxury I currently reside in. I would not have survived this long if I allowed fear to paralyze me with every possibility of misstep. I understand the risks involved with my path, and I choose to walk it anyway, with my eyes open. If I should stumble and fall, then the consequences will be upon my own head. That is the only reassurance I can offer you."

The room lapsed into silence again. Zoe held her breath, waiting to hear what his reply would be. While she waited, the cat appeared in the window sill. Oscar hopped gracefully down to the floor, stalking over and rubbing her orange body against Zoe's legs. She reached down, stroking the top of Oscar's head. It was a strangely comforting motion.

Then Quinton abruptly slammed his glass down and stood, startling Oscar, who jumped up onto the nearby table, abandoning Zoe for higher ground. The man ignored the cat's meowed protests, striding over to a chest at the foot of his cot. The top thrown open with a bang, he rummaged around noisily for another minute or two, all without explanation. Zoe was startled as well, but waited to see what Quinton was doing before commenting.

Finally he found what he was looking for, holding up his prize triumphantly, though Zoe still couldn't make out the object. The only thing she could see was the faint glint of metal in the rays of sunlight streaming through the window.

He strode back and presented the mysterious object to her. "I can't do much about the pressures of society, but if you are going to insist on putting yourself in harm's way at every opportunity, then the least you could do is have some means of protection, for when . . . Brutus cannot be with you."

The object in his palm was a blade, long, thin, and sharp. The handle was gold with an inlay of small pearls—simple but elegant. As Zoe picked it up hesitantly, the weight balanced perfectly in her hands, and she found herself surprised at how easily it became an extension of herself. She knew without asking the knife had meaning, and looked at him expectantly.

"I had a similar one made for Abigail," Quinton continued. "It's supposed to be subtle enough that you can use it as a hat—or hairpin. It didn't do her much good, and hopefully you shall never need it. But it would make me feel better to know you had it."

The image of Abigail came into Zoe's mind—Quinton's childhood friend who had been so tragically killed the year before during the course of their investigation into Lucy's death. The loss had hit Quinton hard. She felt both honored and comforted at this unexpected gift.

"Thank you, Quinton." Zoe swallowed hard. "It's lovely."

He looked away, a faint color on his cheeks. "Just be careful you don't cut yourself with it."

She was grateful Mary didn't pry when Zoe exited Quinton's abode holding the strange prize, though Zoe did note Mary's raised eyebrow. If she had asked, Zoe wasn't sure what she would have said. Her thoughts were still swirling, confused by Quinton's ever-shifting moods.

The knife did prove one thing—Quinton cared what happened to her. As for how that affected her, Zoe realized he might not be the only one with shifting moods.

Chapter Thirty

That stupid, bloody Scot . . . when I get my hands on him . . .
That line of thinking went round and round in Charlie's head. He hadn't taken the news of Rory's arrest well. Only after an excessive amount of swearing, shouting, pacing, and flipping over chairs had he been able to calm down and think rationally about the situation. He was still fuming, but the rage had been reduced to a quiet simmer rather than a boiling overflow. That rage, at some level or another, had been his constant companion nearly all his life. He was used to it by now.

Despite the Scotsman's stupidity, Charlie still felt a sense of obligation towards him. Until Rory hung or was freed, he would still do his best to help him. So here he was, on his way to the bowels of the Bow Street Office, to meet up with John and the toff barrister.

He was rather looking forward to seeing Rory, having silently rehearsed his speech about what an imbecile Rory was over and over again in his head. Why on earth did he leave the house Charlie had provided? Perhaps it was inevitable that Rory would be caught, with the entire city like a pack of hound dogs after the offered reward, but they at least could've bought another day or two to untangle the knots of this investigation if the man had only had the sense to stay put.

The term *investigation* didn't sit well with Charlie—it came a bit too close to law keeping. Never did he think he would use that word to describe anything he was involved in. Justice existed in his world, but it was obvious and swift and usually meted out by him. Investigation was something rarely needed. This untangling of knots was new to him; it fell more into Quinton's or John's territory. Yet investigation was what was needed, so that was what he would do.

The street was alive with a shouting crowd when he turned the corner to approach Bow Street. The men who worked for the newspapers hurled questions at anyone who entered or exited. Other men simply shouted insults and profanity in the general direction of the jail cells. Charlie heard "grave robber" and "devil" among the din, along with several other slurs he couldn't make out. No one was allowed inside the building unless they were known to the magistrate, so he waited on the edge of the crowd for his friend to allow him entry.

It didn't take long for John to appear with the barrister in tow. Charlie had little use for any nobility, but he'd prepared himself to work with this one. There had been a time . . . before the rage . . . when Charlie's British noble father, an officer in the king's service, had stood on a pedestal in his mind. But that was a child's naivety, erased in the blink of an eye after the man brought him and his sister and mother to London, only to abandon them without a backward glance. Now he saw the upper class for what they really were—cowards, given the gift of money and status by an accident of birth but driven only by greed and weakness of character.

That being said, he would tolerate this one. Hugh Dovefield had earned John's and Quinton's respect, and though their standards were lower than his, Charlie trusted their opinions.

Most importantly, according to John, this man had the legal wits to help Rory, which was one thing Charlie couldn't do for him.

Even so, hell itself would grow cold before he called the man "Lord."

The three men nodded at each other, then turned as one to enter the Bow Street office. Shouts were hurled their direction, but no one challenged them as the magistrate was aware they were coming. They entered the building and made their way down to the small jail beneath, where Rory Stewart was held on charges of the murder of one Clarissa Amato.

A jail was a jail, and none were pleasant that Charlie knew of, but this was better than Newgate. That would come soon enough. He took a breath as the iron door to Rory's cell was unlocked, ready to give the man a piece of his mind. But for all his raging, Charlie hadn't remotely prepared himself for the sight of Rory.

Rory was laying on the floor, head resting on his arm. His left eye was swollen, and a nasty black bruise was spreading across his cheek. Dried blood crusted around a gash at his hairline. A sizable split in his lip still oozed blood. The room was devoid of furniture, without even a cot or a blanket for comfort, with only a bucket in the corner for waste. When the door opened with a groaning creak, Rory didn't stir. For a brief heart-stopping moment, Charlie thought he was dead. But when John knelt beside him, Rory's eyes opened and he gingerly sat up.

From the way he winced as he moved and held his arm across his middle, Charlie suspected at least a couple broken ribs. It was jarring to see a man who cared so much for his appearance looking like this—hair unkempt, face pale, and clothes stained with indistinguishable bodily fluids.

Leaning against a wall, Rory smiled weakly. "A sight you all are, that I will say." Even his usual Scottish brogue was heavy and slurred.

Dovefield's eyes darkened, and he abruptly turned and shouted for the jailer, walking out of the cell and towards the man with a determined intensity. He spoke with the man in a low voice Charlie couldn't overhear but with an intensity that was clear. He was a man used to getting his way through privilege, but in this case, Charlie couldn't fault him.

No more than thirty seconds later, Dovefield returned to the cell. "Rory is to be moved to a clean room immediately, with a cot and chairs for his representation. A doctor will be notified to attend him. A meal will be delivered twice a day, water as well for as long as he's here. When he's moved to Newgate, I will make the same arrangements there."

"How'd you swing that?" asked Charlie.

"I told him I'd see to it he was prosecuted for mistreatment of a prisoner under his care."

"Is that a real law?"

"It doesn't matter, as long as he thinks it is." Dovefield shrugged. "I also offered money, which usually smooths over situations such as this."

Charlie was impressed. The lord was more mercenary than he'd suspected.

"Well, don't you have a lecture for me?" The weakly asked question was directed from Rory to Charlie.

Charlie sighed, realizing the steam had vanished from his anger. "Not anymore."

"Mm. That's disheartening." Rory winced again and gave a wry smile. "I must look really bad if you're holding back."

Within minutes they were all escorted down the hallway. Rory leaned heavily on both Charlie and John to make his way, but Charlie was grateful to see that, although he was clearly in pain, his arms and legs all worked. He would recover, given time and proper care. Charlie had seen worse.

The new cell was furnished with a cot, a table and chairs, and water in a jug on the table. Charlie and John maneuvered Rory onto the cot, and he sank gratefully into it. Normally Rory would do the job of doctoring, but John filled the role this time, gently cleaning the dried blood from their friend's face with the water and a rag. He cleaned both filth and blood from the prisoner's hands while Rory closed his eyes and leaned against the wall, supported by the cot.

When John finished what little could be done and had put the water back on the table, Dovefield finally spoke. "I realize this situation is far from ideal, but we need to rally, gentlemen. Mr. Stewart, to do that, we need your help."

Rory's eyes stayed closed, as did his mouth.

Charlie put a tentative hand on his friend's shoulder. "We already know about the rooms the seamstress rented out. It hasn't taken much to deduce you rented them from her for you and a lady friend. That's what the argument was about, wasn't it?"

That got his eyes open. Rory stared at him, and then up at the ceiling, as if weighing his next decision in his head. "Did I ever tell you I was married?"

Charlie choked, sharing an incredulous glance with John. "No. You?"

"No need to sound so surprised." Rory laughed softly. "It seems a lifetime ago now. 'Twas back in Scotland, when I was barely more than a boy myself. Tressa was the village beauty—all the lads were falling over their feet for her. When she chose me . . . I was over the moon. And for a while . . . I was happy. She was sweet and lovely and content with me and our life there. But it wasn't the same for me. It wasn't her fault, but in time, I realized I wanted more. I wanted to have interesting conversations and explore deep subjects and debate things we didn't agree on. Tressa didn't want any of that. She just wanted me to be happy with what we had, and . . . I just couldn't do it."

Rory took a deep breath and Charlie could see the effort it took him to gather his thoughts and continue. "Eventually it got to the point that I couldn't bear it anymore, so like a coward . . . I did what all young men do when they wanna escape their responsibilities—I joined the army. Then one day I received word from home.

Tressa had died while I was gone. Tragically. After that I simply . . . never went home. I couldn't face what I'd done. When my time as a soldier was up, I ended up in London. I won't say I've never been with anyone but Tressa, but the life I built here was meant to be a solitary one. And then . . . everything changed."

"Rory, this is all honestly fascinating." John pinched the bridge of his nose. "Any other time I would love to hear more about all of this. But what does it have to do with your current troubles?"

Rory cracked his eyes open enough to glare at the Bow Street Officer. "I'm trying to give you context, so you'll understand."

"Understand what?" Charlie asked, feeling his impatience rise.

"Why I won't tell you the name of the lady."

"Rory—"

He raised a shaky hand. "You still don't understand. The way I feel with her . . . it's like I've been struck by lightning. She's . . . incredible. The way her mind works and the things we can discuss, so openly and easily . . . I don't think I'll ever meet another like her. We both understand that there is only so much we can have—she's married and will remain married, and believe it or not, I do know my place. But even this small bit that I can have . . . it's enough. I won't betray her, not even to save myself."

Charlie opened his mouth, but Dovefield spoke before he could. "Mr. Stewart, I do understand. If you won't tell us the name of the woman, at least explain the argument with Madame Amato. What was it about?"

Rory sighed and closed his eyes again, but after a moment—to Charlie's relief—answered. "Simply business. She was raising her prices. I was righteously indignant at the higher cost, and she was righteously indignant that I was righteously indignant. I'm quite sure it had nothing to do with her death. She was a good person, and we always got on before. It was just a foolish argument about money."

Dovefield nodded thoughtfully. "I believe you. But there's no one to corroborate your story, and even if there were . . . a conspiracy to help married women cheat on their husbands doesn't exactly cast you in a good light. And a dispute over money is still a motive." Dovefield seemed to be talking more to himself than anyone in the room. That changed when his eyes focused and he leaned towards Rory. "Were you with this woman that night?"

Rory cracked his eyes open again a sliver then shut them. "I don't see how it matters. I wouldn't tell you either way."

"Very well." Dovefield rubbed his jaw. "And the reason you left your hiding place?"

Rory had the decency to blush at this, though it was difficult to discern beneath the bruises. "I had to send her a note, to assure her of my safety, and that no matter what happened, her name would be kept out of this. 'Nothing is so oppressive as a secret.'"

Charlie found it strangely relieving that Rory was still up to quoting Shakespeare. At least not everything had changed. But Charlie knew this was bad. As different as the two men were, one thing they had in common was loyalty. Rory would go to the noose before he betrayed his lover. Charlie both respected and hated him for it.

"It doesn't look good, I know that." When Rory opened his eyes, they were resigned but sad. "I have accepted my time on earth will end sooner than I would have liked. But it does pain me to go out with everyone believing I am a brutal murderer hunted to ground."

"I haven't given up yet, Mr. Stewart, and neither should you," Dovefield replied, a stubborn glint in his eyes.

Despite the bold words, Charlie wondered what more could be done. Discouragement filled his chest, pushing out against his rib cage until he thought it might crack. Purposefully he took a breath and thought about what he had promised when John first came to him about Rory—that he would not hang on his watch. Now he was not so sure.

John had said little in the exchange, but he spoke now. "We're all working on this puzzle, Rory, but no one more than Quinton.

You know how personal this is to him. He's a dog on a bone when it comes to this killer. If I was a betting man, sure as the day is long I wouldn't bet against us."

Dovefield nodded, crossing his arms with a thoughtful expression. "We will work multiple angles. Of course, you will be moved soon to Newgate, but I will send my personal coach to make sure you arrive safely. I know whose hands to grease to ensure you are at least settled there without violence. In the meantime, I will prepare a legal case while the others work on the actual murder." He paused until Rory lifted his head and met his eyes. "The odds are not good, Mr. Stewart. But the chances are not yet zero."

Not the most reassuring speech, but Charlie was grateful for Dovefield's honesty. Anything else would be disrespectful to Rory.

It must've done the trick, because Rory managed a crooked smile. "Seems I have a team. A man can ask for nothing more." He looked at Charlie. "I have a bit put aside to pay Lord Dovefield, and a bit more to perhaps purchase some scotch for the night? It would not go awry, I assure you."

Despite himself, Charlie found himself smiling back. "I can bring what you need, and keep you supplied in Newgate as well."

"And clothes from my home?" A faraway look came over his face. "You have no idea how it pains me to be seen less than fashionably dressed."

That stupid, bloody Scot . . .

Chapter Thirty-One

Simone held the hand of the young woman lying in the bed in front of her tightly. The poor lass squeezed back just as tight, beads of sweat forming on her face, her features twisted into a strained expression.

"Just breathe, dear," she said soothingly.

"Yes, *priy,* you are doing very well. Now after this contraction, we are going to move you to the chair, alright?"

Katy Modi was taking charge of this labor, assisted as usual by her daughter, Savita. Simone had never had reason to regret employing their services. Though, God willing, she was past that point in her life, if a cruel twist of fate were to bestow another child within her, she would want Katy to deliver it.

The state of pregnancy didn't agree with Simone. While many women were nauseous for the first month or two, Simone was physically ill the entire time she was pregnant with Zoe. Even that was bearable, but Simone was then bedridden for months after the birth. She'd been affected by more than just the physical weakness but also a heaviness in her mind, as if a great weight was pressing down on her, smothering her will to do . . . anything.

Eventually she recovered, but she put off having a second child with her husband for years, until it was too late. When Zoe and she fled France, leaving him behind, it hadn't occurred to her she would ever have the opportunity to carry another child. Then she met Hugh.

He was a kind man, and he likely would've been content with just Zoe, even though she wasn't his blood. But Simone understood the importance of a gentleman having an heir, and after everything he'd given them, she wanted to give that to him. So she became pregnant with Walter. The pregnancy was just as difficult as the first, and it took just as long for her to recover. Simone swore she would never do it again.

Phoebe's arrival was unexpected. Though this third child was unplanned, Simone had never been one to whine and moan about the circumstances of life. *Qui vivra verra.* He who lives shall see. This time her confinement to bed was twice as long, both before and after the birth. The heaviness that had weighed upon her mind with the other two returned, this time consuming her in its fog for nearly a year. At one point she could not even lift a spoon to her lips to feed herself. She nearly died.

Fortunately for Simone, her second husband was a rich man who could afford to hire continuous nursing care for her and the babe. She recovered once again, though she knew those years of distance and absence must've been difficult upon her children's formative years. After that, she and Hugh were much more careful, and their efforts had paid off. She was now past the prime of her childbearing years with no fourth child in sight.

However, the young women who came into her care were not. The whole point was to help these unfortunate souls carry their children to term while also providing the mothers with the skills and opportunities to succeed as single parents in a society designed for them to fail. It was an uphill battle, but Simone found she enjoyed the challenge.

Around 3 o'clock that afternoon Rosemary Connor, a girl of

only about sixteen, brought her own child into the world. He was a ruddy cheeked little boy with a healthy pair of lungs.

"Very good work," said Simone with a soft smile.

She and Katy left Savita behind to care for the aftermath of the birth, going through to the small parlor in the house. The pair settled into their plush armchairs, each with their respective beverages—a glass of red wine for Simone and a cup of thick chai for Katy.

Katy took a sip before speaking sincerely. "You have done good work here, Simone."

"I could not do it without you, Katy."

If someone had told Simone a year ago that not only would she be socializing with an Indian midwife but would also be on a first name basis with her, she would not have believed them. And yet here she sat, bonded to this woman by a shared passion to help these girls. It wasn't that Simone had completely forgotten the rules of society and class by which she had lived her life, but here, within these walls, it felt as though those rules carried a bit less weight.

She took a sip of her wine, the tart, fruity liquid going down easily. She had never understood her daughter's affection for whiskey. Give Simone a good French wine any day over that bitter poison.

"Savita gets more skilled each time you visit," said Simone.

"She is nearly as good as I am now, when it comes to delivering babies." Katy said the words with the glow of a mother's pride. "All of my knowledge, she carries."

"She carries it well." Simone took another sip. "She is also more beautiful every time I see her. Does she have any suitors?"

Katy's nose wrinkled. "Not for lack of trying. I've been beating English boys back with a stick ever since she was *bachi*, which is nothing compared to what my son would do to them. But none of them are good enough for my Savita. She deserves someone who sees who she is, not just what she looks like."

"And there's no one she has in mind?" asked Simone.

"Mm." Katy smiled knowingly. "Well, I wouldn't go that far. But we shall see."

Simone sighed, her thoughts turning nostalgic. "If there is one thing I have learned from my children, it's that there's not as much within our control as we would like."

"And how is your own daughter?" asked Katy. "Does she have any suitors in mind?"

Another sigh escaped Simone's lips. "If it were up to Zoe, she would never marry—or if she did, it wouldn't be to someone of my choosing."

"And who would you choose for her? Someone titled, with blue English blood in their veins?"

"Yes." Simone could not deny the truth. "I want my daughter to have the best opportunities available to her, and here, in this day and age, that means the protection that comes with a powerful man. I won't deny the unfairness of it, but I see the world as it is, not as I wish it to be."

"As do I, *saheli*." Katy's voice was without judgment or criticism. "The father of my children, he carried pure British blood. He came from a family with titles and money and land. But when it mattered most, his honor failed him. He abandoned me, and worse yet, he abandoned his children." She paused for a moment, but then continued, dismissing the memory with a wave of her hand. "There are many ways to measure a man's worth. But honor and parentage are not the same. Whatever the circumstances of their childhoods, all my boys are honorable men."

Simone didn't respond immediately, taking time to digest Katy's heavy words. She understood to whom Katy was alluding. She did not know all the details, but she knew Katy had served as a surrogate maternal figure to the constable Hugh was so fond of, John Smith, as well as the current source of her own annoyance, Quinton Huxley.

It was not that she had anything personally against the man. From what she knew of Quinton, Katy was right. He did seem a man of honor. Hugh liked him well enough. Zoe liked him, more than well enough. But it did not change the fact that he was the son of an actress, unclaimed by any father, and though Quinton might dispute the term, a known thief-taker as well.

Nevertheless, what Katy said did ring true. Half the girls in her charity carried the children of blue-blooded noblemen who could not be bothered to take responsibility for their actions.

While Simone would never claim to be a romantic, she did not want the kind of marriage for Zoe that occurred all too often among their class—the kind where a woman turned a blind eye to the roving hands of her husband, settling for a comfortable but cool life of contentment and distance. She wanted her daughter to have a partner, as she did with Hugh.

Simone shook those thoughts from her mind and smiled at her companion. "You are a good mother, Katy . . . and a good woman. I hope your children appreciate you."

Katy smiled broadly. "If they do not, I am always ready to remind them. You are a good mother too, Simone. All we can do for our children is our best. Everything else . . . that is up to fate."

Chapter Thirty-Two

Though Mr. Stewart had only been under arrest for two days, Hugh could see the confinement at Newgate was already taking a toll. The Scot's face was still pale, and the bruise across his cheek actually looked worse than when they had first spoken to him in the Bow Street jail. On the other hand, his clothing situation had decidedly improved. The finely tailored garb suited him. But when Mr. Stewart met his eyes, Hugh saw the real enemy in the room.

The flash of hope he'd seen before was gone. Mr. Stewart had given up.

Hugh glanced at the man next to him and waited for William Garrow to speak.

The retired barrister and current parliament member said, "I'll be honest with you, Mr. Stewart. You look like a rat a cat has been playing with for a day or two, and I can see you are awaiting the final kill." He picked up an empty scotch bottle from the floor and continued. "It is time to rally, my friend, not fade. Perhaps slow down on the scotch and enjoy a clearer mind. That could help us."

Mr. Stewart allowed a shadow of a smile to grace his lips and spoke quietly, his Scottish accent thick. "I appreciate you being here, both of you. But the last thing I want right now is a clear mind. I plan to go to the rope stumbling drunk if at all possible."

William Garrow leaned back, observing the man in front of him. Hugh knew his old friend was already preparing a defense in his mind, as a more brilliant barrister had not yet graced the streets of London. Hugh was grateful Garrow had agreed to help with defending Mr. Stewart, as it could not be a popular choice. At this point in his career, Garrow was more consumed with politics than law, having been elected to Parliament a few years ago. But since his beloved wife's death, Garrow was rarely found in court or at Parliament. It was a fact he was rarely found anywhere but home. The loss had cut deep. Hugh knew it was a sign of the depth of their friendship that Garrow was here at all.

Garrow was well known for establishing a precedent within the court system that accused individuals should be allowed a defense. Prior to his intervention, only a prosecuting barrister was present during a court case. The accused had to present his own case, and naturally most were convicted. Garrow's ideas and relentless drive changed everything—it changed Hugh personally. Hopefully their experience would benefit their current client.

"I will strike a bargain with you, Mr. Stewart." Garrow smiled and met Rory's eyes. "Give us your complete attention, with a clear head, while we prepare your defense. If it does come to the rope, I will give you the bottle of scotch myself, in time to allow the necessary level of drunkenness you seek. Deal?"

That got a hint of a smile. Rory winced at his split lip, but the smile stayed. "Deal, Mr. Garrow. Deal. If it comes to it, I like a good scotch, smoky and smooth. Charlie has supplied me with liquor, and I assure you I am grateful, but the quality has suffered from my usual poison."

Garrow gave a sharp nod. "I have no intention of allowing it to get to that point, but if it comes to it, you shall drink yourself senseless with an excellent bottle. Now, let us get to the matter at hand. Your defense is proving challenging. Walk us through exactly what you said in the argument with Madame Clarissa Amato, and exactly where you went afterwards."

Mr. Stewart nodded, and Hugh watched as he carefully thought about his answer. He hoped Mr. Stewart was past keeping vital information to himself.

The Scot took a deep breath. "I was frustrated with Clarissa, I will tell you that. She seemed to me to have offered a viable solution to our problem of meeting privately, and indeed it was a satisfactory arrangement for some time. But suddenly she claimed she needed more funds, and we would pay more or pay elsewhere. I tried to reason with her, but she quickly became heated. Looking back, she seemed almost desperate." Mr. Stewart sighed. "I think now her need was real. But at the time it seemed based more on greed than necessity. But I certainly wouldn't have killed her over it."

Garrow nodded. "Then what did you do?"

Stewart seemed to pause longer before he answered next. "I left, walking home. I live east and south of her shop, but I walked north for a time, to clear my head, past Dowager Silverington's estate. Eventually I wandered somewhere past Berkley Square and circled around back to St. James Park and on down to my place."

"And you are sure you spoke to no one?" asked Hugh.

"I wasn't in the mood for conversation. Truth be told, I was already regretting my anger with Clarissa. I tossed a coin to a sweeper boy, I think, but I can't even tell you what he looked like." Mr. Stewart's expression had returned to discouragement. "I thought about dipping in for a quick pint, but I just dinnae feel in the mood, so I continued home."

"Very well." Garrow turned to Hugh. "Hugh, could I confer with you for a moment?"

"Certainly." Hugh's brow furrowed as he tried to think of what Garrow could possibly want to confer on in the middle of meeting with a client, but he allowed Garrow to grab him by the elbow and guide him out of the cell.

Garrow lowered his voice. "How certain are you that Mr. Stewart here is innocent?"

Shifting from foot to foot, Hugh considered his answer. Upon getting to know him, he could say with certainty that Mr. Stewart was a likable man—articulate and charming. Zoe and her friends certainly believed in him. And the evidence was mostly circumstantial. But that didn't mean it wasn't compelling. Without an alibi, was there any way Hugh could be completely convinced?

"Aren't you the one who once told me it didn't matter whether a person was guilty or innocent, only what could be proved in court?" countered Hugh, carefully sidestepping the question.

It was the correct response—Garrow grinned and in his eyes Hugh saw a flash of the passionate barrister he'd once known. "Touché, my friend. Touché."

Returning to the cell with renewed vigor, Garrow addressed the prisoner. "It is possible someone did see Mr. Stewart but just hasn't been asked. He no doubt passed countless people, and it is possible someone would remember him. It would take two reliable witnesses. I am afraid a sweeper boy may not count. Do you have a man who could follow Mr. Stewart's path and see if a needle exists in our haystack?"

Hugh nodded. "John has done good work for me in the past, and he is a friend of Mr. Stewart. He can ask the right people the right questions. He's a good hand."

"I'm quite sure that time would be wasted," said Stewart hurriedly.

"It's no trouble, Mr. Stewart. I know your friends are eager to help."

Garrow handed Mr. Stewart a piece of paper and a pencil. The lead utensil was certainly more convenient to carry than a quill these days.

"Draw your path from the coffee shop to your home. John will have to do the rest."

Mr. Stewart hesitated.

Garrow leaned back, watched him, and after a moment spoke. "It's sometimes difficult to recognize wealth, Mr. Stewart. I would say being locked in a cell and accused of a brutal crime might muddy those waters, but you have friends—real ones, who are walking this path beside you and carrying the load you cannot. You are rich, sir. Embrace their worth."

Meeting Garrow's eyes, Mr. Stewart unexpectedly smiled. "To mingle friendship far is to mingle blood. You are right, Mr. Garrow. I am a wealthy man."

As Mr. Stewart began to draw his map, Hugh let out a deep breath. Perhaps it was Shakespeare, Garrow, or God himself, but it seemed a glimmer of hope might be alive in the room again.

Chapter Thirty-Three

Closing the door to his rented room behind him, John tossed the letter he held onto the small table in the corner of the room. The matron always collected and sorted the mail, and had given it to him on his way up the stairs. He hung up his coat and spent a few minutes starting the coal fire to warm his room. He had enough time for a meal before he had to follow the map Mr. Dovefield had given him.

His day had been frustrating. Following Quinton's suggestions, he had spent time looking into Sarah Hammond's love life, but with little success. He had tracked down and spoken to Sarah Hammond's assistant for a second time, but the lass could tell him no more. Miss Hammond had carefully kept her legitimate business venture separate from her private arrangements. He admitted she was a clever woman.

He had tracked down other associates of Miss Hammond as well. Suppliers, tradesmen, even a customer or two. All had the same story. Sarah Hammond was a quiet business woman who paid her bills and kept to herself. According to all he had found, she was not in any discernible trouble and spent no time looking for it.

John sighed and sat down. Perhaps the letter held answers. It was from Sarah Hammond's sister in Yorkshire. John was grateful they had responded quickly. He had written to both inform them of Sarah's death and to ask for information on her life in London. John leaned back in the single straight-backed chair that graced the room in which he lodged. The accommodations were modest, but an absolute palace compared to his childhood. He tore open the envelope.

Dear Mr. Smith,

We are heartbroken at the news of Sarah's death. She was beloved by us all. The news has been especially devastating to our mother, whose health was precarious to start. Sarah's life in London was not a subject we discussed with her, as our mother was opposed to the move. However she was able to provide funds to aid the family regularly, so we know her business was successful. Her last letter held no trepidation, only sorrow for our mother's health. Though it seems unchristian to say, our greatest hope is that the person who took her life suffers for his terrible act, both in this life and the next. People often commented upon Sarah's outward beauty, but her real gift was her beautiful soul. We will miss her forever.

Edith Hammond

John read the letter twice and became thoughtful. By every account of this woman's life she was ordinary, except one thing.

Everyone seemed to agree Sarah Hammond was beautiful.

———————⋅———————

As he looked down at the map in his hand, then back up at the street in front of him, John sighed.

"Do you think this will work?" asked Charlie.

"I don't know. Probably not." John folded the map up and

stuck it in his breast pocket. "But it's Rory's only hope right now. Dovefield's putting on a brave face, but I know his defense is thin. A witness could make all the difference."

"Mm."

John gestured ahead. "Your pick, Charlie. Do you want the right side of the street, or the left?"

Rather than give a response, Charlie just grunted then walked to the left side without a backward glance. John couldn't help but smile.

Charlie's skill set didn't generally include looking for witnesses. John had been genuinely surprised when he asked to go along. He suspected Charlie was just wanting to help, and there was little else he could do.

They had agreed to meet here at the coffee shop about the same time of night Rory would have been walking home that fateful day. John carefully watched the comings and goings of the street as he walked slowly along. He was looking for someone who was a mainstay—a constant on the street. They needed someone who would be watching and remember a finely dressed handsome Scottish man. It was a long shot, but it was all they had to go on.

<hr>

Two hours passed with nothing to show for it. The sun had long since set, and he knew it was time to call it a night. John had long ago lost track of Charlie, but he figured he would catch up with him soon enough.

No one had remembered Rory. A few urchins thought they might've seen someone like him, or at least were willing to say they did for enough coin. But it didn't matter—the word of an urchin wasn't worth anything in court.

Suddenly Charlie materialized beside him and John jumped.

His friend smothered a snicker. "Hold your horses, John, it's only me."

Clearing his throat, John forced a laugh himself. "Wool gathering, I'm afraid. Did you have any luck?"

As Charlie smoothed his shirt, he spoke easily. "I might have. A couple of the boys told me an older man usually sits in front of his flat in the evenings and has a drink. He wasn't there tonight, but I'll come back and talk to him tomorrow night. Maybe he saw Rory."

"Which street? I can go back myself."

"It's probably not worth your time." Charlie shook his head as he began to walk away. "I only know the house. I'll let you know what he says. Up for a pint at the Black Swan? I've had good news about a certain business venture. I'll buy tonight."

John didn't miss the evasive way Charlie changed the subject. Knowing Charlie's disdain for the law, he was almost certainly hiding something. Charlie liked to think he was very smooth, but John saw through him more often than not. As he watched his friend walk toward the pub, John made a conscious decision to not pursue that particular line of thinking, instead following after him. After all, it wasn't often Charlie offered to buy.

Chapter Thirty-Four

As the energy of the crowd filled Hugh, his own energy rose to match them—in intensity, if not bloodthirstiness. He never tired of being in a courtroom—the roar of the crowd, the battle between the two barristers, the passion for justice, and the anticipation of never knowing what would happen next. At one point in his life, he had lived for nothing else. The energy of court gave him purpose when he needed it. Though his life had changed drastically since that time, he still loved his work.

That didn't mean he was blind to the less desirable parts of the system. The section in the Old Bailey for spectator seating was overflowing in any major case. Even though that had been true for years, it still amazed him how every crowd was hoping, not for justice, but for blood—for entertainment. As if somehow the injustices in their own lives were leveled by the distraction of seeing someone else suffer. Hugh couldn't help but be reminded of another occasion in history—when ancient Rome had ruled the world, providing entertainment in the form of combat to the death in an arena. Did that make him one of the gladiators?

Glancing up at the crowd, he easily spotted Zoe and Mary. Both looked more than a little forlorn. Hugh knew these feelings were not due to where they were seated but to what they were dreading. A large figure parted the masses, and he could make out Quinton moving his way to their side. He reached out a hand, placing it on Zoe's arm. John was with him, and Hugh watched him and Mary have a similar exchange. Clearly no one expected this to go well.

The one face he'd been expecting to see was strangely absent. Their friend from India who had been so involved in the whole affair was nowhere to be seen. Hugh wasn't sure what that meant, but he didn't have too much time to dwell on it, so he made a mental note and returned to the task at hand.

The Old Bailey courthouse was situated along the original bailey or wall of the city. It had only one courtroom, but recent remodels had added more comfortable facilities for court personnel. Hugh thought it especially noteworthy that witnesses had a space to wait to be called, instead of waiting at a nearby pub as had been the case in the past. Newgate was located conveniently close, with a passage to bring prisoners through.

He watched as Mr. Stewart was brought in, standing tall as Garrow had instructed him, though with one arm pressed against his side in a futile but instinctive effort to stabilize his cracked ribs. As promised, Mr. Stewart was putting his best—sober—foot forward. As he was escorted to his place in the dock, directly facing the witness box, he looked around at the shouting mobs, his expression unreadable. The jurors sat in their box to his right, their reactions ranging from intimidated by the frenzy to joining in the shouting.

Hugh himself sat at a table below where the judges sat. His solicitor sat with him, and space was made for Garrow as well. The well-known barrister's presence added to the excitement, as he was so rarely seen in court these days. As for the man himself, he looked at home, as he always did once the performance started. Hugh was grateful to have him at his side.

The judge called to order once Mr. Stewart was settled in, and the prosecution started to speak. James Armstrong was about Hugh's age, with a receding hairline and a stout waistline. He was the kind of man one could easily overlook, but Hugh knew not to underestimate him.

"Before you lies a brutal murderer, gentlemen. This trial won't last long and you won't wonder if I am right. Rory Stewart makes his way as a grave robber to be sure, and cutting up and selling bodies has bought him fancy clothes and a fancy life. But fancy clothes can't change a man's nature. He went too far when it came to Clarissa Amato—strangling her to death in the shop where they were lovers."

Garrow stood with a loud scoff. "There is absolutely no indication that Mr. Stewart and Ms. Amato were anything more than patrons of the same coffee shop. I can appreciate Mr. Armstrong's fanciful imagination, but perhaps he should save it for his own bedroom, instead of speculating about the defendant's."

The watching crowd, already abuzz with whispers, burst into loud jeers. It took a firm shout from the judge to settle the mocking laughter.

Mr. Stewart had given them strict instructions to mention nothing of his liaison, and Hugh knew Garrow would honor that promise.

"Let's see what the witness says," Armstrong countered. "Agnes Barnes, come to the witness box."

It took only a moment for the sturdy coffee shop worker to make her way to the witness stand and quietly face Mr. Stewart.

Armstrong barked questions. "Tell us, lass, have you seen this man before?"

Agnes shifted nervously, but when she spoke, it was with conviction. "Yes sir. This man was arguing with Madame Amato in the coffee shop where I work."

"Would you say they were friends, lass, or maybe something more?" Armstrong waggled his eyebrows at Agnes as if to convey his meaning, but she needed no cues.

"I don't know, sir. I couldn't hear—"

"But what was the dynamic between them? Was the argument passionate?"

"Well, I suppose, but—"

"As lover's quarrels often are. And do you remember the night this argument occurred?"

"Yes sir." The girl swallowed hard. "It was the day . . . the day they found the lady dead."

As the crowd erupted, Armstrong smiled. He had them on his side . . . for now.

"Is that all you have? An argument?" Hugh stood this time, shouting to be overheard above the din. "Haven't you ever had an argument, Armstrong?"

"I have an argument with a well-known resurrectionist, Dovefield. A resurrectionist with no one to vouch for his whereabouts during the murder." The prosecutor puffed out his chest. "That's more than enough."

The squabbling continued with each witness. The prosecution didn't have much more to offer, but Garrow and Hugh had arranged for several people to speak in Mr. Stewart's defense when it came to his character. Three people testified that Mr. Stewart had saved their lives with his medical knowledge, even though they were unable to pay. Since so much of the prosecution's case rested on the negative assumptions about the moral uprightness of a grave robber, they hoped it would help establish Mr. Stewart as a man of good character. But Armstrong made sure the crowd and jurors were aware that the capacity for good in a man did not erase the capacity for evil. It was a good argument, Hugh had to admit.

"And then there is the manifest," boomed Armstrong.

Garrow leapt to his feet. "That manifest has nothing to do with the current case. If you wish to try him for a different crime, I suggest you charge him with it. I would love to hear your other evidence."

"It is well established in the papers that there is a so-called connection between this murder and several previous," countered Armstrong. "I do not need to prove he killed the other women, only that he could have."

"That's ridiculous—"

"It establishes opportunity, as well as a pattern of behavior—"

"I will show you the pattern of my boot—"

"Order in the court!" shouted the judge, interrupting the tirade. "The barristers in question will behave as gentlemen in the court, or else I will have you both removed."

"Apologies, your honor." Armstrong's voice was smooth—he no doubt understood he'd won that round. He turned to the jurors, holding up the piece of paper. "This manifest is from a ship, originating in Edinburgh and bound for London. As the men of the jury will note, it is clearly dated 1792, and shows the defendant's name—Rory Stewart—plainly. The first of these so-called series of murders took place in 1793." Armstrong paused for effect, letting the jurors and the crowd process the information.

Hugh seized his chance. "And where were you in 1973, Mr. Amstrong?"

Blinking rapidly, Armstrong furrowed his brow. "I fail to see how that pertains to evidence at hand."

"Well, if you were in London in 1973, according to your own reasoning, that would make you suspect." Hugh stood, gesturing around the room. "It would make nearly every man here a suspect! Should you fail to convict the defendant, do you plan to accuse all of them?"

Loud whispering filled the room but was cut short at Armstrong's snapped response. "So then you maintain his presence in London at the time is simply another coincidence?"

"Of course it is." Hugh said the words with confidence, but he couldn't help the disquieting thought that he had just walked into a trap.

The crowd stilled as Armstrong pointed to Mr. Stewart.

"Are we to believe this is just another coincidence?" Armstrong shook his head. "How many coincidences can there be surrounding the defendant before we come to the natural conclusion—that they are not coincidences?"

That statement got a reaction from the onlookers. Shouts and jeers swirled, all echoing the same sentiment—hang him.

An increasingly disquiet feeling took root in Hugh's stomach. It did not look good for Rory Stewart. Though the Scotsman's face remained stoic, Hugh couldn't fail to note the whites of his knuckles as he gripped the rail in front of him.

The last thing to be done was for Mr. Stewart to speak for himself. The judge gestured for him to do so. The crowd, Armstrong, and the jurors all became quiet to hear what the man had to say. Hugh knew it would almost certainly sway no one, but it was his right.

Mr. Stewart took a moment to look around the room, then spoke to the jurors. "You will follow your heart in this, I know each of you will. You don't know who I really am, or how my life has led here, but I want to make it clear. I have lived a life I am proud of. I have loved and lost. I have gained knowledge which helped heal sick people who had nowhere else to turn. I have both been a good friend and gained good friends. These are things that cannot be taken from me, no matter what happens here today. But what I am not is a killer and what I have not done . . . is kill Clarissa Amato."

The crowd immediately broke into a frenzied shouting.

"Order! Order!" shouted the judge. "I will expel anyone who cannot control themselves in this courtroom!"

As the blanket of quiet fell, Mr. Stewart continued. "Clarissa Amato was a friend, but nothing more. I mourn her passing. I did not hasten it. Although there is precious little to prove it, I did not kill her."

"But I can prove it, sir." Everyone turned to see the source of the voice that echoed from the back of the courtroom. "I saw you, on Baker Street, the night the lady was killed."

If the crowd was in an uproar before, it was nothing compared to the anarchy now. As the crowd shouted, Hugh leapt to his feet and scanned the mass of people, searching for the source of the bold statement. Finally his eyes came to rest on a man standing in the back, the calm expression on his face contrasting with the chaos of the room.

The judge shouted again for some semblance of order—this time the crowd quieted but did not still. The restless movement caught Hugh's eye, and he noticed his stepdaughter and her friends again. This time the young Indian man, Charlie, had joined them.

"Bring this new witness forward," said Garrow.

"Absolutely not!" Armstrong sprang to his feet, his face red. "We can't allow this man to testify—he isn't on the witness list, and there's no way to know if he's credible."

"We won't know if he's credible unless we hear him out," countered Hugh. "Please, Your Honor, in the interest of justice, we must hear what he has to say."

A tense pause filled the room as the judge considered the conundrum. "It's highly unusual, but I will allow this . . . witness to speak."

The man was escorted to the witness box, making his way with a slight limp.

"What is your name, sir?" asked Hugh.

"Me name is Lincoln Johnson, but everyone calls me Jack." The man spoke with confidence. "And I know I saw this man walking past me that night she were killed."

Armstrong began to rise, but Garrow glared with a force that would knock even the most stubborn mule backward. "Could you at least wait your turn, Mr. Armstrong, before calling him a liar?"

With evidently great reluctance, Armstrong sat back down. Hugh turned back to Jack. "Tell us what you saw that night."

"I live over on the East End, but I haven't been able to work steady since the war." He nodded towards his foot and continued, his expression still calm. "I pick up some odd jobs here and there, and sometimes I find a corner off Bond Street to rely on the kindness of others. That night I was on a corner off St. James, and this man gave me a coin, enough for a hot meal, and I was grateful. That's why I remember him."

This time Armstrong did stand. "He gave him a coin? So he only saw Mr. Stewart for a moment? Even if this is true, there would still be plenty of time left in the night to kill Ms. Amato."

"But here's the thing, sir." Jack spoke again, never raising his voice. "I took 'is coin, and was goin' to The Two Cats for a pork pie, but I saw this man head on toward Green Park. I dunno why, but I was curious, and I followed for a minute. I saw him stop and find hisself a bench in the park. He sat quiet like, so I popped into the Two Cats, which is right there near the park, and had me a couple ale and a good pie." He turned to Mr. Stewart. "Thank you for that by the by. It was right welcome."

Mr. Stewart stared, blinking slowly, and then giving a slight nod.

"Anyways, when I was finished, I walked back to the park. It weren't far, and I wanted to look for the man on the bench. He were still there, sittin' and thinkin' I reckon. It were a good two hours I spent in the pub, and that man never moved. You can reckon for yourselves if he coulda gotten over to kill the lady after that." Jack sat back and looked satisfied.

It was a subtle gesture, but Hugh noticed Mr. Stewart lifting his gaze to the spectators, eventually fixing his eyes on his friend—Charlie. The look was met with an unwavering stare.

Garrow was quick to act. "Madame Amato was discovered slain just after midnight. The well-established dispute between her and Mr. Stewart confirms she was alive late that evening. A reliable witness accounts for Mr. Stewart being away from the murder scene at the time it occurred. What more is there to consider?" If he was aware of the glances happening between Charlie and Mr. Stewart, Garrow seemed to be choosing to ignore them.

Leaping to his feet, Armstrong faced Jack. "You swear by all you hold holy that this man before you was the man you saw, and he was in Green Park for over two hours that night? I remind you, sir, if you are lying, not only will God hold you accountable, but so will the law and the family of the next murdered lass."

Despite the heavy words, Jack met the prosecutor's eyes without flinching. "I know what I saw, sir, and it was this man—this man in front of me—in that park for hours. I am positive."

Everyone turned to the judge for direction. He looked almost ill, but he waved his hand and shouted above the din. "This goes to the jury. Let them decide."

━━━◆━━━

Hugh watched as the twelve men of the jury began to consult. They were seated in the rows of the courtroom reserved for them, six men to a row. In order to discuss the case, they had to lean across each other or turn in their seats to face the men behind, whispering their opinions fervently.

One man in particular seemed to take charge, arguing forcefully to anyone near him. Hugh noticed Garrow watching the same man, a thoughtful expression on his face. As the debate continued, the crowd murmured and shifted, though an occasional shout from the judge had a quieting effect, at least for a few minutes.

It wasn't Garrow's first court trial, or even his hundredth, no doubt. He seemed calm and settled, watching the jurors bicker back and forth.

It wasn't his own first case either, Hugh reminded himself, attempting to calm his own racing heart. He too had conducted hundreds of jury trials, first as a prosecutor and then in defense of the accused once they were allowed more representation. In his own heyday he had sat with as many as eight trials in a single day, each being discussed by the twelve men chosen to be jurors, followed by a verdict, with the accused either released or taken back into custody. It was not uncommon for the jury to take only a minute or two to come to a decision if all were in agreement.

That was not the case this time. These twelve were taking longer than expected. The loudest man continued to make his point, even physically moving down his row to speak to the men seated above. He leaned in, whispering in one man's ear. Whatever he said seemed to satisfy his fellow juror, as the man nodded and sat back.

Hugh leaned forward at that, but he felt a firm hand on his arm. He glanced at Garrow and the other man shook his head.

"If you really believe the man is innocent, I suggest you hold your tongue, my friend," said Garrow.

Hugh hesitated. Did he believe beyond a shadow of a doubt that Mr. Stewart was innocent? He glanced up at the Scot. Perhaps the better question would be, did Hugh believe beyond a shadow of a doubt that he was guilty? That was easier to answer. And if there was any doubt that he could have done it, then how could it be justice to hang him?

He held his tongue.

Moments later the loud man signaled to the judge their decision was made. The judge shouted again for quiet and asked the man if the decision was agreed upon by all.

"Aye, we all think the same, your honor." The words were spoken with conviction.

Hugh held his breath. This was the pinnacle of every trial—the culmination of the anticipation. It could swing either way, and nothing remained but to wait for the next words to be spoken. He thought his heart would beat out of his chest.

"What say ye, then?" The question from the judge echoed like thunder in the tense courtroom.

The chosen juror looked up without flinching. "Ain't no proof he did it, judge. We say let him go."

Chapter Thirty-Five

The crowd exploded as John made his way down to the courtroom floor. Just moments before the surprise witness appeared, Charlie had joined them on the balcony. The glance exchanged between him and Rory did not escape John's notice.

John was no fool; he knew what Charlie had done wasn't legal. Yet, it was justice, and that was enough for him. However, someone needed to get Rory out of there quickly before the crowd descended upon him.

He seized Rory as he exited the dock, Lord Dovefield joining them swiftly. Together, they dashed toward the street, Rory panting in agony with each stride.

"My coach is around the corner." Lord Dovefield's voice was low in his ear. "I was optimistic."

As the three clamored inside, John turned back to see the crowd spilling out of the Old Bailey, their thirst for violence unabated. No doubt they would find it, but he was content to let the other runners deal with the fallout of the brawls and drunken melee to follow.

The carriage raced at breakneck speed until stopping outside of Lord Dovefield's home. The lord headed inside while John helped Rory out of the carriage with more care. Two footmen met them at the stairs, taking over, and Rory leaned heavily on them both as they dragged him within, John following close behind. Lord Dovefield directed the footmen to his study.

"I have already sent the boot boy to find Dr. Lewis," said the lord. "Fortunately, I requested he stay close in case we needed him. I have no doubt Zoe and her clan will find us soon enough. Now, if you'll excuse me for a moment, I need to go tell Lady Dovefield the news."

It wasn't long before Lord Dovefield's prediction came true. The clatter of a second carriage echoed on the cobblestones outside, promptly followed by Zoe and Mary dashing indoors. John directed them to the study before stepping out to await Charlie's arrival. He knew Charlie would come, though he was just as likely to slip in through an open window as the front door. John preferred the latter.

Only a few minutes passed before his friend appeared beside him, though he never heard the sound of horse hooves or carriage wheels. John wondered at Charlie's means of traversing London's streets—if it involved the wings of a royal raven, he wouldn't have been surprised.

The two of them exchanged a look, but there was no need for words—not yet. John clasped Charlie's shoulder and guided him inside the residence. They entered Lord Dovefield's study, but stopped uncertainly at the threshold—it seemed wrong to continue uninvited.

"John, you know where the whiskey and glasses are." Lord Dovefield came up behind them. "Can you see that everyone is served? I don't want any curious ears overhearing whatever conversation ensues."

Dovefield cast a glance at Charlie while he spoke, yet Charlie's black eyes betrayed no guilt. His confidence was unwavering, though whether that was real or a facade was anyone's guess. John understood that any effort to uncover his secrets would be futile. As tempted as he was to push, John reminded himself that this time justice carried more weight than legality.

As John found glasses and poured whiskey, Dr. Lewis entered the room. He examined an ashen Rory behind a convenient screen in the corner of the room. The group was silent, waiting, the only sound the occasional clink of a glass onto a table. After some minutes Dr. Lewis reappeared, followed slowly by Rory, still awkwardly buttoning up his shirt, which remained untucked from his pants. Zoe and Mary both blushed, but at this point propriety wasn't the priority. Every person here just wanted Rory to recover from this nightmare.

The physician leaned in to speak to Lord Dovefield.

"Excuse me," interjected Zoe. "We are all eager to hear your report."

"Ah, of course." Dr. Lewis glanced at the lord, but when Dovefield didn't correct his daughter, the doctor directed his speech to group. "Three broken ribs, which will take some time to heal. A strong sprain in his wrist, which I have wrapped. Multiple bruises, and that gash on his head should have been stitched. At this point it has already begun to heal and stitches would do more harm than good, but he can expect a significant scar. As he is still mobile and, well, alive, lends to the conclusion of a lack of internal-type injuries. The lack of a fever indicates minimal infection. Either this man is uncommonly fortunate, uncommonly healthy, or simply an enigma. In any case, with care, he will recover completely."

John breathed a deep sigh of relief. "That is excellent news."

"Quite." Dr. Lewis cleared his throat. "The ribs will take the longest to heal, obviously. I've given him something for the pain for now. He should have a great deal of rest to allow those to heal. For a few weeks he will need care."

"Very good. Thank you, doctor." Lord Dovefield gave him a firm handshake and then escorted him out.

The rest of them pulled chairs around Rory. He smiled and then spoke, his voice soft and his accent tamed again. "I thank each and every one of you. Without you I could even now be at the end of a rope, not sipping good whiskey in a fine house surrounded by true friends." He paused and his eyes met Charlie's. "Good on ye, Charlie, for finding such an impeccable witness to my hours at the park. A soldier, no less. I hope he has a long and comfortable life."

"I have a feeling his winds have changed for the better." Charlie said the words casually and without remorse. "But there is no way to know for certain."

"And one of the jurors seemed uncommonly convinced as well." Rory raised an eyebrow. "A smart man, no doubt."

"I wouldn't know about that." Charlie spoke without hesitation. "But it does seem to be the season for favorable winds."

Rory met his gaze evenly, but said nothing further, instead leaning back with a slight sigh. His face was lined with signs of exhaustion, and John suspected he didn't feel the conversation was worth pursuing further.

"What counts is the rope did not find an innocent neck, can we agree?" said John, reflecting the same sentiment.

Nods all around greeted his words, and a comfortable silence filled the room. But it couldn't last, though John would have liked it to stretch a little further.

"'Tis true, I am pleased to have my neck still intact." Rory sighed. "But the truth is, until the real killer is unmasked, there will always be some who believe it could be me."

John was quick to protest. "Not anyone who knows you, Rory, and that is all who matter."

"Easy words to say." Rory glanced at those seated around the room, his gaze intense. "But can any of you honestly say ye never doubted me?"

An uneasy atmosphere settled over the room as most of them shifted in their seats, stealing glances at the others. John felt heat bloom on his own cheeks, and he had nothing to say in his defense.

"I never did." The bold statement came from Charlie, his arms crossed as he squinted at the other members of the party. "Didn't know everyone else was in the same boat."

Rory chuckled, reaching out a hand to pat Charlie's forearm. "Thank you, Charlie. But I wouldn't have blamed you if you did. Once the seed of doubt is planted . . . it can be mighty difficult to uproot. I can't honestly say what I would have thought if the roles were reversed."

Quinton leaned forward, his cheeks mirroring the blush on John's. "You're right, Rory, and I am sorry. We need to unmask the true murderer, as much for your sake as for justice."

"We've gathered a great deal of pieces about these murders. We seem so close." This was from Zoe, who then glanced at Quinton, meeting his eyes squarely. "For the sake of all those left behind, as well as Rory, can we finally put the puzzle pieces together? Can we finish this thing?"

Chapter Thirty-Six

As Zoe spoke the words, her stepfather returned to the room and took a chair. Rory had already dozed off, prompting Charlie to reach over and slip his glass from his hand. Quinton leaned back, content to let the others discuss the case before offering his opinions.

Dovefield was the first to respond to Zoe's question. "What do we know and what still remains unknown?"

"Well, to start, it likely all began with Annie Huxley," said Mary.

"Agreed. For reasons we still don't understand, she seems to be the key to all of this." John leaned forward, hands clasped together. "The one thing we do know is that most of them at least looked like her—beautiful and dark haired. Magistrate Holdsworth agrees. Until I pointed it out, he hadn't realized all the victims had such a similar appearance, but he thinks it can't be a coincidence."

"But Margot Anderson was not," objected Dovefield. "Dark haired that is. She had red hair—auburn, as Simone would say."

John nodded. "That's true. Margot was killed differently too. The others, at least the ones we know of, were killed with a thin chain, and then the cloth was left wrapped round their necks . . . almost like . . . a gift. But Margot was strangled with the cloth itself."

"Another thing—Margot survived the initial attack, succumbing to her wounds later. It's almost like he didn't follow through." Zoe threw back her whiskey in one motion before refilling the glass herself. "What would make a killer like that—someone who's so comfortable with violence—change his approach? Did he hesitate, or was he interrupted?"

"Perhaps he was fonder of her than the others," suggested Mary. "Maybe she had a second lover, this mystery killer."

"That doesn't seem likely," Zoe countered. "The girl was only beginning her first season, and pretty as she was, she didn't have the worldly experience to juggle two lovers."

Her stepfather raised an eyebrow at her comment, but before he could say anything in response, Rory grunted. Quinton nearly jumped in surprise; he'd been so sure his injured friend was sleeping.

"Must have been a different killer." Rory's voice was soft, only barely audible, and his eyes were unfocused as exhaustion drained the last bit of strength he had left. "Sometimes a man kills more than once in his life. If a man was in the war, any war, he likely killed multiple times, God rest their souls. But this is different. It's not killing out of necessity, it's killing for pleasure. When someone falls that far . . . becomes a hunter of men and women, they also become driven . . . like a kind of compulsion. They tend to do things the same way. For all the discrepancies in Miss Anderson's case—she looked different, she was left alive, and killed with the cloth instead of the chain . . . well, it doesn't make sense. I think she died by a different hand."

The uncharacteristic rambling slowed at the end, as if he needed a moment to recover his strength to speak. The group took the moment of silence to glance at each other uneasily. Quinton sipped his whiskey, letting the liquid warm his throat while he considered Rory's words. Rory was very dear to him, and he trusted his counsel, but he was ignoring a very clear piece of information.

"But what about the red cloth with the elephants, Rory?" Quinton finally said. "It was from the same bolt as the cloth at my mother's death—and the others. How could a different killer have access?"

"It is a conundrum, Quinton. They must be connected. But I believe it was a different hand . . ." The last sentence trailed off as Rory's eyes finally closed again.

Quinton waited until his friend's breathing evened out before he said, "Regardless, as Mary already said, it goes back to my mother. We just need to figure out the connection."

"Do you still keep in touch with anyone from the old days? From when you lived at the theater?" It was the first time Charlie had said anything since the initial questions about the surprise witness. While the others had been debating the facts of the case, he'd been quietly sipping his whiskey. Quinton knew this place was well outside of Charlie's comfort zone, despite his facade of nonchalance. But one of Charlie's strengths was his adaptability; no matter the situation, he would figure out how to survive—to thrive, even. His was a clever mind and the wheels were always turning.

"No, not really. Not since . . . not since Abigail died." The thought of his friend still gave Quinton pause. He cleared his throat and continued, "And she was the only one before that for ages."

"What about Old Arthur?" pressed Charlie. "You ever seen him around?"

"Old Arthur? The odd jobs man?"

"Yes. He used to give us sweets whenever you took us back around there. Bit touched in the head, but a constant fixture of the theater. People like that, they get overlooked, but they see and hear more than most. Perhaps someone should ask him what he remembers." Charlie's eyes had taken on a faraway look, as if lost in the past.

Quinton nodded slowly, grateful he had friends who shared his boyhood. "I haven't thought about Old Arthur for years. Perhaps I can pay him a visit, if he's even still alive."

As he and Charlie had been having their exchange, Zoe's features had taken on a thoughtful expression. Quinton knew her well enough by now to recognize that look, so he waited for her to speak her mind. He didn't have to wait long.

"There is something else that has been bothering me." Zoe glanced at Quinton, before turning to Mary. "We know that Madame Amato—Miss Hammond—was hosting affairs in her upper rooms. We also know at least three of the women using those rooms. At least, we think we know. It seems likely. Lady Soarington, Mrs. Lorant, and Lady Brightlingsea. At the time we talked to them, they kept their involvement with the whole thing a secret, understandably."

"I recall." Mary nodded, clearly comprehending where Zoe was going with this.

"Given that they wouldn't want to confess to anything that might portray them in a scandalous light, it's likely they're withholding information," Zoe mused, biting her lower lip. "I believe we should pay at least one of them another visit. I know Lady Soarington well enough to call on her. If Mary and I approach her together, with our current knowledge, we might convince her to reveal more details to us. And if not her, then we'll find a way to approach one of the others."

"Agreed." With that, the two women were united in their next course of action.

Through all of this, Dovefield had been listening quietly. but now he leaned forward to speak. "I'll tell you how we stand legally. Rory was not declared innocent. It was determined there was not enough to prove him guilty. The last-minute witness certainly threw a horseshoe into the prosecution's plans. Fortuitous." He paused, glancing thoughtfully at Charlie, but Charlie didn't acknowledge the look. Instead he stared down, as if fascinated by the bottom of his empty glass.

Quinton glanced between the two men, wondering whether

Lord Dovefield would say anything more and what Charlie would say in response. The Lord's intense gaze rested on Charlie for several tense moments, as if doing the calculations in his head, weighing what needed to be weighed. Finally he sighed, reaching for the whiskey and filling Charlie's glass. A gesture of acquiescence and acceptance that Charlie was sure to understand. He met the Lord's eyes without flinching, nodding in acknowledgment.

Dovefield continued. "So Rory is a free man, but the taint of this will remain. There will be little consequence in his line of work, but know this—he will have to watch his back for the foreseeable future, possibly forever. Many will always believe he is a murderer, and they will not be satisfied unless another candidate is put forward."

Quinton knew the lord wasn't wrong. He finished off his whiskey with a sigh. "Then for my sake, for Rory's sake, for Miss Anderson's sake, we must press on. As Lady Demas said, let us end this."

Agreement murmured among them, and a few glasses were raised to show accord.

"Now to settle Rory," said John with a glance at the sleeping man.

"The Dowager. Good choice. She'll have me." Rory's eyes were still closed and his mumbled words were barely discernible, but the intent was clear.

The general reaction of the room was astonishment, but after a few moments, Quinton couldn't help himself. He laughed out loud. "You're not going to Lady Theo's house, you mad dog," he said to Rory, swatting gently at his friend.

Rory, more awake now, scowled at him. "Don't be ridiculous. I don't mean anything untoward."

"Of course you don't," said Zoe with an amused expression. "After all, people have inherent value outside of romantic interest."

Mary laughed at this, though she seemed to think it was funnier than Quinton did, not that he disagreed with the sentiment. He squinted, glancing between Mary and Zoe. Perhaps there was some inside joke between the two he wasn't in on.

"You may be correct, Zoe," interjected Hugh with an air of authority. "But in this case, I think it might be best for Mr. Stewart to convalesce at our home instead."

The solution seemed to suit those involved, though Quinton couldn't help but wonder if the mild-tempered barrister would regret his decision once Rory regained enough of his strength to be a nuisance.

Chapter Thirty-Seven

The unlikely tribe parted ways late in the evening—too late for an uninvited visit to the Soarington household. Zoe and Mary agreed it would be best to wait until the next day, though Zoe did so reluctantly.

That night she tossed and turned, her mind unable to settle. The evening's conversation played over and over in her mind, occupying her thoughts so that sleep eluded her. The use of time was not productive, but despite the exhaustion weighing her body down, Zoe could not still her overactive mental faculties long enough to slip into the void of unconsciousness she craved.

Brutus's snoring didn't help either. She was very fond of the beast curled in a large lump at the foot of her bed, but he was not known for his quiet disposition. When Zoe drifted off quickly it wasn't a problem, but on nights like this . . .

Finally she gave up altogether on sleep, quietly slipping out from under the covers so as not to disturb Brutus, and donning her dressing gown. She made her way down the stairs with as little noise as possible, hoping not to wake the other members of the household. But when she reached the landing, Zoe was surprised to find she wasn't the only one who'd had trouble finding rest.

The light of a fireplace flickered eerily in the shadows of the staircase. Zoe found herself drawn toward the warm glow, tracing the source of illumination to the parlor.

Her mother sat on the sofa in the room, her legs tucked up under her petite frame and a glass of red wine in her hand. Her long soft blonde hair was loose, falling like a waterfall down her back and shoulders. Firelight danced across her striking features as she stared off into the middle distance, obviously lost in thought.

Zoe's presence suddenly felt like an intrusion. As she turned to leave, a floorboard creaked under her weight. She froze and glanced back at her mother.

"Ah, *ma fille*." Simone patted the cushion next to her own. "Come sit."

"Sorry, Maman. I didn't realize anyone else was awake."

"No apology is necessary. I always have a hard time sleeping when I have things on my mind, but I don't mind the company."

"I must get it from you then." Zoe went over and sat next to her mother.

Simone placed a soft hand on her arm. "What things are keeping you awake tonight?"

"Oh, it's nothing. I'm just overexcited about everything that's been going on these last few days, and my mind doesn't know when to quit." Zoe considered her mother. "What about you?"

She was silent for a moment before answering. "Believe it or not, I was thinking about when I met your father."

"Really?" That was a surprise. "I didn't think you still thought about him. You don't . . . you don't talk about him often."

"Of course I think about him. Every time I look at you, I think about him." Simone smiled. "You look more and more like him with each year that passes."

Zoe returned her smile. After a moment, she decided to take advantage of this rare state of openness. "Would you tell me, how did you meet?"

"It wasn't terribly romantic, if that's what you were hoping for," said Simone with a soft chuckle. "My parents arranged the marriage with his parents, as was usually done. We were both young . . . I think I was fifteen when I actually met him, and he wasn't much older. We were probably in the same room twice before the wedding."

Pausing to contemplate this new information, Zoe chose her next words carefully—she wanted to keep the dialogue going. "What did you think of him when you met?"

"I thought he was handsome, even if he was a bit full of himself. And I knew it was a good match, for both our families. *J'étais contente.*"

Zoe laughed. "I suppose that sounds right." She rarely found her mother in such a talkative and open mood. Zoe decided to push a bit farther while she had the opportunity. "Did you stay . . . satisfied?"

Simone was silent again.

"Sorry, you don't have to answer that."

"No, it's fine." Simone cleared her throat and took a sip of her wine. "My relationship with your father was . . . complicated. I did love him, in my own way, and I think he felt the same about me. But that didn't mean we always liked each other. However, on the days when it was harder to like each other, we had the most important thing in common—you."

Zoe reflected on this. Some of her earliest memories were of her father, seen through the innocence and naivety of childhood, where parents are heroes who can do no wrong. As she grew older, however, she'd learned that people were far more complex. She supposed that would have to include her father as well.

"What was it about him that made you not like him sometimes?" Zoe's voice held no judgment, just genuine curiosity.

Her mother raised an eyebrow. "Are you sure you want to hear this, *ma fille?*"

She thought about it for a moment, knowing that once the box was opened, she wouldn't be able to close it again. "Yes. I think it's time."

Simone took another sip of her wine and looked back into the flickering light of the fireplace. "Your father was a complicated man. He was raised to be impulsive and indulgent, with no consequences, as most men of his station were, but he wasn't malicious. He was just . . . self-centered, at times. He enjoyed drinking, and cards, and on occasion women. He lived his life in the moment, focused on pleasure rather than practical concerns. That left me to deal with many of the more practical aspects of life. So sometimes it was hard for me to like those parts of him."

It was difficult to think about her father in that way. Zoe had always held him up in her mind as a perfect figure of her childhood—made hazy with time, but ideal in her memory. The things she remembered about him were strong hands lifting her high into the air and a wide smile and the smell of fresh-cut grass as they walked hand in hand through the garden. But she wasn't a child anymore, and part of growing up was recognizing the imperfections of one's parents. Her mother's imperfections were apparent because she was present, involved in Zoe's life every day. Her father, in contrast, remained a martyr, forever unchanged and beyond further scrutiny in death.

Zoe leaned her head on her mother's shoulder, hoping to offer comfort. "I am sorry, Maman. That must've been difficult."

"Thank you, my dear." Her mother's head rested on her own for a moment before she pulled back, looking her in the eyes. "I don't mean to paint him as a villain. Your father was many things, but he wasn't a bad man. He was handsome and cheerful, usually in a good mood, and surprisingly generous. He loved art and architecture and literature. And of everything in his life, there was nothing he loved more than you."

Zoe smiled sadly. "I loved him as well."

Simone returned her smile and patted her gently on the hand. "I know."

"So what made you think of him tonight?"

"Nothing in particular." Simone's tone was nonchalant, but she had turned to look into the fire again. "I've just been thinking about marriage in general recently."

"Are you and Hugh alright?" asked Zoe, squinting at her mother.

Her mother laughed. "Of course. Hugh and I are fine." The wine glass clinked as Simone placed it on the table. She rose to her feet, wrapping her dressing gown a little tighter around her petite body. "I think that is enough reminiscing for one night, *ma fille*." As Simone walked toward the door, she paused in the entryway. "You know I love you, my dear, more than anything, right? Everything I do, I have done for you, even when it might not seem like it."

"Of course, Maman." Zoe was surprised at her mother's uncharacteristic frankness. "I love you too."

Chapter Thirty-Eight

Zoe didn't dream when she finally did go back to bed—her eyes simply closed while it was dark, and when they opened again, sunlight was streaming through the window. Her limbs felt heavy with exhaustion as she rose, and for once she was grateful when Camille came in to help her dress.

Coffee was her only saving grace. She consumed multiple cups before Hugh finally intervened, claiming he could hear her heart beating from across the table.

It was now much too early in the day to call on the Soarington household, so Zoe was forced to wait, the hours dragging by slowly. She and Mary twiddled their thumbs, the anticipation too consuming to turn their attention to anything productive while they waited.

Mary did manage to amuse herself by schooling Camille in the art of a lady's maid. The young lady was still spending days with the Dovefields and evenings at The Haven with her own baby. She was proving a good fit for Zoe, and Mary's extra instruction on Zoe's curls was carefully put to practice. It was on the second hairstyle that Zoe remembered the hairpin Quinton had given her. Camille wove it in firmly, and it truly added a lovely touch.

Finally the time arrived when social convention would allow them to show up at the Soaringtons' home uninvited.

"Are you bringing Brutus?" asked her mother as she opened the door.

Zoe took a moment to contemplate the great beast sitting by the door, his head cocked to one side and his tongue lolling out of his mouth. "It's just a social call. I think his presence might hinder rather than help our cause in this case."

She gave the beast a quick pat on the head as she dashed outside, Mary hot on her heels. The coachman was waiting, the carriage ready to go. It didn't take long to reach their destination— Ruth Soarington's new husband was a titled lord with land and money and a house in the most prominent part of London, just down the street from Theo on Piccadilly and not far from where the Dovefields resided at Grosvenor Square.

Zoe presented her card to the butler at the door, and she and Mary were soon granted entry to the parlor. The Countess Soarington joined them shortly thereafter.

The countess was a woman of composure, but Zoe could tell she was surprised. She couldn't blame her—Zoe wasn't known for her social calls. They had once been peers of a sort, although never quite friends. They had been grouped into the same category that all single women in their society were grouped into, but Ruth was several years older, approaching thirty, and quiet by nature. When she married and joined the circle of married women, Zoe had hardly noted her absence.

"Lady Demas and Miss Fletcher, what a pleasure to see you." Ruth gestured for them to sit, her good manners too well ingrained in her to ask the direct question—what on earth were they doing there?

They made pleasant small talk for a few minutes, but patience had never been one of Zoe's strong suits. As soon as the tea was served and the servants had departed, she made her move. "Forgive me for my directness, Lady Soarington, but there's something I would like to discuss with you." Zoe hesitated. "Something of a somewhat delicate nature."

Rush shifted in her seat, eyes on her tea cup. "I see. I can't imagine what such a delicate matter could be."

"Countess, we have no desire to embarrass you or to make you uncomfortable." Zoe meant that, and she didn't want to say anything a servant might overhear and then get back to her husband, so she chose her next words carefully. "I've recently learned some information about Madame Amato and some of the services she provided. We know there was a select group of clients for whom she performed certain special requests, such as after-hours ordering and tailoring. We have reason to believe you were one of those clients."

The statement hung there in the air, heavy with the shared understanding of what was being implied without being said.

Mary filled the silence. "We would not intrude into your business like this, my lady, unless 'twas very important. But if there was anyone, such as yourself, there at the modiste's shop later than most would expect, it's possible they saw something incriminating . . . something they might not have come forward about on account of wanting to avoid any awkward questions about why they were there themselves. If they did . . . this might be a good time to discuss it."

Lady Soarington quietly contemplated this, taking the two of them in with an intelligence and shrewdness that Zoe hadn't credited her with before. Finally she sighed and set her teacup down. "Madame Amato was a very talented seamstress." She paused, obviously choosing her words just as carefully as Zoe had. "I had used her service for after-hours tailoring before, but recently her prices became too expensive for me. So I was searching for other accommodations."

"Oh." Zoe felt her stomach drop with disappointment. "So you didn't have an appointment with her that day?"

"I had an appointment during regular hours for additional alterations on one of my gowns," Ruth corrected her. "But I did not see her after that."

"I see."

Ruth cleared her throat and shifted in her seat. "I know a man's life was at stake in this matter. If I knew anything about what happened to Madame Amato that night, I would not have kept silent."

Zoe swallowed her disappointment. "Well, thank you so much for your time, Lady Soarington. We won't take up any more of it."

As she and Mary rose to leave, Ruth stood as well. Her expression was appropriately sober for the subject, but Zoe realized she was a prettier woman than she'd once thought. Her wheat blonde hair was pulled back into a loose bun, revealing large hazel eyes and pleasantly arranged features. Her gown fit her slight frame well— the image of a small sparrow came to Zoe's mind.

Ruth's expression was neutral—again, good breeding and manners prevented her from showing too much emotion to mere acquaintances, but Zoe recognized a stoic melancholy that seemed to envelop her. She knew of some of the woman's story—Ruth came from a family with all the right bloodlines but no more money. Season after season she was passed over, until she was approaching the age when most women would accept that their future was that of a spinster, grasping on to the coattails and good will of richer relatives.

That all changed for Ruth when her parents managed to make a match with Lord Soarington, Count of Liverpool. He was a man with more money than sense, approaching the twilight years of his life but, after a string of wives, was still without a living heir. Their marriage seemed like a saving grace to both families, with the only loser being poor Ruth. Zoe could hardly blame her for seeking comfort elsewhere.

"I am sorry I couldn't be more help, Lady Demas." Lady Soarington shook her head. "Lord Fairfax and I were just reflecting on how strange it was to see poor Madame Amato one day alive and well and then the next to hear of her death. It seems unreal."

"Lord Fairfax? Do you mean Lady Fairfax?"

"No. Lord Fairfax is a friend of my husbands. I had several appointments with Madame Amato that week due to a particularly difficult gown issue, and I happened to cross paths with him when he was dropping his mother and her maid off the day before Madame Amato's death."

"Really?"

Zoe thought back to the soiree. She thought Lady Fairfax had told them she'd taken a hackney to her appointment—in fact, she was sure of it. Why would she lie about her son being the one to drop her off?

"Thank you again for the tea, Lady Soarington."

As they walked out of the house and into the soft afternoon sunlight, Zoe and Mary exchanged a meaningful look.

"It might be that she just forgot. She is on the older side," suggested Mary.

"Maybe. But I still think we should ask her about it." Zoe started off toward the carriage.

"Very well, I agree. But let's stop by Theo's for a moment and just let her know where we're headed. I don't want your parents to worry since we're going to be out later than expected."

It was a good idea, so Zoe quickly agreed, but her thoughts were already racing ahead. She was eager to get to the Fairfax home and see what the old bat had to say for herself.

Chapter Thirty-Nine

The back door of Covent Garden Theater was opened without objection to Quinton. This wasn't the same building where he'd spent his early childhood—that structure had burned down and been rebuilt several times over. But most of the people were the same, and though he didn't come around like he once had, he was known to them.

As Quinton approached the stage, a stooped man sweeping the floor of the stage looked up and turned to face him. His hair was thin, and he remained stooped, favoring his knee. But his face broke into a smile as he saw Quinton.

Old Arthur.

The old odd jobs man had been such a fixture in the background that he had become invisible, to the point that even Quinton had overlooked him. However, as soon as Charlie brought up his name, Quinton immediately recalled the man—a silhouette paused in a doorway, always with a broom or some tool in hand, seldom speaking, yet ever observant.

Hopefully he was not as touched as he made out to be.

Quinton returned the old man's smile. "Hello there, Arthur.

Do you remember me?"

The old man's head bobbed up and down. "Annie's boy! I remember you! You got big. Annie's boy."

"I did, Arthur. I grew up. How is life treating you?"

Arthur's smile faded. "Life treating me. Not good. Not good, Annie's boy. I have bad knees and my back is hurt. Bad knees. And no sleep. No sleep."

The curious habit of repeating himself and then repeating what he heard transported Quinton back to his boyhood. The feeling was only strengthened when Old Arthur reached into the pocket of his sweater, fishing out a barley sugar candy and holding it out to him. "I remember you like candy. You and your friends. Candy."

Quinton accepted the candy with a nod. He popped it in his mouth. The flavor lingered, extending the surreal moment, as though the child he once was remained alive, relishing the barley sugars.

"Thank you, Arthur," Quinton said sincerely. "I haven't had a barley sugar since . . . well probably since you last gave me one."

That was true. The streets had no place for luxuries, and sweets were only for the children with homes. That was the way of the world, and Quinton wasn't bitter. But, Lord Above, the sweet was good.

It took effort to pull himself from his boyhood memories and back to the purpose for his visit. He gestured for Old Arthur to sit on a bench just to the back of the stage, and he pulled up a nearby chair for himself. "Arthur, how long have you worked here at the theater? Seems I can't remember a time when you weren't around."

"I been here. But not at first. First Drury Lane. Drury Lane." Arthur's eyes darkened. "Bad man there. Bad man."

It was left to the imagination to picture what had happened those years ago at Drury Lane to the younger version of Arthur, but after a moment the darkness left his eyes and he continued, "Good people here. Good people." His smile returned, as if seeing Quinton again for the first time. "Annie. I like Annie. You're Annie's boy."

That was the opening Quinton had been waiting for. "That's right. My mother was Annie. Do you remember when she died?"

"She died. She died," Old Arthur responded sadly.

"That's right." Quinton leaned forward. "Do you remember men from before she died? Men who liked her?"

Arthur bobbed his head again. "All the men liked Annie. All the men. Annie pretty. Annie good. Good men."

It seemed to Quinton that Old Arthur put people in one of two categories, like a boy sorting apples. They were either good or bad, with little in between. Understanding this, he asked the obvious question. "Arthur, did Annie know any bad men?"

"Shhhh. Bad man." Old Arthur stood up and looked around sharply. "I don't like bad man."

The question had clearly struck a nerve. "Do you know if the bad man hurt Annie?"

"Hurt Annie. Hurt Annie." Arthur started back towards the stage and grabbed a broom.

It wasn't clear if he was parroting the words back or if he really knew a specific bad man. Quinton sighed—perhaps this was a waste of time. Suddenly Arthur stopped, as if he'd heard what Quinton was thinking.

He looked as if the tune of a long-forgotten song had just come to him. "Annie say no. Annie say bad man. Bad man say meet later. I heard them. Then Annie hurt. Bad man, bad man." Arthur stopped and looked at Quinton. "Annie's boy."

"Yes, I am Annie's boy." Quinton clasped the old man's shoulders. "Did the bad man have a name, Arthur? What was his name?"

"Name. I know his name. Name. Name." Each word became a note in a tune, set to the beat of the sweeping broom. "He liked Annie. But Annie did not like him. He had a name. Bad man."

As his frustration and anticipation built, Quinton sighed. He was so close and yet nowhere nearer. The information was there but trapped in the addled mind of an old man. He doubted Arthur would be able to give a reliable description. When the frustration built to anger, he realized it was time to go.

Maybe he would never find the answers he needed. Maybe he followed an endless maze—just going on and on but never leading to any answers. But he kept his voice calm. This wasn't Arthur's fault. The man could give no more. "That's alright, Arthur. Sometimes, life isn't fair."

As he turned to go Arthur smiled broadly.

"Fair. Fair. Bad man had a name." The tune in his head finally reached its conclusion. "Fairfax. Bad man Fairfax. Bad man hurt Annie."

Chapter Forty

"Thank you for your hospitality, Lady Fairfax." Zoe sipped the bitter brew, gazing over the rim of her cup at the woman across from her.

She frequently likened Lady Fairfax to a rodent, not because of any distinct flaw in her appearance but rather due to the constant sour expression etched on her face. Well, and the small beady black eyes that darted about, tracking every movement.

At times such as this, Theo would remind her to be kind in her opinion. After all, Lady Fairfax's life hadn't been an easy one—she'd endured a son living his life in the navy and a husband's life cut short well before his time. Felix had never taken a wife, so there were no grandchildren to dote on either. Now she was old, living alone most of the time with a son who was only around when his ship was in port. One could hardly blame her for being a bit sour.

Nevertheless, knowing her story didn't make her company any more pleasant. If someone had told Zoe she would ever voluntarily pay the woman a social call, she would've laughed in their face.

"Of course, my dear." Lady Fairfax took a sip of her own tea. "Forgive me if this seems impertinent, but is there a reason for your visit today? I'm always happy to entertain Theodosia's niece, but I would assume you have better things to do with your time than visit an old woman like me."

Zoe forced a thin smile. "I always have time for Aunt Theo's friends." That was a lie. "But you are discerning, Lady Fairfax. I do have an ulterior motive for calling on you today."

She perceived a creaking sound in the hallway outside the room, dismissing it as a servant walking by. But she saw Mary glance over, her frame suddenly tense, and her fingertips brushed against Zoe's forearm. But they had no opportunity for discussion between the two of them; Zoe needed to focus her attention on Lady Fairfax.

She took a breath and continued, "I've taken an interest in the death of the Madame Amato."

Lady Fairfax frowned. "That doesn't seem an entirely appropriate interest of a young woman to take."

"You're not alone in thinking that." Zoe brushed past the obvious statement. "You said earlier that a hackney dropped you off at your modiste appointment. But Lady Soarington mentioned in passing that she saw your son when he was dropping you off."

Lady Fairfax's face twisted into an even more sour expression. "She must be mistaken."

"I don't think so. She distinctly remembered having a conversation with him. He's a friend of her husband's, you see."

"Ah. Well, I am getting up there in years . . . I do on occasion get confused." The expression eased into what Zoe assumed was an imitation of a smile, though somehow it was more unsettling than her frown. "This tea is a little bitter, isn't it? Would either of you girls like some sugar?"

Without waiting for a reply, Lady Fairfax dumped a spoonful of sugar into each cup, the spoon clinking against the sides as she stirred to mix it in.

Zoe smiled back politely and took the cup back into her hands. The growing frustration she felt resulted in putting aside the social niceties of a dainty sip and instead taking a gulp of the sweetened tea.

The intense sweetness was a surprise. As she started to take an actual sip, she felt Mary's hand again on her forearm. Her friend shook her head. Zoe squinted at her in confusion, but she did set the cup down. Mary sometimes felt things she couldn't quite understand, but Zoe had learned last year to put stock in Mary's feelings.

The creaking sound came again, and then the door opened. A figure stood in the doorway, silhouetted by the light behind them. Zoe squinted, trying to make out a face. It took her far too long to recognize Felix Fairfax, the very man they'd been discussing.

"Hello there!" he said with a wide smile. "If I had known there were two lovely ladies in here, I would've made an appearance earlier."

"Lord Fairfax." Zoe blinked, wondering if her words sounded slurred to anyone else. "When you dropped your mother off at the modiste, did you meet Madame Amato?"

"You know what, I did. Very compelling woman." Fairfax cocked his head. "Why do you want to know?"

"I'm interested in her death."

"Not a very ladylike interest."

"So I've been told."

The room seemed to shift around her. Zoe swallowed hard and blinked again, trying to steady her vision. Her hand grasped the arm of her chair, desperate to hold on to reality. Much too late, it dawned on her what was happening.

As her mind had been processing her predicament, Felix Fairfax had closed the distance between them. He knelt down in front of her, his face woozy. "Why is it women like you always feel the need to stick your noses where they don't belong?" His hand reached out, pushing her hair out of her eyes. "I've never killed a noblewoman before—too much attention, you understand. I've often thought how much you remind me of her—the same blue eyes and dark hair and arrogant attitude. But I always resisted that urge . . . until now that is."

Mary. Where was Mary? Zoe's head was so heavy. Her heart pounded in her chest and she wanted desperately to run. Her last few threads of conscious thought were enough for her to understand she was in terrible danger, but her head was so heavy. She tried to speak again, but the sound that came out couldn't be understood as words.

As her neck finally gave into the heaviness, Zoe's head lolled back against her chair. Her eyelids slid shut, despite every instinct in her body screaming for them to stay open. Finally her mind slipped into the darkness and there was nothing.

• • •

Mary knew what was happening with her first sip of the tea. She had been on high alert ever since that floor creak. The uneasiness that sometimes affected her had rolled in fully then. She could sense the evil behind that door, but she hadn't been able to act on her instinct to get herself and Zoe safe. She would wait for her chance. While Fairfax interacted with Zoe, she let her own eyes close and her head fall back as if asleep.

"Well, this is a fine pickle we've gotten ourselves into, mother," said the lord.

The old woman harrumphed. "I did what I had to do. She was getting too close—"

"I know, mother. You did the right thing." Fairfax sighed. "But this does complicate things. Someone will come looking for these."

"We can keep them here in the house until dark."

"Yes, we'll have to do that. I'm going to go get some rope—tell the servants to stay out of this room."

The sound of footsteps grew distant as the pair left the room. As soon as the door closed, Mary's eyes opened. Her heart raced—she knew she didn't have long. They would be back soon, and though she'd barely tasted the tea, she could still feel whatever drug it was affecting her as well.

Mary snatched a piece of paper off Lady Fairfax's end table as well as the quill. She paused, thinking about what to write. The drug was slowing her thoughts . . . she needed to leave a message that Quinton or John or whoever came looking for them would understand.

Finally Mary scrawled out the only words she could think of before crawling back to her chair and settling into the same position, shoving the paper into the crevice between the cushion and the arm. Her breathing shuddered as she drifted off into the void, the message she'd written going round and round in her mind.

We are still in the house.

Chapter Forty-One

The blood rushed to Quinton's head as he stared at Arthur. "You're certain? His name was Fairfax?"

Arthur nodded slowly. "Fairfax. He wasn't fair. Wasn't fair. Annie was good."

"Very well. Thank you, Arthur."

The words were an ordinary response, but internally Quinton was soundlessly screaming. After all this time, he had a name.

What did he know about Lord Fairfax? From his brief sighting of the man at Whites, the man seemed to be about the same age as his mother. He recalled Lord Colville saying the man's own father had sent him away by buying his navy commission. Surely there was more . . .

He could think of only one person to turn to for more information . . . and for advice. Quinton quickly found his way out of the maze of the theater and flagged down a hackney, directing the driver to the Dovefield residence. At his urging, the carriage took the turns at breakneck speed, but Quinton felt as though he was in a dream, with everything hazy and slowed down. As soon as they were approaching their destination, he jumped clear while the wheels were still turning and tossed the fare to the driver.

After only a short wait, Quinton was brought into the parlor where Lord and Lady Dovefield and were enjoying their tea. Zoe was absent, but a third person was present.

"Aloo there, Quinton!" Rory greeted him cheerfully. The single night in a real bed not surrounded by bars or mold or guards with ready fists had already made an improvement in his friend's appearance. He looked at Quinton with a glimmer of his old twinkle, though not quite the same.

Some might find it easy to point at Zoe as the eccentric of the family, but as Quinton took in the scene of the husband and wife readily breaking bread with a known resurrectionist who was barely acquitted of a brutal slaying, he reflected that it wasn't difficult to see where Zoe got here unusual proclivities.

"Please, sit down, Mr. Huxley," said Lady Dovefield. "At your height, there's little difference between hovering and looming. Would you like some tea?"

Quinton blushed, the gentle reprimand restoring him from his dreamlike trance and bringing reality back into sharp focus. "Yes, thank you, Lady Dovefield." He took a seat in an oversized armchair, accepting the saucer from her delicate hands.

"You're always welcome, Quinton, but is there a reason for your visit this afternoon?" asked Hugh, his gaze appraising.

The words rushed out, tumbling from his mouth like boulders down a hill. "I just came from Covent Garden, my lord. I spoke with Old Arthur. He's still a bit touched in the head, but after a fashion he was able to tell me of a man who met with my mother. According to him, my mother did not like him and this man hurt her."

Hugh leaned forward, his eyes bright. "Did he have the where-withal to give details?"

"Not much helpful. But he did come up with a name." Quinton took a deep breath, letting it out slowly. "Fairfax."

"Bloody hell." Rory cleared his throat, turning to Lady Dovefield. "Begging your pardon, milady."

"There are more pressing issues than lack of manners," said Lady Dovefield with a slight wave of her hand. "I take it from your reaction that you know this man, Mr. Stewart?"

"Unfortunately, milady, we have crossed paths, though I doubt he remembers. Bad form, that man. Very bad form."

"You sound like Old Arthur. Give us details, man," Quinton said, barely holding back his frustration.

"I've also had the misfortune of witnessing Felix Fairfax's bad form." Hugh frowned, his tone bitter. "You first, Mr. Stewart."

"In war, things are different." Rory took a moment to gather his thoughts. "It's difficult to explain to those who haven't been a soldier, but standards are different. Every man who faces battle does things he would never do in peacetime. We all live with the knowledge we did what we had to do to survive, but it still haunts us . . . the good ones anyway."

Throughout the years of conversations with Rory, where Quinton often shared his deepest feelings, he had remained unaware until now of the profound regret harbored in Rory's heart—a subject Rory never mentioned. If he wasn't so impatient to get to the bottom of the Fairfax mystery, he might ask Rory to elaborate. As it was, his friend couldn't speak fast enough for his liking.

Rory continued. "But there are always bad ones too. The worst is when any of the bad ones has a position of authority. Fairfax was one of those, and his reputation preceded him. I was an army grunt, and he was a Navy officer, but there are places where the two kinds mix. I encountered him in person at the port of Madras, in a club which pandered to British servicemen. The men under his command gave him a wide berth, and that shoulda been my first clue. But I was young and foolish, and I just saw the chance to take an officer for all I could in a game of cards. At first it was fine . . . but as he lost, he got angrier and angrier. It was a quiet temper, but drunk as I was, the darkness building behind his eyes still chilled me. When I finally left the table, I thought he was going to explode right there. But he didn't." A sigh escaped Rory's lips, his eyes distant. "The last I saw of him he was leaving the club with one of the local working women. The next morning . . . she was found beaten to death. I was working under the army medic, and we examined the body. I saw his work with my own eyes. It was . . . truly despicable. When I went to my superior officer, he just shrugged it off. The locals were plentiful and expendable, and no one wanted to deal with prosecuting a lord. So he got to sail off into the sunset without so much as a reprimand, and I was left there, fantasizing about him falling overboard with an anchor tied around his neck." He blinked, the haze in his eyes clearing for a moment, and he nodded again at the Lady. "Begging your pardon, milady."

"You forget, Mr. Stewart, I lived through *la Terreur.*" Lady Dovefield spoke matter-of-factly, but Quinton could see the whites of her knuckles as she gripped her saucer. "When Zoe and I fled France, we both saw things no one should see. A tale of a man's debauchery has little power over me."

Lord Dovefield glanced over at his wife, his expression thoughtful, and Quinton wondered if even the lord knew all his loved ones had endured. Quinton made a mental note to give Zoe more respect.

"My tale corroborates the man's character." Lord Dovefield features had taken on a dark countenance. "A case was brought against him here in London a few years ago, and I represented those against him. His money kept it quiet, but it also involved a woman. Mr. Stewart has provided enough details, so let us just say that I agree with his assessment. He is a nasty piece of work."

Quinton leaned forward, eager to take action. "It must be him. Hugh—Lord Dovefield—what is our next step?"

"I am of no use with the legal aspect. I believe my bed is calling me." Rory rose, exhaustion clinging to him like wet linen. He turned to both the Lady and the Lord and spoke sincerely.

"My lord. My lady. I thank you again for all you have done. I will of course pay my legal debts to you when I am able to again access my funds, and reimburse you for the care you've hired. But there is no reimbursement I can offer for the rest of what you've done. I owe you my life, and I cannae tell you how grateful I am." With that, the Scotsman departed, moving slowly, but on the mend.

Hugh turned his attention back to Quinton, contemplating his answer. "If we could have arrested, convicted, and hung the man for being a terrible human being, we would have done so years ago. What we need is proof. We must ascertain his guilt beyond a shadow of a doubt. We can access his docking records to show he was in London for the known murders. We can call many who would happily testify to his brutal character. We may even be able to place him near the scene of the murders on an occasion or two." Hugh sighed. "Clarissa Amato is long dead and buried, but, as he is a commanding officer and an Earl, we almost need to catch him in the act to truly put his neck in a noose."

As the words were spoken, Quinton felt a strange, uneasy sensation creep up his spine. His mother would have said someone walked over his grave, but whatever it was, something told him those words would come back to haunt them.

Chapter Forty-Two

"This just arrived from the Dowager's boot boy, my lord." Quaid had entered so quietly Quinton jumped when he spoke. As the butler handed Lord Dovefield a note, Quinton caught a whiff of the Dowager's signature lilac perfume.

The change in Hugh's countenance was instantaneous. He leapt to his feet, eyes wild, and cursed under his breath. "Zoe is at the Fairfax manor. We must leave immediately."

Simone stared at her husband, her expression one of bewilderment mirroring his own. How had Zoe managed to find herself in the lair of the man they had only just identified as the probable murderer?

If Hugh was as dumbfounded as them, he didn't let it slow him down. "Have the carriage brought around immediately," he snapped at Quaid. "Send me a boy to take a note to the Runners."

The butler was out the door faster than Quinton would have thought the old dodger could move, and the lord turned to him.

"Hopefully we will find Zoe and Mary happily sipping tea, as was their intent according to Theo's note. But Fairfax is clever and evil, and if he suspects they are on to him . . ." Hugh shuddered.

"Normally I would advise waiting for a constable, but I do not believe there is time. We will leave as soon as I can send word to Bow Street."

Noting that the lord never asked if he would accompany him but rather simply assumed he would, Quinton nodded. Glancing over, he observed Lady Dovefield as she arose, her expression transformed from shock to one of resolute determination. Hugh also noticed his wife's steely gaze.

"It would be best if you remained here—" he began to say.

"Of course it would be," she said, cutting him off. "There is no need for you to tell me my place. I'm not a fool, Hugh, and I know my strengths as well as my weaknesses. I would be of little use in hand-to-hand combat. As you said, everything may be fine and they will return here unharmed. If that is the case, I will send word to you." She paused and spoke softly. *"Mon cœur."*

Her eyes were dark with a mix of barely contained terror and fury. Quinton recognized it because the same potent combination swirled in his own mind like a thunderstorm, threatening to drown him in despair. Hugh also seemed to understand the source of her sharp tongue, going over and taking her in his arms briefly, murmuring words only she could hear, before turning to go.

During their embrace, Quinton glanced away. It was a private moment and he just happened to also be in the room. When Hugh finally stalked out, he soundlessly followed.

<hr>

The Fairfax manor looked deceptively peaceful when Quinton and Lord Dovefield arrived. The lord led the way, pounding hard on the door. A middle-aged butler answered, but Hugh shoved his way past before the man could speak. As Quinton too brushed past the butler, he wondered briefly how they would know where to go. But Hugh didn't hesitate, as if some homing instinct in the nobility gave them prior knowledge of every large home's floor layout. He stalked down a hall past several doors, ignoring the butler's protests, before throwing one open.

Lady Fairfax sat sedately drinking tea in her parlor, appearing unperturbed, as if men burst uninvited into her home all the time. Almost as if she had been expecting them. Quinton's heart sank as he realized Zoe and Mary were nowhere to be seen.

Lord Dovefield wasted no time on introductions. "I understand my daughter and her companion paid you a call today, Lady Fairfax. I find myself concerned over their whereabouts."

"You understand wrong, Lord Dovefield." The old woman didn't even raise an eyebrow. "I have had no such visit from your daughter. Why would such a pretty young thing visit an old woman like myself?"

Taking a seat in an armchair facing Lady Fairfax, Hugh began to ask her a string of questions, demanding answers. Quinton could hear the conversation, but it was as if he was listening from under-water. He found himself drawn to the window, staring out at the manicured gardens, his mind drifting to all the thoughts he hadn't allowed himself to dwell on earlier.

What if something had actually happened to her? What if she were already dead? How would he tell John his favorite cousin was gone?

His thoughts drifted back to the first time he had laid eyes on Zoe Demas. Quinton remembered her blue eyes darkening with anger over something rude he had said—eyes like her mother's. They had not been friends at first, verbally sparring at every turn. But things had changed. Despite his best efforts, she had managed to weave herself into the fabric of his life, so much so that he now couldn't imagine life without her there.

Even at their worst, he had never been indifferent about Zoe. He now wondered just how long he had been in love with her.

Finally Quinton forced himself back to the present and the task at hand.

Lady Fairfax was speaking, her face sour and her pitch high. "All I can do is assure you—once again, I may add—that your daughter has not now, nor ever, darkened my door. As you continue to insist on this nonsense, I will have to ask you to leave."

"On the contrary, Lady Fairfax," replied Hugh. "I will remain here until we receive answers. Zoe left word she was coming here, and come here she certainly did. If you will not disclose their location, perhaps you would be good enough to tell us where your son is?"

Pulling a chair around to join the conversation, Quinton sat heavily. An unexpected crinkling sound caused him to jump back to his feet. Stopping mid-sentence, Lady Fairfax stared at him, for the first time showing a glimmer of alarm.

Reaching down, Quinton felt around the seat cushion. This particular chair had a space between the cushion and the arm, and moments later his hand brushed against something smooth and distinctly non-fabric. He pulled it out, revealing a crumpled piece of paper.

Unfolding it, Quinton read the hastily scrawled words aloud. "*We are still in the house.*" He paused. "It's Mary's handwriting."

Hugh was at his side in an instant, snatching the note to read for himself, before whirling back around to Lady Fairfax. "Where is my daughter?" The words were shouted menacingly as Hugh closed the distance between himself and the lady until he towered above her, shaking the note in her face. "Clearly they did indeed arrive. Where are they now?"

His tone became louder with each word, but Lady Fairfax regarded him with the same composure she'd shown since they first arrived. "You will never find them, Lord Dovefield. It is too late for them already."

For a fleeting moment Quinton thought Hugh would strike the older lady, and he took a step forward to restrain him. But the moment passed and instead, the enraged father simply sat down. "Bow Street will be here in force soon. This house will be searched until they are indeed found. And then, *Lady* Fairfax, I will see that justice is administered to the absolute fullest extent of the law. You should pray they are found alive, as you will hang alongside your son if they are not."

The sound Lady Fairfax made was shrill, bordering on shrieking, and it took him a moment to realize she was laughing. Now that she had no reason to pretend, the glint of madness filled her eyes. "You are full of your own pride, Lord Dovefield, but you are about to realize how helpless you are in the face of genius. You may have me, but you will never find Felix. Search all you want. Your girl is gone, but I hope you are forever tormented by never knowing all that she endured before her demise. My Felix can be so very . . . inventive."

This time Quinton knew if he hadn't stepped in front of him, Hugh would have physically attacked the woman. Holding the typically calm barrister by his shoulders, Quinton locked eyes with Hugh. He wondered how he himself was not equally affected, but the truth came out in his next words. "She's alive, sir. I know it. We will find her."

In his heart, despite all his worldly knowledge telling him otherwise, Quinton knew Zoe was alive. He couldn't explain how—perhaps it was simply a belief in the woman herself. Zoe did nothing quietly, and dying would be no exception. She was clever and resourceful and determined, and she had an equally intelligent partner in Mary. They would do what it took to stay alive until help could arrive—until he could find them.

The distinct clatter of horses and carriages broke the moment, and he felt Hugh relax. Quinton released his grip as Hugh straightened up, still glaring at Lady Fairfax. "I'll brief the magistrate," Hugh muttered as he turned on his heel to leave the room.

Quinton let out a shuddering breath as he turned his attention back to Lady Fairfax. He couldn't help but wonder how such madness could affect both a mother and son. Of course, after another few moments of reflection, the answer became obvious.

She had passed down her madness to her son, as surely as Lady Dovefield had given Zoe her blue eyes.

Lady Fairfax met his pondering gaze without hesitation. "Felix was always a fine boy, but his father never understood him."

"Is that why he bought Felix a navy commission? Because he didn't understand him?"

"Rubert did that because he was weak." The old woman scoffed. "He couldn't handle the truth of Felix's genius, and instead of dealing with it like a man, one way or another, he just sent him away. What kind of father sends his only son away like a piece of defective furniture? A weak father, that's what. Felix deserved better than that, and I made sure Rubert knew before he died what a weak and useless excuse for a man he was."

Quinton swallowed hard; the longer he could keep her talking, the more he might learn. "What do you mean before he died? Did you . . . did you kill your husband?"

She smiled at him, the expression unnatural on her sour face. "He shouldn't have sent Felix away."

He was still staring at her when Lord Dovefield reappeared, followed by John and the magistrate himself. Soon men were searching every room in the house, with Hugh and Quinton joining in.

<hr>

Well after midnight, Quinton found himself sitting alone in Lord Fairfax's small study. Though others were still searching the house, Quinton had begun to feel hopeless with the endeavor. He'd hoped that sitting in the madman's study would give him some insight into where he might have taken Zoe. Unfortunately, the study appeared to be little used.

Hugh joined him, sitting down in a nearby chair and leaning back with a defeated sigh. The poor man already looked older.

Finally the barrister spoke wearily. "There is nothing more to be done here tonight. We have searched every inch of this house, and apart from the note, there is absolutely no sign of them. The magistrate has started to expand the search and is seeking out Fairfax's ship as well. But he could have a property we know nothing of, or access to any number of buildings." He paused, running his fingers through his hair. "I must go home to Simone. She'll be fraught with worry by now. We will have to sleep on it and resume the search in the morning."

He wanted to protest, but Quinton knew Hugh was right. The note had given him hope—something to grasp at in his desperation, but he could feel the hope losing substance, dissolving to mist in his hands.

As they departed, John caught him, clasping his shoulder. "Don't worry, Quinton. Me and the constables will keep looking. You go get some sleep."

$$Chapter\ Forty\text{-}Three$$

Silence hung heavy in the carriage ride back to the Dovefields' home. An exhaustion stemming from constant worry enveloped the two men like the thick fog which blanketed the street outside. Quinton stared out the window, too consumed with his own disquieting thoughts to offer any comfort to Hugh.

As the carriage pulled to a stop, Hugh jumped down and disappeared into the depths of the house, still without a word. No doubt he was thinking of Lady Dovefield, wishing to give her what news he could. Quinton alighted as well, but hesitated as he stood there at the bottom of the steps, feeling very much like the lost boy he had once been. Should he go home or should he go in?

Suddenly he felt, rather than saw, movement at his side. When Quinton turned to look, he saw Ezra had materialized in the darkness as if out of thin air.

"What are you doing here?" he asked.

The boy moved his hands quickly in the poor light, but Quinton could still make out his meaning. *"The lady sent for me. Gwen needs me. Did you find Zoe?"*

Ezra had assigned each person in his life a one-handed gesture to symbolize their name. By this time, Quinton knew 'the lady' was Lady Dovefield, and he recognized the gestures for Gwen and for Zoe.

"No. No Zoe. Not yet," he responded.

The words were acknowledged with a nod of the head. Ezra was a child of the street, and with that came a certain practicality. People came and went. No point in getting too upset about that inevitable fact of life. Quinton had just been living in a cozy home with a comfortable life for so long that he'd forgotten.

Quinton glanced up at the large Dovefield residence. Lady Dovefield had been wise to send for the boy. Whatever the rest of them were to Gwen, Ezra was her family. In the midst of this ordeal, Quinton was grateful to have some kind of assignment that made sense. Ezra wouldn't stay with the Dovefields, but Gwen could come home with them for the night.

"I'll go retrieve Gwen for you," Quinton told the boy.

When Quaid admitted him into the house, Lord Dovefield was nowhere to be seen. The butler directed Quinton to the shared breakfast room, where Gwen sat on the floor with Brutus. He wondered, not for the first time, how a dog bred to fight could be so gentle with a little girl.

The beast's fondness for children was evident, and his interaction with Oscar the other night clearly indicated that was not his first meeting with a cat. Possibly Brutus's early years weren't as grim as previously imagined. Regardless of the path that had brought the dog to Westminster Pit, Quinton hoped that the beast retained at least a few distant memories of affection and gentleness.

At the sight of Quinton, Gwen unfurled herself from the floor, standing uncertainly. Tears streaked her face, betraying the frightened child she was. She had weathered many losses but had finally found a foothold in this world with Zoe and her family. The thought of another loss was clearly too much too bear.

Glancing back at Brutus, Quinton could see he was anxious as well. The hound surely couldn't understand what was happening, but he could feel the emotions of those around him. All he could know for certain was his beloved mistress wasn't there and something was wrong. Brutus stared at him briefly, then looked over to the sofa, bathed in shadow. To Quinton's surprise, he made out a figure perched on the edge. A moment later, Walter Dovefield stood and took a step forward, shifting uncertainly from foot to foot.

Meeting his eyes, Zoe's half brother spoke, his voice surprisingly firm despite his uncertainty and young age. "I did not want Gwen to have to wait here alone. You will take care of her?"

Quinton had met Walter briefly last year on one of his visits with Lord Dovefield, and their paths had crossed from time to time but never for more time than it took for a passing greeting. This was an odd time for their first private conversation. An odd subject as well.

"I will." Quinton had intended to do so anyway, though he was surprised at Walter's concern for the girl.

Walter wasn't done. "Maman is beside herself, but I heard her send for Ezra. Papa will tell me nothing except to stay out of the way and it will be alright. This is enough for Phoebe. I need to know. Is Zoe coming home? "

No easy answer to that question, and Quinton wasn't sure it was his place to provide one. But the young man deserved more than platitudes. As he took a deep breath he noted Gwen watching as well, waiting for his answer. He knew they both deserved honesty. "I cannot tell you for certain that she is, but I can tell you this," Quinton finally said. "She is a fighter, and she has Mary as well. Together they will not give up. And neither will your father, or your mother, or I. Tomorrow will give us answers."

It wasn't much of a response, but it seemed to satisfy Walter. He nodded before turning on his heel, walking toward the door. He paused for a moment in the doorway, catching Gwen's eye one last time. Then just like that he was gone.

Shaking his head, Quinton turned back to Gwen. "Do you want to come stay with Ezra tonight? I can only offer you a blanket and a hearth."

Gwen managed a watery smile and nodded. "I've slept without either many times."

"I know."

As her hand found the dog's head, she paused. "Can Brutus come too?"

Quinton reckoned no one here would miss the beast, with both Zoe and Gwen out of the house. Oscar would not be pleased, but he would make it up to her later. "Very well. Come along quickly."

The young girl took his hand, her small fingers clinging to his large ones tightly. As they made their way out of the house, Quinton pulled Quaid aside and asked him to inform Lord Dovefield of Gwen and the dog's whereabouts.

He suspected sleep would elude him that night, but being there for Ezra and Gwen gave Quinton a sense of purpose he was craving in the midst of the turmoil. There was little else he could do for Zoe or Mary right now, but he could do this one thing, and that determination grounded his racing thoughts.

Once they stepped outside, Ezra again materialized, falling into step with them. All four headed east, disappearing into the dense fog in the direction of his own home.

Chapter Forty-Four

"Abigail, wait up!" Quinton dashed after his young friend, her long blonde hair cascading behind her as she ran. They were playing in the depths of Covent Garden, a place as familiar to him as the back of his own hand. For Quinton and Abigail, who had grown up in the theater, the district was their version of a garden.

"Abigail, wait!" he called out once more.

But she didn't stop, nor did she look back. Quinton hastened his pace, chasing her around a blind corner in the hallway, but when he rounded it, she was gone. In her place stood Zoe, not as a child but as an adult.

"Come along, Quinton," Zoe said, smiling. "I'll fix you some luncheon."

"Where's Abigail?" Quinton spun around, searching for his friend. When he turned back, Zoe had vanished as well.

Then he heard another sound.

"Help! Quinton, help me!" Abigail's voice was so faint, it was almost inaudible.

"Where are you?" he shouted. "Abigail, where are you?" He sprinted down the hallway, peering behind each door, but found nothing. The more he ran, the more distant her voice became. At last, he flung a door open, and there she was.

She appeared just as he remembered—expressive green eyes taking up most of her face, framed by perfect bouncing blonde curls. They were both nine years old—his favorite age—just before his life turned for the worst.

Beside her stood Brutus, nearly reaching Abigail's shoulders. However, Quinton's gaze was drawn past them to a second room, where Zoe and Mary lay on the floor, eyes open but lifeless. He was too late.

A silent scream tore through his throat. Quinton tried to call out Zoe's name, but no words came out.

He gasped and sat up abruptly. Quinton took several deep breaths, returning to reality as the nightmare's dark tendrils receded. He peeled away the sweat-soaked blanket and swung his feet over the edge.

He made his way over to his desk, pulling open the top drawer and taking out a bottle of whiskey. Pouring himself a generous draft, he sat down, trying to calm his pounding heart. As he glanced over at the hearth, the sight of Gwen and Ezra, both curled up in blankets and sleeping soundlessly, grounded him. Their presence made the dream he'd just had less real, but also somehow sharper.

As his heartbeat gradually calmed, he reflected on the dream. He and Abigail had indeed explored the tunnels, doorways, and rooms beneath and surrounding the theater. They were familiar with every twist, turn, and secret the theater concealed.

The theater did have secrets. Sometimes a door would lead nowhere, passed by when a room was added on. Occasionally a room would be lost, sealed over and forgotten. Not lost, but hidden. But he and Abigail would always find their way in.

A revelation suddenly slammed into his brain like a bullet. Quinton straightened up, slamming his glass on the desk.

A hidden room. That must be the answer. He thought back to Fairfax's cozy study lined with books. It was a fine room, but upon reflection he recalled something strange about the dimensions . . . it was shorter than it should be. Could there be a hidden room within?

Many old houses had priest holes—small rooms where a priest could be hidden from days not that far gone by. What if a clever, maniacal man somehow repurposed the hiding place, enlarging it for his own evil uses?

A nudge at his hand broke his train of thought. Quinton looked down, thinking it must be Oscar. However the massive head under his hand belonged to Brutus instead. The dog looked up at him, and Quinton thought he could see a hint of pleading there. He made a snap decision.

He was still fully dressed, so he only needed to grab his coat as he headed out the door, motioning the beast to follow. He would need Brutus to try his plan.

As he stepped out into the cold night air, Quinton uttered a rare prayer to find Zoe and Mary alive.

Chapter Forty-Five

The feeling came back to Zoe's body a little at a time. First she was aware of an aching on one side—she was lying on a hard surface, certainly not her own bed. Then she realized her arms were pulled behind her back and she couldn't move them. Something rough and scratchy was wrapped around her wrists, keeping her hands bound. Finally, she opened her eyes.

She blinked, trying to focus her eyes in the dimly lit space. Mary was lying in front of her, eyes already open wide. Her friend glanced over to the other side of the room, then back to Zoe.

As Zoe turned, her eyes caught a figure in the corner. Bent over, it was hastily stuffing items into a small chest. The figure then stood upright, turning to reveal his face, and Zoe's breath hitched as a flood of memories returned to their rightful place.

Charlotte Fairfax, of all people, had drugged them. Being outwitted by someone as irritating as her was humiliating. Zoe strained to remember what had happened next. Felix had arrived just as she was fading into unconsciousness, Zoe recalled. What had he said? That he had never killed a noblewoman before? That didn't make sense, yet Zoe was certain that, even if her recollection of his words was inaccurate, the implication that he intended to kill her was unmistakably present.

Despite their predicament, a part of her was proud of figuring out who the killer was. More than a decade spent murdering women, and she was the one to find him. It was just too bad she would be dead before anyone knew of the accomplishment.

As Felix's eyes locked with hers, a wide smile bared his teeth. "Good, you're awake."

No point in playing coy. Zoe used her elbow to push herself up, leaning against the wall for support. She still felt lightheaded, so she took a deep breath to steady herself before replying.

"Is it better for you, Lord Fairfax, when your victim is awake? You need to see the fear in their eyes as they die?"

"Please, call me Felix. I think our relationship has progressed past such formal niceties." He cocked his head, considering. "In answer to your question, Zoe, yes I do like to look into their eyes. I think there's no more intimate connection than to be present at one's death, don't you agree?"

"I wouldn't know."

"I suppose not." He took a menacing step towards them. "Maybe I'll do your friend in first, and that way you can experience it."

A cold spike of fear ran down Zoe's spine and her breath caught in her throat.

Fairfax smiled again. "There it is."

He turned back to his box in the corner, as if having lost interest, and continued his rummaging. Zoe realized now that he wasn't putting things in, but rather was taking things out, as if searching for something.

She took a moment to study the room they were in. It was cramped but large enough for three people to inhabit without crushing each other. The ceiling was low enough that their captor's head just narrowly avoided brushing against it when he stood straight. The only light came from an oil lantern hung by the door, providing dim illumination.

The room had little in the way of furniture. The only thing other than the box of undetermined objects was something in the far corner. It appeared to be a blanket, covering a formless lump beneath it. Zoe couldn't make out any details beyond that, but something about it chilled her to the very core.

"One of my first." Felix had caught her staring. "First people, anyway. That was what turned Father against me. He tried to ignore the rats and the cats and the dogs, but he couldn't seem to ignore that one."

Zoe forced herself to look away, turning her attention back to Fairfax. "Where are we?"

"Wouldn't you like to know."

"There's no harm in telling us now, Felix. We're going to die anyway, right?"

By this time Mary had also pushed herself up and was sitting next to Zoe along the wall. She glared at Zoe after her nonchalant remark, but Zoe stared straight ahead, avoiding eye contact with her companion.

"You are relentless, aren't you?" said Felix with a chuckle. "Very well, if you must know, this is a priest hole. I found it when I was a boy of fifteen."

"I thought priest holes were small?" said Mary, gaining courage.

"Normally you would be correct—it would be just big enough to hide a man during a search. But in this case, the hole was enlarged into a room so the poor Catholic sod could stay back here permanently." He laughed again. "It's just good luck that I happened upon it. Haven't used it in a long time—haven't needed to. But there's no beating the convenience when I have needed it."

The reality finally dawned on Zoe. "So we're still in your house?"

"Correct," he said, as if she was a favorite pupil. "Mother was right about you. You are a sharp one."

"Well, I do aim to impress." Zoe considered her next words.

"Your mother must love you very much. I don't know if mine would cover up multiple murders for me."

"Mother understands me. Father never did, but Mother . . . Mother understood."

"Did she understand when you killed Annie Huxley?"

His face darkened at the mention of that name. "You are sharp, Zoe Demas—too much so for your own good. You like to show off—you like people to think you're smarter than them—better than them. Just like Annie."

Zoe kept pushing; the longer she kept him talking, the more time someone had to find them. "I've been told it's a failing. Did Annie make you feel stupid?"

"Annie made me feel like I was flying."

"Really? Is that why you strangled the life out of her?"

"Flying is the best feeling in the world . . . until you fall." Fairfax shook his head. "You know, I've had just about enough of your questions. You're stalling, hoping against all odds that this isn't your tomb."

He was right on that count, thought Zoe desperately. "What about the others? Did they make you fall, too?"

Fairfax took a step closer and glared down at her.

"All the others were Annie's fault. They all had that same beauty, a beauty that calls a man. Like Annie. But they all looked at me like they were better than me, with their arrogance." He paused, his breath becoming shallow.

Zoe could see she was getting to him. That might be a mistake, but she reflected she had little to lose.

He continued, his voice angry, "They all thought they had their pathetic little lives in order, that they didn't need a man to lean on. That look in their eyes, independent, proud. Contrary to the nature God gave them. Unbecoming of a beautiful woman, calling to me, then walking away. Just like Annie. That seamstress looked down her nose at me, laughed when I suggested she and I go upstairs to that bedroom she rented out." Fairfax's voice became more and more agitated. "Laughed at me!" His voice had risen to the level of shouting, but then he abruptly turned away. Zoe could see him taking deep breaths, standing perfectly still. When he turned back towards her, he had regained his composure and his voice was controlled.

"She wasn't laughing when I came back." He leaned down toward Zoe, close enough she could smell the alcohol on his breath. "You have that same look. Proud. Confident. I'm looking forward to seeing that pride drain from your eyes with your life."

Refusing to give in to the fear coursing through her veins, Zoe glared up at him. "People know where we were going. They'll know to look for us here."

Fairfax snorted. "Ah yes, your barrister stepfather and the whore's son? You've been asleep longer than you think. They've already come and gone and found nothing."

The sense of deep dread that had been looming over her finally crystallized in her chest at those words. "You're lying."

"They've given up and gone home. No one is looking for you anymore." He leaned forward until his face was only inches from her own, his breath hot and rancid. "You are going to die here, and no amount of questions will save you."

It suddenly seemed very hard to breathe, as if her lungs were being constricted. Zoe forced herself to push past it—she wouldn't give him the satisfaction of seeing her cry. "You fancy yourself a monster, Lord Fairfax, but I see you for what you really are—a sad, pathetic creature who has to hurt those weaker than himself just to feel like a man."

The punch surprised her, even though she should've expected it. Pain exploded like a thousand stars in Zoe's skull as his fist slammed into her cheekbone, and then again when her head recoiled, smacking against the wall. She tasted blood as her teeth cut into her cheek.

"Don't you touch her!" screamed Mary.

"What are you going to do about it?" he replied with a scoff.

Blinking through blurred vision, Zoe saw him straighten back up. "You're lucky, Zoe Demas, that I seem to have misplaced my spare pocket watch chain. If that seamstress hadn't broken the original, you'd already be dead."

Zoe thanked poor Sarah Hammond in her head. "Good for her."

"Don't get too comfortable, ladies. I'll be back before you know it."

With that, Fairfax pushed the door open and swept out of the room. As the door slammed shut again, the flame in the lamp flickered. Zoe's didn't dare exhale, anticipating being plunged into complete darkness, but the determined little flame recovered. It wasn't much, but it was better than nothing.

She let out a deep sigh of relief. "Mary, quick, is my hairpin still in my hair?"

"What?"

"My hairpin. Do you see it?"

"Um . . ." Mary craned her neck. "Yes, it's still there. Barely hanging on, but it's still there."

Zoe shook her head, worsening her intensifying headache. She shook it once more, attempting to dislodge the object. It might be their only chance.

Finally her efforts were rewarded with the sound of metal clattering against wood. She felt around for it blindly, uttering a curse as the sharp end sliced her finger open.

"What are you doing?" hissed Mary.

"It's a knife," replied Zoe. Fumbling around until her fingers finally closed around the handle, she began to work the blade against her restraints. Clutching it tightly, she moved her hands back and forth, driving the blade in a clumsy sawing motion. With every pass, Zoe winced as the knife's edge bit into her palm.

"You're cutting yourself." Mary's voice was aghast.

"I'm aware. But there's nothing else to be done." Taking a deep breath, Zoe kept going, ignoring the sharp pain as much as she could. She could only hope it would be enough.

Chapter Forty-Six

The Fairfax house was quiet in the moonlight as Quinton and Brutus made their way around to the servants' entrance. No doubt the frantic activity yesterday had scared most of the staff away, with the arrest of Lady Fairfax being the final straw. The servants' door was locked, but that wouldn't stop Quinton. Retrieving his lockpick set from his coat pocket, he had the door open within two minutes. His soft footfalls through the house went unchallenged as he made his way to the study.

Despite the ominous sign in his dream, Quinton remained hopeful that he wasn't too late. John and the Runners had departed, but he couldn't have been far behind them. Certainly their presence would have discouraged even a madman like Fairfax from taking the risk of harming the girls while they were present.

Moonlight streamed through the study's window, providing just enough light for Quinton to locate and light the oil lanterns near the door. The lanterns' flickering glow cast ghostly shadows across the room, revealing the books lining two walls and the wood paneling on the others. Portraits and framed maps decorated the paneled walls. Following Quinton, Brutus entered, his shaggy, misshapen ears perking up as he made his way to the room's center. He seemed to listen intently, turning his head from side to side, before ambling towards a bookshelf and starting to scratch at it.

As Quinton examined the shelves, he noted a thick layer of dust settled on the tops of the books. He wasn't surprised. Many of the upper class liked the intellectual look of lots of books, thinking it made them seem well read, but didn't want to actually crack their spines. Lord Fairfax was also often gone for long stretches in the Navy, so even if he did read when he was home, it wouldn't be for months at a time—long enough for a considerable layer of dust to gather.

But shouldn't a maid still clean them? As Quinton looked around the room, he realized almost every object was coated in dust. He hadn't noticed it when they were searching the house earlier. Even in a barely used room, the maids should've kept it clean. Unless there was a reason to forbid their entry.

Returning to the bookshelves with renewed interest, Quinton skimmed through the titles, not sure what he was seeking. Finally, his roving eyes stopped when he saw one book with fingermarks trailing through the dust. He tilted his head to read the title— *Hamlet*. Quite fitting, indeed.

Placing his own fingers in the marks, Quinton pressed down and pulled back towards himself. As he did so, he was rewarded with a soft clicking sound. Grasping the book firmly, he yanked on it with all his might. The bookshelf swung open with a loud creak, revealing a dim light on the other side.

Swallowing hard and steeling himself for what lay ahead, Quinton crossed the threshold with Brutus at his side.

As he took in the interior of the hidden room, a wave of relief washed over him, so powerful it nearly brought him to his knees.

Zoe and Mary sat in the room, disheveled yet alive. Their arms were bound behind them, and Zoe sported a burgeoning bruise across her face, but they were indeed alive.

He took a step forward, opening his mouth to speak, but the shift from relief to sheer horror on Zoe's face stopped him.

"Behind you!" she screamed.

The warning came too late. As Quinton started to turn, a heavy blow struck the back of his head. The impact brought him to his knees as a sharp burst of pain radiated through his body, and he stumbled into Brutus, eliciting a yelp from the beast. He instinctively raised an arm, trying to shield himself from further blows. Pain surged through his arm as another hit connected, and he caught sight of a cricket bat shattering into splinters.

The first strike had blurred his vision, so Quinton's retaliatory swing was blind. Luck was with him, however, as his longer reach proved advantageous. His fist found its mark, propelling the other man against the wall with a resounding thud.

Quinton attempted to get back on his feet, staggering backwards as he struggled with his uncoordinated weight. His head throbbed, and he could feel warm liquid seeping down his neck.

Through his blurry eyesight, he could make out the shape of his attacker standing up. He couldn't quite make out his features, but it could be no one else than Felix Fairfax himself. Suddenly, another form hurtled towards Fairfax, pinning him to the floorboards with a fierce snarl—they'd both forgotten about Brutus. The great beast, having shaken off Quinton's fall, entered the fray with vengeance.

Fairfax let out a scream, an understandable response to being attacked by a dog the size of a small horse. Despite his age, Fairfax was a strong man and remained on his feet, using his free arm to strike Brutus's head, each blow landing with a disturbing crunch.

In his panic, Fairfax was so fixated on the dog that he failed to take into account the other people in the room. Before Quinton could regain his composure, he saw Zoe rise to her feet. Disheveled, with her curly hair cascading over her shoulders and her gown smeared with grime, her eyes held an intensity Quinton had never seen before. Her gaze had harbored storms, yet those were mere squalls compared to what he saw now. This was raw fury—a tempest filled with such rage that it would tear across the open sea and drag any living thing it encountered down into the watery abyss without mercy or conscience.

In her hand was the knife Quinton had gifted her. A trickle of blood stemmed from her palm down the blade, dripping off the tip in crimson droplets. Her fingers tightened around the handle as she crossed the distance between her and Fairfax, moving too fast for Quinton to process what was happening.

Fairfax never saw it coming. Zoe plunged the blade into his back, in the meaty part where the shoulder met the neck. As he screamed, she pulled backwards, ripping it out of his body. Blood droplets flew off the blade, splattering against the wall as she swung it back, preparing to strike again.

Her arm froze, the blade still held aloft, stopped by a force not her own. Quinton's feet had finally found solid ground beneath him, and he held her wrist firmly. Fairfax slumped to the floor in a rumpled heap as Quinton gently pulled the knife from her fingers. She didn't resist, but she didn't look at him either—she just stared straight ahead.

"You got him." Quinton grabbed Brutus by his collar, yanking him off the now unconscious man. "He's beyond hurting you now."

"He deserves to die." The words were said evenly, without emotion.

"Yes. But you don't deserve to have to live with it. A man like that isn't worth having on your conscience. Trust me."

Zoe finally looked at him, the storm calmed, but with a hollowness left behind in its wake. She stared silently, but Quinton knew what she wanted. To get out of that hellhole.

"I'll take you home." Quinton realized he was still holding on to her wrist but couldn't find the will in himself to let go. He met her gaze, hoping his eyes would convey all the things he couldn't bring himself to say out loud.

The silence stretched as they both let themselves exist in that moment for as long as they could. Sometimes a moment was all one got. Sometimes it was enough.

"Hello. I'm still here, thank you very much." Mary's voice snapped both of them back to reality.

"Of course. Don't just stand there, Quinton, untie her." Zoe glanced over at the prone figure of Fairfax and spoke firmly. "We need to find a surgeon if we want him to live to see the noose."

Chapter Forty-Seven

When Quinton shouted and banged on the door, Quaid opened it, still ramrod straight and dressed impeccably. Zoe sometimes wondered if he ever slept. His carefully crafted decorum was forgotten for the first time in memory when he placed his hand on her back to usher her inside.

Hugh had heard the commotion and rushed into the hallway to meet them, his dressing gown open, revealing his sleeping clothes. But despite appearing to be ready for bed, Zoe saw immediately her stepfather had known no real sleep since her disappearance. Hugh already looked older, his beard unshaven and dark circles beneath his eyes. When she met his eyes, he enveloped her with a tight hug that said more than words.

Another set of arms joined the embrace, her mother somehow wrapping her tiny frame around them both, murmuring in French. Zoe could feel the fear and tension ease from their bodies as they held her.

With his arms still wrapped around her, Hugh spoke to Quinton. "What of Fairfax?"

"He's in custody. The constables are handling it," Quinton responded in a low voice. "We were allowed to leave. The magistrate will no doubt have questions that need answering, but they can wait for the light of day."

"Very good, very good." Hugh's voice was calm, but Zoe knew him well enough to discern the undertone of barely contained emotion.

When they finally released her, Zoe's own tension drained in the form of tears. She started to sob uncontrollably. Simone placed a gentle arm around her shoulders as Hugh barked orders. "Get Doctor Lewis here," he snapped at a footman.

"But, my lord, it's the middle of the night—"

"I don't care! Roust the man if you have to, just get him here!"

"Of course, my lord."

But before the man could leave, a familiar voice broke into the fray. "I dinnae mean to intrude, but I'm able to look the girls over now." Rory Stewart stood in the entrance to the parlor. He pointed at Zoe's hand, still seeping blood through the makeshift bandage Mary had fashioned. "Pretty handy with a needle and thread too."

"Yes, yes. Thank you, Mr. Stewart. Very good, very good." Hugh sighed with relief and herded the whole group into the parlor after Rory.

If the British believed in one thing, it was food in times of distress. Quaid soon reappeared with cold meats, cheese, and crusty bread. Zoe was surprised to see Quinton help himself, heaping a plate, with Hugh following suit. She wondered if anyone had eaten a bite in the last day and a half.

As Rory began stitching up her wound, Zoe distracted herself watching her hungry companions attack their plates, including Mary. As her tears waned, she felt herself a bit peckish as well.

Not long after, Quaid appeared with another laden tray, and Zoe saw him catch Mary's eye. The two had yet to become fond of each other, following an unfortunate incident last year involving a midnight foray for biscuits while Mary was wearing her face cream. Quaid's embarrassment at having mistaken her for a ghost had been too much for his British disposition to handle. But now, Zoe saw him smile ever so slightly at Mary, nodding distinctly to the very biscuits on the tray that had caught her interest last year.

Nothing like a near death experience to bury misunderstandings.

"All done now," said Rory as he patted her hand and placed the needle and thread aside.

"Thank you, Rory." Zoe turned her attention to the cold cuts, her own stomach grumbling. "Is that . . . salami?"

In between mouthfuls, Mary and Zoe told their story. The others listened in disbelief. Rory muttered darkly about Fairfax's soul, while Hugh looked appreciatively at Quinton when Zoe explained where she got the hairpin knife. In his own turn, Quinton told his view of the knife encounter with enthusiasm, adding Brutus's part in the battle. The way he told it, it she was some kind of shining Valkyrie of legend.

As he spoke, Simone took Brutus's face in her hands and whispered something to him. Whatever it was, his tail thumped happily.

As the words slowed, Quinton rose to his feet. "I believe it is time for me to take my leave. Gwen and Ezra will no doubt be eager to hear the news."

Hugh stood as well, his eyes welling with emotion. "There are no words, Mr. Huxley. You have given us back our very soul."

Quinton nodded stiffly, the rising color in his cheeks betraying his embarrassment, before walking out into the night.

Zoe watched him go, thinking back on the one moment none of them had relayed to the group. She rubbed her wrist with her other hand—for some reason it felt cold where his fingers had once grasped it tightly.

"Are you alright, dear?" asked Simone.

"Yes, of course." Zoe cleared her throat. "My wrist is just cold is all."

Rory nodded sagely. "Blood loss, no doubt."

Staring at him mutely, Zoe realized Rory was somehow right.

She had lost not only blood, but very nearly her life, and for better or worse she was now intricately tied to the man who had just walked out the door. Her whole body felt colder without his nearness.

As the silence stretched, Zoe numbly responded. "Yes. No doubt."

Chapter Forty-Eight

The interview with Zoe and Mary was a formality at best. Having been caught and with little hope of avoiding the noose, Felix Fairfax decided to take advantage of this last opportunity to brag about his . . . accomplishments. He spoke willingly of Madame Amato and the others, admitting to killing them and expounding on their last moments and his motivations.

On only two counts did he remain silent, much to John's chagrin.

He claimed responsibility for Annie Huxley's death but refused to share any details, despite John's persistent inquiries. Furthermore, he strongly denied any connection to Margot Anderson's demise.

As frustrating as his stubbornness was, it would not change his fate. Lord Felix Fairfax would hang without additional testimony.

As Hugh escorted the magistrate out, Quinton followed. John could see the exhaustion etched into his features—this whole ordeal had taken a toll. In truth, it had taken a toll on all of them, but John wasn't ready to leave just yet.

He pulled Mary aside. "I've been getting an earful from your mama about you, Mary. She must have heard about some of what's been going on, and she wants to hear it direct from you. Says you haven't returned her messages. For my sake, make up while you can."

"There hasn't been a falling out, John. More like a falling apart." Mary's dark eyes were troubled. "I haven't returned her messages, that's true. But every time I'm in a room with her, it just reminds us both that things are different now. She resents me, and has for a while now, and in my own way I resent her. We just don't know how to talk to each other anymore."

This wasn't news to John. Tension had been brewing in Mary's family for a long time. Lord knew he'd had more than a few conversations with her mother, his Aunt Cherry, about her part in it. But because of that, he also knew Cherry had regrets and that she did want to patch things up with Mary. But knowing something and saying something were two different things. It wasn't John's place to explain Cherry's feelings or actions. He pondered what to say next.

"Your mama's not perfect, I'll give you that. She's made her fair share of mistakes. But I tell you this, Mary." John sighed, stroking his chin thoughtfully. "Life's not easy on any of us. We all just make the best decisions we can in the moment, and sometimes looking back, it wasn't the best after all. I'm not trying to excuse what she's done, I'm just saying it's not always as black and white as it seems at the time. She's your mama, for better or worse. I'd give all I have for a single extra day with mine. Quinton too. Maybe you should make the most of the time you still have with yours."

His words had struck a chord, John could see that. But no matter what he said, Mary wouldn't be bullied. Best to leave her to mull.

Zoe had been patiently waiting for them to finish their discussion, but now that they were done, she had something to say. "What do you make of Margot's death? Rory thought she was killed by a different hand, and Fairfax says it was not him."

"We cannot take what Fairfax says at his word," said John quickly. "He's a killer—a man who murders innocents without remorse. Lying is hardly a sin compared to such depravity."

"I make no claim that he is above lying, John." Zoe leaned forward. "But why would he do so in this case? He has admitted, even bragged, about the other killings, according to Magistrate Holdsworth and yourself. Save for Annie Huxley, he has provided details of his work without holding back. Why would he stay silent in regard to Margot Anderson? It makes no sense."

Mary frowned. "But it makes no sense someone else did the killing, either. The details might differ, but she was killed with the very type of cloth used with the others. It has to be him."

"That is true, Mary. The same bolt of cloth was used." Zoe stood suddenly, clearly restless in her musings. "Maybe someone else somehow had access to that bolt. We know his mother was involved—why couldn't someone else be part of the madness?"

Shaking his head, John protested. "Magistrate Holdsworth is convinced Fairfax worked alone, and he should know. He has fixated on these murders for years. No one knows more about the cases." He paused for a moment, a sudden feeling of uneasiness coming over him. "He always said no one paid any heed until Miss Anderson was killed. He said it was a terrible gift that a nobleman's daughter was a victim, as it brought light to what was happening."

"But why would Fairfax leave Margot alive?" Too late to head off the conversation; Mary was engaged now. "She must have seen who attacked her. She spoke after she was found even, but was not understandable. Why would he take that chance, when he told Zoe and I he actually enjoyed watching the life drain from his victim's eyes?"

"He wouldn't have. Whatever else Felix Fairfax is, he's strong and ruthless. He would have dispatched a little bird like Margot with ease." Zoe swallowed hard, speaking her next words hesitantly. "You said there was only one other person who cared about the murders at the time of her death."

A silence deep as the Thames engulfed the room. John watched in horror as the women exchanged a glance, a wordless understanding passing between them. He knew what they were thinking—the same notion had surfaced uninvited in his mind, like a corrosive worm.

Magistrate Holdsworth.

An uncharacteristic anger filled John's veins. "You cannot be serious. The magistrate is a good man who has worked tirelessly to stop these killings. He would never kill an innocent. The man sitting in prison right now—that is a man who kills without conscience."

"Calm down, John." Zoe raised her hands deferentially. "We are just working through our thoughts out loud. But you said it yourself, Margot's death was a kind of terrible gift. It brought attention to these killings for the first time, even if it didn't quite lead to the capture of Fairfax at the start."

"And she wasn't killed the same," offered Mary. "Rory said the others were killed by a chain—but not Margot. She was strangled with the cloth itself. Why the difference?"

"Well then, what about Chedrose? If Holdsworth really did—and I don't think he did—kill a girl to get people to take these killings seriously, why would he let someone like Chedrose take the fall? There's no way that boy could be the killer of Annie Huxley, and Holdsworth would have known that if he was the killer."

"He had little choice, once those up the chain settled on Chedrose as their man." Mary shook her head. "But when we spoke with Thomas Chedrose in Newgate, he said it was the magistrate who kept him from hanging. Maybe a guilty conscience was behind his generosity?"

"Or maybe he just didn't want an innocent man to hang!" John found himself growing angrier. "It proves nothing. In fact none of this proves anything."

"You're right." Zoe sighed and fell back into her chair. "In the end, whatever our private musings may be, there is a glaring flaw in our logic. Magistrate Holdsworth didn't have the elephant cloth. There's no way he could have done it without that."

An icy coldness started in the pit of John's stomach, spreading its icy arms to wrap around his heart. The cloth—Holdsworth told him he saved the cloth from one murder to prove that it was the same killer when he killed again.

He did have it.

All of a sudden the room seemed terribly small, as if the walls were closing in on him. John couldn't breathe. With a swift turn, he walked out without another word. Mary's voice trailed after him, calling out his name, but John couldn't stop. He was desperate for a breath of fresh air and space to think.

It could not be. John wholly believed what he told Mary. Ackerly Holdsworth was a good man. A bit full of himself, and perhaps a bit obsessed with the killings. But he was committed to justice for the victims, so how could he not be?

John couldn't help but recall the man's words: *A shame it took a noble man's daughter to die for people to listen to what I have been saying for years. A terrible gift.*

Was Holdsworth capable of crossing that line? Would he actually take a life if he thought doing so meant saving countless others?

His mind was in a haze, but his feet knew where to go. John walked straight to Bow Street, heading into the magistrate's office without a word to anyone else.

⁛

Holdsworth had returned from interviewing Mary and Zoe and was just lighting a cigar when John walked in. He took a deep puff, motioning for John to sit down. "Something on your mind, John?"

He almost didn't say anything. Once the words were spoken, there would be no taking them back. If he was wrong, it could destroy his career. If he was right . . .

"You told me once you saved one of those pieces of red elephant cloth," said John finally. "I'd like to see it, sir."

"For what purpose?"

John met his gaze evenly. "I think you know why, sir."

After a few long heartbeats, Holdsworth sighed. He pulled out the gin bottle from his desk, pouring two glasses, and motioned to a chair. "I don't think I ever told you of my time as a soldier," said the magistrate finally. "In fact, I know I didn't. I don't speak of it often. But the truth of the world is there's always a war, and always young men who think it is their duty to fight them. That was me, full of love for God and country. And of course, knowing whatever we did it was on the side of right—that we were right."

Taking a long drink from his glass, Holdsworth swirled the remaining liquid in a small circle, his eyes trained on the circular motion. "But in the heat of battle, right and wrong get blurred. The choices you have before you are often choices of which wrong is less wrong, but none of them are right. So I made the choices, and I lived with them. Like every soldier."

His story mirrored what Rory had said. People did things in wartime that they would never do in peacetime. But this wasn't war. John held his tongue, waiting for his next words.

"I ask you this, John: which would you say is less wrong, trading one girl's life for dozens of others, or turning a blind eye to the suffering of those to come?"

Bile rose in John's throat, not because of the terrible truth he had uncovered, but because, in a way, he understood the twisted logic. But that didn't mean he agreed. "I trusted you—she trusted you—and you betrayed everything this office represents."

"Yes, you are right." Holdsworth's eyes were distant. "She did trust me. I'm a good friend of the family, did you know that? Known the girl since she was a lass. So when she got into that fight with her father, she came to me—asked me to reason with him. Even when I took her to the alley, she never suspected anything . . ."

"How could you?" asked John in horror.

The magistrate shook his head. "It was harder than I expected, truth be told. I'd killed before, of course, but looking into her big, frightened eyes . . . it was different. I held tight until her eyes closed, but I didn't double check—I was in such a hurry to get out of there. That's the one thing I do regret . . . that she lingered on, suffering needlessly."

"That's what you regret?" Taking his gin in one swig, John placed the glass on the desk and stood. "The way I see it, Magistrate Holdsworth, ain't none of us have a right to play God, not when it comes to taking a life. I myself have never stood on a battlefield, so I can't judge any man for choices made there. But in the streets of London, with an innocent lass, I do make judgments. This wasn't war and you had no right.

"All of life is a war, John." Holdsworth sighed, placing his empty glass on the desk as well. "We stand on one side, holding back the darkness with any means necessary. Surely you understand this."

"If that's true, then by doing what you did, the war has already been lost." John shook his head in disgust. "If there's no difference between us and a madman like Fairfax, then the darkness has won."

Holdsworth smiled sadly. "I'm well aware."

That took John aback. "Then what are you going to do about it? If you think I'll stay silent—"

"No one could ever accuse you of being less than a man of honor." Holdworth stood. "As am I. Give me a day and I will see to it justice is done for poor Margot Anderson as well."

John weighed his limited options. Who would trust his word if he did raise the alarm? And despite this terrible thing his mentor had done, he still saw the magistrate as a man of integrity. After a moment's hesitation, he nodded and departed. It was time for the magistrate to demonstrate his honor, if he had any left.

Chapter Forty-Nine

Venturing to the Anderson home, Zoe was once again alone. After parting ways with John, Mary had said something about going to see her mother, leaving the responsibility to go see Mabel to Zoe. She didn't mind though. What was to come was an intimate conversation, one that was best had between the two of them.

Mabel didn't take long to join her in the parlor. This time she wore a day dress in the color of lavender, symbolizing her transition to half-mourning. The color didn't particularly favor her pale complexion and auburn hair, seeming to wash her out even more, but it was a sign of improvement.

Mabel embraced her with the familiarity that came with genuine friendship. If someone had told Zoe a year ago that she would count this girl as a close friend, she would have laughed in their face.

The two of them settled onto a love seat as the tea was served. Zoe took hers as she usually did, with honey and cream, and snatched up a scone with clotted cream. It was one of the few things British food had gotten right in centuries of blandness.

"I'm sure you've heard the news," said Zoe, taking a bite of the delectable treat.

"Yes. Felix Fairfax will hang for the murders of five women . . . including my sister." Mabel's eyes shone with emotions too complex to express aloud. "I cannot thank you enough for your help."

Zoe squashed any private doubt she may have allowed to arise. "Of course, Mabel. I'm just glad a murderer is caught and poor Mr. Chedrose won't have to spend another day in that horrible place."

"Margot would be glad of that too. I hope now she can rest in peace, knowing justice was done."

"What about you, Mabel? Are you at peace?"

She considered her answer. "No. But I think I will be, one day."

Zoe patted her hand affectionately. "I have no doubt, my friend."

"And what of you, Zoe? What is next for you, now that you're a lady investigator?"

A laugh escaped her lips. "Lady investigator? That's a bit far-fetched. I'm sure my life will return to some semblance of normal."

"I wouldn't be so sure, Zoe." Mabel's eyes were serious as she replied. "You're gaining something of a reputation. I wouldn't be surprised if others sought your help before long."

"My mother will be thrilled about that." Zoe hesitated. "I have found a certain satisfaction in what I have been able to do. A certain purpose." Zoe surprised herself by confiding in Mabel. Uncomfortable, she changed the subject. "And how are your parents handling the news?"

Mabel clearly noticed the change in subject, but after a moment she replied, "They would prefer it was never brought up again. In fairness, they thought all of this was put behind them a year ago. Now our family's private grief has all been dragged up again, and it's the talk of every society gossip mill. It's not pleasant, I'll give them that, but I think it's a small price to pay for justice." Mabel shrugged. "I'm not sure they'd agree."

"Everyone handles grief differently. Perhaps they'll come around."

"Perhaps. Right now they're bemoaning the fact I've only just entered half-mourning, which means I'll have to wait another year for my next season." Mabel sighed and took a sip of her tea. "It's for the best, I think. I don't know that I could focus on balls and suitors and impossible expectations at the moment."

"Things will work out for the best, Mabel, I'm sure." There was really no way to know that, but it seemed like the right thing to say. Zoe hesitated again before continuing. "Mabel, I hate to bring it up, but . . ."

"Of course, of course." Mabel reached behind her and retrieved a reticule. "The final payment, plus expenses. It's not all in pounds—I had to throw in some jewelry to fill it out. I hope your agent won't mind."

"Oh, I'm sure he'll figure out a way to make it work," said Zoe with a wry smile.

Chapter Fifty

When Rory was recovered enough to return to his own home, Lord Dovefield offered to have his carriage take him over, but Rory declined. The Dovefields had already been more than generous, and Rory was able to pay for his own hackney. More importantly, he had business to attend to before he went home and he didn't want anyone to be able to report back on his activities, even unintentionally.

The hackney took him over to the west side of Hyde Park. It was quieter there, mostly for horses rather than foot traffic. Rory had the driver drop him off at the entrance, paying him a generous tip before venturing inside.

She was waiting for him just past the gate. Her back was to him and she was wearing her lady's maid's clothes, but Rory would recognize her anywhere.

"Hello, Ruth."

As Lady Ruth Soarington turned to face him, Rory experienced the familiar sensation he always felt upon seeing her—as if he were laying eyes on her for the very first time. The sunlight filtering through the tree leaves dappled her face, illuminating the golden flecks in her hazel eyes. Her dark blonde hair was pulled back loosely, showing of her delicate features. Those who didn't know her might miss the quiet strength defined in her stance. She was a small-boned woman, but the gown she was wearing emphasized her curves in ways he hadn't noticed before.

"Rory." She glanced around nervously before grabbing his hand and pulling him back into the thicker foliage. No one else was around to see them, but secrecy was a force of habit for those in their position.

Placing a gentle hand on his face, she looked him over. "Are you well? You seem thinner."

"I dinnae know how much weight I coulda lost in just a few days," he replied with a laugh.

"It's not funny." Ruth turned a way, tears in her eyes. "You could have died."

"But I didn't." Rory pulled her closer. "Everything is well and as it should be."

For a moment they stayed that way, two people entwined in an embrace, oblivious to everything else around them. Rory could have built eternity in that moment. But such perfect things couldn't last, not in this world.

Ruth pulled back, still looking away. "Everything is not as it should be, Rory, and you know it. The reason you were nearly hung is because you couldn't be honest about where you were that night . . . you couldn't tell them you were with me."

"I certainly wasn't meditating in a city park, despite what an impeccable witness said." Rory hoped to raise the mood with humor. He was not successful.

"No, Rory. It's time." The tear she'd been holding back finally slid down her cheek. "What we've had, it's been . . . lovely. But we've been flying near the sun for a while, tempting fate, and it's only a matter of time before one of us gets burned. It's time."

This wasn't the conversation Rory had been expecting to have.

But that didn't mean she was wrong. Their days had always been numbered—in truth, it should never have happened to begin with.

Their first meeting had been just a chance encounter. Her new marriage gave her slightly more freedom in society, and she chose to spend that freedom at a scientific presentation detailing the newest advancements in steam engine development. Rory had been there out of interest in the subject, not to meet a woman—certainly not a married one.

That first meeting was nothing remarkable, just a few words spoken in passing. Then it happened again at the following soiree, this one about birds of the Amazon. He stood next to her that time, offering commentary and listening to hers in return.

But again they parted ways, this time as friendly acquaintances but still nothing more. Not until a particularly interesting meeting detailing something called a "vaccine"—something which would no doubt change the world as they knew it—had things changed. The subject was so exciting, and they were both so intrigued by it . . . he just couldn't resist continuing the conversation over coffee.

From there a friendship grew and continued to grow into something else. She was lonely and unhappy in a marriage that was never meant to be anything but a transaction. He was content in his life, but that didn't mean it wasn't a solitary existence, and he was grateful for the company and conversation. Rory wasn't sure one could call it love, but they filled a hole in each other's lives. The time spent with her was the happiest of his life, at least as far as he could recall.

Yet he had always been aware that it couldn't last forever. It was not a thought he had wished to linger on, but deep down, he knew the truth. "You're right, as you usually are." Taking her chin gently, Rory turned her face back towards him. "I wish you nothing but the best . . . Lady Soarington."

As Rory watched her walk away, he realized two things at the same time. One was that his relationship with the woman was no mistake. It was a decision they had both made fully conscious of the repercussions. He had no regrets on that front. The second was that letting her go now was a mistake he already regretted. But as he himself turned to walk the other way, Rory also knew that in this world, it was a mistake he would have to live with.

Chapter Fifty-One

When Zoe suggested she and Mary go to spend a few days with Theo, Hugh knew what she intended. She wished to parlay with her strange little tribe without stirring up controversy in their household. He'd been prepared to look the other way and allow her this freedom. He hadn't been prepared for his beloved Simone to suggest that, before Zoe left for her aunt's, they should invite the tribe over for an informal dinner in their own home.

The suggestion had shocked both father and daughter. The idea of having her mother's hawklike gaze watching over the proceedings clearly made Zoe uncomfortable, but there was no way to wriggle out of it once Simone made up her mind. So here they were, three days later, awaiting the arrival of their unusual guests.

When he'd asked his wife about it in the moment, all she said was, "I am a woman, Hugh. I'm allowed to be as contradictory as I wish."

That was her usual response when Simone wasn't ready to discuss a matter, so Hugh let it lie then. But as he watched her glide through the room, directing servants and rearranging seating, his curiosity got the best of him.

"Simone." As Hugh said her name, he took his wife's hand in his own and guided her away from the busy servants and over to the relative privacy of the fireplace. "My dear, what exactly is your scheme with all this?"

She sniffed. "What makes you think I have a scheme?"

"You do little without purpose, my dear. Although I will admit I am unsure what your intention is here. Perhaps to keep a closer eye on our daughter's new friends? To exert some control over the situation?"

"You make me sound like an overbearing general, darling. I hardly think a little parental influence in our children's lives—"

"Of course not," soothed Hugh. "You are a wonderful mother, Simone."

"I have always done what I thought was best for them." She paused, considering her next words. "But recent events have caused me to reevaluate what actually is best."

Hugh frowned. "What do you mean by that?"

"That perhaps it's not as simple as I once thought. I've always wanted Zoe to have access to every opportunity she could, and there is no denying that opportunity is tied to power and privilege. It's a game all mothers in society play, maneuvering their children here and there, all with the end goal to secure them the best possible position on the board. It's complicated and delicate and the stakes couldn't be higher. It's easy to get so consumed by it that all you see is the game and not the individuals. Zoe . . . Zoe deserves a chance to choose for herself what kind of life she wants, without the pressure of disownment from society hovering over her."

"Simone, I'm still not sure what you mean."

She sighed. "I'm speaking of Mr. Huxley, obviously."

To say Hugh was stunned would be an understatement. "Surely you can't be saying you would endorse a match between the two of them?"

"It wouldn't be my first choice. But he is a good man and an honorable one. He may not come with a title or an estate, but he is hardly without a means of earning a living either. And whatever else you may say about him, he is clearly devoted to Zoe. That doesn't come easily or often in this life."

There was no way Hugh could have been prepared for how this conversation would go. To think that Simone, of all people, would lose her senses over this . . . she was usually so rational and logical. He couldn't believe he was the one who would have to talk her back around. "Simone—my darling, beloved Simone—we cannot go down this path. I don't disagree with you about Huxley's merits, but there is no escaping the fact he is the illegitimate son of an actress with a method of earning a living that is dubious at best. The scandal would ruin us—we must think of Walter and Phoebe, and even my brother and his family."

His wife's blue eyes appraised him with an icy glare. "You don't have to explain the implications to me as if I were a child, Hugh. I'm well aware of the stakes. But you know as well as I that a scandal is only a scandal if you acknowledge it. Think of your good friend William Garrow and his beloved Sarah. They lived in sin together for nearly two decades, bearing both their children out of wedlock. Yet today he is the most famous barrister in all of England, a member of parliament, not to mention the likely future Attorney General for the prince himself. And did either of his children have trouble securing a match?"

"Well, no, but—"

"Exactly. Whatever anyone may have thought or said behind closed doors, in public no one batted an eye. What do you think was the secret to their success?"

Hugh sighed—he hated arguing with his wife. "I'm sure you will tell me."

"They weren't ashamed." Simone paused to take a breath, as if to calm herself. "I cannot know for certain what the future will hold. But I do know that whatever Zoe decides to do, we will set the tone for how it is received by society. It might be bumpy at first, but I believe with time and the proper attitude, we would come out the other side relatively unscathed."

"Hmm." Hugh was eyeing the decanter of whiskey across the room. "Your reasoning is flawless, as usual, my dear. But even if all that is true, you forget one small detail. Mr. Huxley has a voice in the matter as well, and as you said, he is an honorable man. He would never allow Zoe to throw her future away, no matter what her feelings on the matter."

"Then he is a fool and unworthy of her."

Hugh started. "I am surprised to hear you say that."

"My darling husband, I hope the day never comes when I cease to surprise you." She laid a gentle hand on his chest. "I will leave it at this for now—the past year has changed me. It has changed Zoe. If nothing else, it has helped me to realize that if we are the road-block to Zoe's happiness, then I don't know if that is something she can forgive anymore. I don't know if it's something I can forgive."

With those words Simone walked away, returning to her duties as hostess and leaving Hugh was a great deal to think about. Preferably over a glass of whiskey.

Chapter Fifty-Two

Looking in the mirror as Camille put the last few pins in her hair, Zoe felt a sense of satisfaction. Her curls were under control, while still leaving soft tendrils to frame her face. The dark mass was piled high in the back, with decorative pins strategically placed to keep everything contained. Few would suspect a knife hid among their ranks. After the ordeal she'd faced . . . Zoe liked having it with her, especially with the blood washed off. It made her feel safer, even though she knew logically that she was safe in her own home.

"Does it please ya, milady?" Camille's tone was uncertain, as if Zoe held power over her and would use it to her detriment.

Zoe felt a rush of empathy. Hers was not the position of a servant, but she did have some idea what it was like to have her future dependent on the decisions of others. "I love it, Camille. You have a gift with hair."

The flattery was not empty. Mary had taken some hours of concentrated schooling to teach Camille the ins and outs of Zoe's rebellious curls. Without the right touch, within an hour they would find themselves free of confinement and doing as they pleased. Not unlike the head upon which they rested . . .

The gown Camille had already helped Zoe into was a deep green, which favored her slender figure. It was cut lower than she usually wore, but she was feeling daring that evening. A simple strand of pearls, a gift from her stepfather, adorned her neck, while matching pearl earrings shaped like droplets completed her jewelry. Stepping back from the vanity mirror to take in her full appearance, Zoe saw a beautiful, mature woman reflecting back at her. It was a strange sensation to perceive herself that way.

Leaving Camille to straighten up the room, Zoe made her way downstairs, Brutus at her side. The guests would come soon, and she wanted to be settled and ready for their arrival.

As she entered the formal parlor, she noted her mother and stepfather already there, talking to each other easily near the blazing fireplace. The weather had turned distinctly colder over the week since she and Mary had come so close to losing their lives to Felix Fairfax. The warmth was welcome.

Hugh's smile radiated almost equal warmth when he caught sight of Zoe. He looked rested again, the haggard fear which had marked him when she came home that night replaced by his customary easygoing demeanor. The whiskey in his hand likely added to the glow.

Her mother smiled as well. "*Les petits* wanted to attend tonight, *mon chou*. The stories you told them have enthralled them. I trust you left out the near-death part?"

"I have some sense, Maman," said Zoe, returning her smile. "I made it out to be a fairy tale of sorts, focusing more on Brutus and Quinton's rescue more than the reality of our situation. Now Phoebe is quite taken with Quinton, and gets dreamy-eyed every time she hears his name."

Her stepfather chuckled. "I've grown fond of him myself, Zoe, as has your mother. He risked his own life to save yours. We will never be able to repay what he did for us. That being said, I do think I'm a tad less dreamy-eyed about the man than the Dovefield ladies seem to be."

Zoe laughed at the joke, but her mother merely gave an enigmatic smile.

"That cannot be argued, Hugh," said Simone. "But at least we can host a gathering for him, and the little tribe Zoe has found. All of them played a part in taking a very evil man off the board."

As if on cue, Quinton entered the parlor, followed by Quaid. Given the eclectic backgrounds of their guests, Hugh had asked the butler not to announce each one, to give an air of informality. Quaid had reluctantly agreed, but drew the line at allowing them to wander in unescorted. He caught Hugh's eye and gave a careful nod before stepping out to wait for the others. Zoe couldn't help but smile fondly.

Quinton took a drink from the carefully balanced tray offered of the footmen. He then approached the three of them with an easy smile.

It was impossible not to notice how impeccably Quinton was dressed. With his perfectly tied cravat, fine single-breasted waistcoat, and a jacket that could only have fit his broad shoulders so well if it was tailored to do so, he looked the part. To top it off, his smile transformed him.

Clearly her throat and glancing away, Zoe wondered just how dreamy her own eyes were. "Good evening, Mr. Huxley."

"Good evening, Lady Demas."

John entered next alongside Mary, with Quaid trailing behind. The two cousins were chatting cheerfully, with Mary doing most of the talking. John laughed at something she said, and Zoe found herself smiling at his good-natured entrance.

Within a few minutes, Rory entered as well, also dressed flawlessly. He still moved a bit gingerly, but the color had returned to his flesh and he stood tall, a smile fixed on his features. Zoe noted it didn't quite reach his eyes.

As Mary made her way to Zoe's side, it was Charlie's turn to enter, accompanied by his younger sister Savi and his mother Katy. Zoe noticed a difference in him. Charlie seemed more relaxed, less stiff. Given he was at a nobleman's home as a guest, Zoe considered the sense of ease unexpected. Perhaps a leopard could change his spots.

But he would always be a leopard, Zoe reminded herself.

Aunt Theo was behind them, but it was not in her nature to simply enter a room—she was one to make an entrance. Dressed in a lovely gown of sky blue, her gray hair in a simple but elegant updo, Theo entered without pausing and spoke immediately. "I want the story in its entirety, nothing left out. Seat me by the fire and tell me everything."

A smattering of laughter echoed through the room, but the effect was purposeful. Soon all of them were gathered around the seating area near the fire, ready to listen to the harrowing events of the night when Zoe and Mary nearly died. Before they started, Hugh instructed the footmen to refill the trays of food and drink, and then leave them at the table near the door before departing. This wasn't a story that needed to spread to every noble family in the vicinity.

Most did not know all the details. Quinton spoke of his talk with Old Arthur and the revelation that caused him to come to the Dovefield residence. Theo, never one to feel excluded, added her own flavor by recounting how Zoe and Mary had requested her to inform the Dovefields of their visit to Lady Fairfax. At the time of their request she was hosting tea, so she promptly relayed the message before returning to her guests, thinking nothing of the encounter.

Taking the story further, Mary recounted their tea with Lady Fairfax, with Zoe interrupting periodically to add detail. Mary told about her strong feeling of evil when she heard the floor creak, and then how she left the note. Hugh and John spoke of the search of the Fairfax home, Hugh's voice conveying their utter despair when their search proved fruitless. As the story moved towards its ending, Quinton revealed it was in a dream that he first thought of a hidden room, and how he and Brutus went back to search again.

At his description of Abigail leading him there, an eerie feeling came over Zoe, and she couldn't help but wonder if it was just a dream after all. But however he had reached the conclusion, she would be forever grateful.

The story reached its climax with the battle. Zoe showed everyone the hairpin knife which was instrumental in their escape. A not-so-subtle look passed between John and Charlie as one handed the blade to the other, which Zoe didn't miss.

When the words finally ran dry, silence settled over the room. Some got up to seek refills of food or drink before drifting into smaller groups. Zoe found herself with Mary, John, and her stepfather.

Hugh was thoughtful in what he said next. "Fairfax will swing next week, but it's truly an injustice that Magistrate Holdsworth won't be there to see it. His death was a tragedy, so close to seeing the work of years finally pay off."

Zoe expected John to add something, knowing how close he was with the magistrate, but the officer stayed silent. His usual cheerful countenance seemed muted as he stared at the liquid in his glass. Perhaps the grief was too fresh.

Zoe took the moment to ask a question she'd been curious about. Plus she wanted to see John's reaction. "How exactly did he die?"

Hugh shook his head sadly. "Such an unfortunate accident. According to his housekeeper he felt poorly and was having trouble sleeping, so he had acquired some laudanum to help. Somehow he took too much and slipped away in his sleep. The poor woman found him dead in bed the next day. Such a tragedy. We can only hope his spirit finds some peace knowing Fairfax would not have been brought to justice without his efforts."

Standing abruptly, John bowed his head. "The whole affair is a tragedy. If you'll excuse me."

"It's a loss for the lad," Hugh said wisely once John was out of earshot.

As she watched John stalk over to where Savita and Katy stood, Zoe wasn't so sure of the source of John's distress. She had her suspicions. But whatever was bothering him, it was for him to say or not. She stood as well, making her way to Quinton, who sat staring contemplatively into the fire. Charlie sat nearby, but when he looked up at her, Zoe was surprised to see, not disdain, but something akin to respect. It might not be camaraderie, but she would take it.

As she sat down, Charlie spoke. "You know who killed your mother, Quinton, and that's worth something. But I cannot understand why you don't wish to know more."

Groaning, Quinton turned from the fire to face Charlie. Though Zoe felt like an observer, she knew it was an act of trust they spoke openly in front of her.

"Because I cannot bear to speak to him." The words were soft, but the feeling ran deep. "I wish him to burn for all eternity for what he did to my mother, and Margot Anderson, and all the others. But I do not wish to speak with him before the fire is lit."

It was a sentiment Zoe could understand to a degree. There were questions in her own life she was only now willing to pursue for answers. But she still had her mother to ask for answers. Time was on her side. Quinton would get no second chance.

"Quinton . . . you don't have to do anything you don't want to do." Zoe reached out a hand, but then quickly withdrew it. "But if there's anything else you need to know, now is the time."

Rising to his feet, Quinton rested his arm on the mantle, staring again into the flames. Zoe tried to think of something else to say, searching for words to help ease his discomfort. But a chuff of laughter from Charlie made them turn to follow his gaze.

The source of his amusement was John, who was engaging in an animated conversation with Savita. She was laughing, her brown eyes twinkling with unsaid emotion. The way John was looking at her . . . it was not as a friend of her brother's. It was a way a man looks at a woman.

"John? And Savi?" said Zoe with a gasp.

To her surprise, Charlie leaned back, seemingly satisfied. "Savi has always liked John. As a little girl she would want to tag along with us, moon-eyed at John. He all but lived with us for a spell. He was always very tolerant of her, as a child. But then, when we got older, and each took our own path, John stopped coming to the house as often and they didn't see much of each other for a while. Savi held on to those feelings all these years, but I think it's only just occurred to John there might be something there."

The romantic drama having pulled Quinton back to reality, he glanced at Charlie. "And you're okay with this? Your little sister and one of your best mates?"

His wry smile made Charlie almost handsome, despite the scar that would forever mar his features. "Savi isn't a child anymore. She's spent enough long nights bringing new life into the world and making families complete; I think she's ready for a life and family of her own. For his faults, John is a good man with decent prospects." He glanced back at Quinton. "At least he doesn't owe me money."

Quinton had the decency to blush, but he held Charlie's eyes. "You will be paid in full this week."

"I don't mean anything by it, Quinton."

"I know, but you're right. It's time for me to pay back my debts." As Quinton grinned, Zoe's heart skipped a beat. "I'm back, Charlie. Back among the living and back to work." Turning suddenly to Zoe, he said, "Thanks to you, Zoe, I have funds again, and the mind to earn more. I'm in your debt as well."

Feeling herself begin to drown in Quinton's grateful brown eyes, Zoe glanced away, taking a deep breath. Before she could say anything else, someone unexpected entered the parlor.

Alexander Dovefield stood uncertainly in the doorway, his eyes searching faces until they rested upon hers. He strode over without a word, but much to her surprise, Quinton rose to block his path, hands clenched into fists at his side. Charlie stood as well, but only after Quinton, clearly uncertain as to what issue they had taken with the newcomer but ready to back his brother up.

Quickly looking past Quinton, Alexander addressed Zoe. "Lady Demas. May we speak privately?"

Of all the shocking things which had happened in the past few weeks, nothing could have prepared Zoe for the shock of Alexander calling her Lady Demas. Zoe did not remember him ever addressing her by her name in such a respectful manner. The best he'd ever done was call her "my French stepcousin, not actually my blood" one time at a soiree. Usually it was just Cousin Zoe said in the most sarcastic way possible.

"Of course. Come with me," she said as she stood.

Quinton didn't move, his glare unforgiving. "Do you wish me to accompany you?"

It occurred to Zoe for the first time that the men must have some kind of a past outside of their interactions with her.

To make the moment even more surreal, Alexander answered for her. "She will come to no harm, Huxley. You have my word. Whatever else you think of me, you must know I would never harm my cousin."

This whole interaction was bizarre, but if there was one thing Zoe wasn't going to stand for, it was men deciding things on her behalf. "Thank you, Quinton, but I am perfectly capable of talking to Alexander." She glared at her cousin. "You better have a good reason for this."

Reluctant but respectful of her wishes, Quinton nodded and stepped aside. Following Alexander out of the room and into the hallway, Zoe gestured for him to get on with it.

He leaned in close, as if afraid someone else would overhear them. "First of all, I am well aware I have been an arse to you, Zoe. I offer no excuse. I hope you can put that behind you for a moment, and listen to me."

She raised an eyebrow. "Hmm. That depends on what you say next."

"I need—I need your help." Alexander let out a slow breath, his tone having taken a desperate edge. "I have gotten myself into a situation in which I no longer see a way out."

Zoe raised an eyebrow. "What kind of situation?"

"I need your help . . . and probably your agent's as well. If he will indeed help me."

Chapter Fifty-Three

There was quite literally nowhere on earth Quinton wanted to be less than where he was. He had put this off until the very last moment, but in the end he hadn't been able to stay away.

Lord Felix Fairfax's trial had been swift and final. If all the other evidence wasn't enough, what they found in his priest hole sealed his fate. Underneath the blanket in the corner had been bones. Most were the remains of animals, just like his mother had said. But among the pile, a skull had been found—the skull of a child. There was no way to know now who it had once belonged to—an urchin perhaps, who disappeared one day, with no one to notice their absence.

He was sentenced to hang for his crimes, the date set for his death almost immediately following the trial. The sooner the nobleman was executed, the sooner the rest of society could put the whole unfortunate affair behind them, so no one was eager to drag things out.

If there's anything else you need to know, now is the time.

Three days earlier, Zoe Demas had uttered those words. Quinton had deliberately disregarded them, doing everything in his power to divert his thoughts elsewhere. Yet as the appointed time drew nearer, it became the only thing he could think about. Unable to hold back any longer, he finally found himself back in the grim confines of Newgate Prison, peering through the bars at the man responsible for his mother's death, just hours before the condemned's final march to the gallows.

Recent events and accommodations had taken a toll on the doomed man. Where Quinton had once thought of him as over-groomed, those weren't the words he would use to describe him now. Fairfax's graying hair was matted to his skull, his skin pale in color and appearing clammy A surgeon had stitched up his wounds, but Quinton suspected if the noose wasn't going to claim his life, the infection likely would. It wasn't a thought that would keep him up at night.

When he'd stopped Zoe from killing the monster, it hadn't been out of a moral objection to his death. If he had been the one holding the knife in that emotionally charged moment, Quinton knew he would've finished him. No, his intervention had been for Zoe. She didn't deserve to live with another person's death on her conscience—even the death of a man like him.

"Ah, the whore's son." Fairfax gave a dark chuckle. "Come to gloat?"

Squashing the boiling rage within him, Quinton clenched his jaw so tight he could've sworn he heard a tooth crack. Any insult paled when compared with imminent death. It didn't matter what this man said—Quinton had already won. "I don't want to be here at all," he replied. "But if you have anything to say before you leave this mortal earth, now is your chance."

"What makes you think I have anything to say to you?"

"Fine." Quinton shrugged. "Spend your final hours staring at the wall then."

As he turned to leave, he got the reaction he was hoping for.

"Wait." Fairfax sighed. "You must've come here with a question. What is it you want to know?"

That was a good question. What did he want to know? Quinton sighed—he knew the answer. In the end, there was only one question that mattered.

"Why?"

As Fairfax forced out a chuckle, he pushed himself up straighter with a wince. "Why? You don't want to know if she suffered or what her last words were?"

The man was lucky the bars were between them. Quinton let out a slow, furious sigh. "I know she suffered. What I want to know is why."

"Ugh, boring." Fairfax hauled himself to his feet, his balance unsteady but his gaze focused. "Fine. The truth is your mother was a whore who would spread her legs for any man with money, then acted like she was better than them. The world is better off without women like that."

Stepping closer to the bars, Quinton balled his hands into tight fists. "So you're just providing a public service then? No, I don't think so. My mother wasn't perfect, but she was no whore. You're just a pathetic liar."

"How would you know?" Fairfax smiled. "You weren't even born when I knew her."

That was new information. Quinton had assumed they'd met shortly before her death. But if Fairfax had known her since before he was born . . . that was over a decade. That was more than a passing acquaintanceship.

"Ah, I see you didn't know that," Fairfax continued. "There's a lot about your mother you don't know."

"Perhaps. But I can hazard an educated guess regarding your significance to her. My conclusion . . . utterly nothing." Quinton crossed his arms. "Indeed, I'd wager that's what tormented you through the nights. She dismissed you outright, and you were unable to deal with it like a man. The puzzle for me is why it took you over ten years to finally address that fury."

Fairfax's eyes glittered with fury. "You've clearly never been betrayed by someone you love."

Quinton scoffed. "You aren't capable of love. Whatever twisted notion you have of what love is, I can assure you, my mother would never have reciprocated it."

"You actually sound just like her." Fairfax tilted his head, his eyes narrowing. "So arrogant. So sure you're better than me. Be careful—that attitude might get you killed one day."

"One day. But not today." Quinton leaned in closer, lowering his voice. "I wouldn't want to steal your spotlight on your special day."

For a moment he thought Fairfax would come at the bars like a rabid dog—the fury in his eyes was almost palpable. But then the moment passed and he did something even stranger—he laughed. "Not just Annie . . . you sound like him too."

"Him?"

"Your father."

Quinton's breath caught in his throat, his brain struggling to process this information. "My father? You knew my father?"

"Well we did run in the same circles after all." Fairfax rolled his eyes. "It would be hard not to know him."

"Then is that why you killed her? Because she loved him but not you?"

"Annie was an actress who came from nothing. The only thing she had was her looks and that silver tongue. But I was young and foolish and willing to throw everything away for her. I asked her to marry me, just before my father sent me away. But was she grateful for the opportunity I was offering? No. She turned me down like I was just nothing—like I was just a meaningless face in the crowd."

"So you killed her because she rejected you?"

"No. I was angry, but I didn't kill her then. Around the same time, my father and I had a frank exchange of opinion over some of my . . . unorthodox activities. He bought me a commission in the navy and sent me away and I stayed away for a long time. I didn't see Annie for years."

Frustration boiled in Quinton. "Then why? Why did you do it?"

"I thought that moment, when she turned me down . . . I thought that was the most humiliating moment of my life. But it wasn't. I came back, just to see her. To see if she regretted her decision. I even brought her a bolt of cloth, all the way from India, as a gift. But then I found up what she'd been up to in my absence." Fairfax's lip turned up, as if disgusted. "I saw you."

Quinton's blood ran cold. "You killed her . . . because of me?"

"Don't be ridiculous. I didn't care about you beyond the fact your parentage was clear. I knew she'd been with him. I asked her to meet with me and she agreed. I was angry at first, but I was willing to look past it because he was already dead. Then she told me the truth."

"What truth?"

"That she hadn't just spent her nights with him and borne him a child." Fairfax leaned in. "She'd married him . . . after she told me she would never marry anyone. And that . . . after that, I just couldn't let it go. I made sure my gift to her would be her last."

"What? My parents were married?" Quinton shook his head, trying to steady himself as the floor seemed to crumble beneath his feet. "That doesn't make any sense."

"It's what happened, whether it makes sense or not." Fairfax pointed past him. "Now, if you'll excuse me, I think that gentleman is here for me."

He'd been so absorbed in Fairfax's story that Quinton hadn't even heard the prison guard coming up behind them. They were both out of time.

"Wait." Quinton turned back to Fairfax. "Who was my father?"

"You know what?" Fairfax stepped back from the bars, a smug expression on his face. "I think I'm done talking to you. But don't worry. I'll tell the whore you said hello."

"I wouldn't worry about that," Quinton snapped as the guard walked Fairfax out of the room. "I doubt you'll cross paths where you're headed. But I'll make sure to tell your mother you said goodbye when the asylum allows her visitors."

Quinton left the prison immediately, not bothering to wait and watch the execution. He'd seen men die before, and it wasn't something he enjoyed. Besides, he had better things to do with his time than spend any more of it on that monster.

The hackney made good time to his destination, so it wasn't long before he was standing in the ornate parlor of his host's home. When Lady Theodosia Bexley entered the room, he didn't hesitate. The last time she had offered to give him information on his heritage, he had flatly refused. But his conversation with Fairfax had changed the game. It was time.

"I'm ready to know." He swallowed hard before continuing. "I'm ready to know who my father was."

About the Authors

Sandra and Taylor Preisler share a love of reading and writing, an obsession with foster kittens, and of course DNA. *The Wounds That Linger* is the mother daughter duo's second novel and somewhat surprisingly, both survived the experience. Most of the time they even enjoyed it. While both are from Casper, Wyoming, Taylor now lives in Phoenix, Arizona with her sister, roommate, two Pit Bull's and probably some of those pesky fosters. Sandra and her husband Ken split their time between beautiful Wyoming and equally beautiful Arizona. Their two cats love the change every time and have never complained.

Follow us on social media at:
Facebook: www.facebook.com/sandraandtaylorpreisler
Instagram: www.instagram.com/taylor_and_sandra_preisler

Other Books in the
Regency Mystery Series

The Ties That Divide:
A Q & Z Regency Mystery
Book One

In the heart of Regency London, where the gulf between the opulent upper class and the squalid streets is as wide as the Thames, Zoe Demas, a young French woman entangled in two worlds, finds herself at the center of a chilling mystery.

When her lady's maid, Lucy, is found dead in the notorious district of Whitechapel, Zoe refuses to accept the verdict of a tragic accident. Determined to uncover the truth, she enlists the help of Quinton Huxley, a man whose expertise lies in navigating the murky waters between legality and the underworld.

Alongside a cast of characters as diverse as they are mysterious—Zoe's stepfamily, a Bow Street runner, a resurrectionist, and a gangster among them—Zoe and Quinton unravel a tale of forbidden love, jealousy, and betrayal that threatens to consume her.

Available at Amazon.com in paperback, hardcover and Kindle.